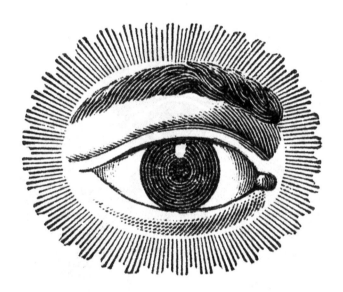

Hypnotism in Victorian and Edwardian Era Fiction
Volume II.

The Hypno-Ripper

or

Jack the Hypnotically Controlled Ripper

Containing

Two Victorian Era Tales
Dealing with
Jack the Ripper
and Hypnotism

Edited by

Donald K. Hartman

THEMES & SETTINGS IN FICTION PRESS

Buffalo, New York

©2021 Donald K. Hartman

THEMES & SETTINGS IN FICTION PRESS

Buffalo, New York

First Edition, 2021

Layout, cover design, and
Liston knife separators by

David J. Bertuca

Cover and original artwork by

Rob Sajda

Publisher's Cataloging-in-Publication Data

Names: Hartman, Donald K., editor | Oliver, N.T. | Frost, Rebecca
Title: The Hypno-Ripper or Jack the Hypnotically Controlled Ripper
    Containing Two Victorian Era Tales Dealing with Jack the Ripper
    and Hypnotism / edited by Donald K. Hartman.
    Series: Hypnotism in Victorian and Edwardian era fiction ; 2
Description: First Edition. | Buffalo, N.Y. : Themes & Settings in
    Fiction Press, 2021. | Includes bibliographical references.
    Summary: Two stories on Jack the Ripper by N.T. Oliver
    (pseudonym), also known as "Nevada Ned" and Edward
    Oliver Tilburn, plus a biography of the author.
Contents: Preface — Foreword: Explaining the Ripper / Rebecca
    Frost — The Whitechapel mystery; a psychological problem
    ("Jack the Ripper") / Dr. N.T. Oliver — The Whitechapel horrors /
    Charles Kowlder — Conjectural note — Biographical Information
    on Edward Oliver Tilburn — Acknowledgements.
    Identifiers: Library of Congress Control Number: 2020947789 |
    ISBN 9780960082308 (print)
Subjects: LCSH: Hypnotism and crime—Fiction. | Hypnotism in
    literature. | Mesmerism in literature. | Jack, the Ripper—Fiction.
    | Animal magnetism—Fiction. | Murder—Fiction. | Oliver, N.T.
    —Biography.
Classification: LCC PN6071.H9 H76 2021 | DDC 813.08 D43--dc23

Contents

✠MPUT✠TING.

ANTISEPTIC KNIVES.

For Division of the Soft Parts in Major and Minor Operations.

Esmarch has devised Antiseptic Knives made of one piece of steel, so as to afford no lodgment for septic germs, which might possibly adhere to ordinary knives. One objection to these is, that the handles become quite slippery if wet with blood; in order to obviate this, we have made antiseptic knives of which the handles are baked on, of hard rubber, but contain no crevices whatever. Any instrument constructed in this way is as if made of one piece, and affords the perfect customary hold.

Liston's Amputating Knives.

FIG. 1502.—Long.   FIG. 1503.—Medium.   FIG. 1504.—Small.

Catlings.

FIG. 1505.—Long.   FIG. 1506.—Medium.

FIGS. 1507, 1508.—French Finger Knives.

Bistouries.   Scalpels.

Tenotomes.

FIGS. 1509, 1510, 1511.   FIGS. 1512, 1513, 1514, 1515, 1516.   FIGS. 1517, 1518, 1519, 1520.

Preface

Peple of the Victorian age were fascinated with hypnotism—the fear that someone could manipulate the will of another person to commit a crime—possibly even to murder—left folks, understandably, quite anxious. Given their fascination with all things hypnotic, it's not surprising that some Victorians would have coupled the Whitechapel murders with the idea that hypnotism may have played a part in the crimes. Take, for example, the following article that appeared in the July 29, 1889 edition of the *Edinburgh Evening News*:

"JACK THE RIPPER" A MESMERIST.
A THOUGHT-READER'S DREAM

In his curious weekly, *The Mirror*, Mr. Stuart Cumberland gives a picture of "Jack the Ripper," as revealed to him in a dream. He says: "The face was thinnish and oval in shape. The eyes were dark and prominent, showing plenty of white. The brow was narrow, and the chin somewhat pointed. The complexion was sallow—somewhere between that of a Maltese and a Parsee. The nose was somewhat Semitic in shape, and formed a prominent feature of the face. The formation of the mouth I could not very well see, it was shaded by a black moustache. Beyond the hair on the upper lip the face was bare. It was not a particular disagreeable face, but there was a wild intensity about the dark full eyes that fascinated me as I gazed into them. They were the eyes of a mesmerist!" From which Mr. Cumberland concludes that the murderer first mesmerises his victims before dispatching them.

[Source: *Edinburgh Evening News*, July 29, 1889, p. 2]

This article summarizes a column written by Stuart Cumberland in *The Mirror*, in which Mr. Cumberland provides a picture of Jack the Ripper that was revealed to him in a dream. Cumberland's dream furnished him with a physical description of the Ripper and he was especially taken back by the killer's eyes: "but there was a wild intensity about the dark full eyes that fascinated me as I gazed into them. They were the eyes of a mesmerist!" Mr. Cumberland concluded that Jack the Ripper first hypnotized his victims before he killed them.

Who's to say if such a dream did, actually, appear to Stuart Cumberland, the editor of *The Mirror*, a sensational publication which dealt in occult subjects such as Theosophy and eastern mysticism, and he no doubt knew that fear and criminal titillation were topics that excite the reading public, and that fervor tied to a murderer with hypnotic powers could lead to increased sales of his periodical. (Cumberland did in fact flood the streets of London with men carrying advertisement boards for *The Mirror*; the ads announced that Jack the Ripper was a mesmerist.)

Victorian era magazine editors weren't the only individuals who tried to capitalize on the possibility that hypnotism had a role to play in the Ripper murders; at least two late 19th-century writers of fiction also put forth that theory, and those two authors' works are reprinted here. These two stories are among the earliest fictional accounts of the famous serial murder case, and interestingly, both of these stories have Jack the Ripper being an American, who travelled from New York City to London to commit the murders. But these stories differ from Cumberland's dream in the role hypnotism played in the Whitechapel crimes: Cumberland has the Ripper casting his hypnotic powers over the victims and then killing them, whereas Jack the Ripper commits his crimes while under the influence of hypnotism in the stories presented in this book.

The first story is a novel, *The Whitechapel Mystery; A Psychological Problem ("Jack the Ripper")* which was published in 1889, as part of the *Globe Detective Series*, by the Chicago based Eagle Publishing Company. The title page of the novel lists N.T. Oliver as its author—"N.T. Oliver" was a pseudonym for the highly interesting Edward Oliver Tilburn. Besides being an author, Tilburn was a minister, lecturer, traveling thespian, secretary for several cities' Chambers of Commerce, snake-oil salesman, sharp-shooter for a Wild West show, Christian psychologist, as well as an accused embezzler, shady real estate broker, and a self-proclaimed medical doctor (for more on Tilburn see the biographical information about him at the end of this book.) *A* New York City detective named John

Dewey narrates *The Whitechapel Mystery.* Dewey is investigating a bank robbery which a Dr. Westinghouse has perpetrated by the use of hypnotism. Westinghouse flees to England and is pursued by Detective Dewey. Westinghouse turns out to be Jack the Ripper, or rather, half of the Ripper because Westinghouse gains hypnotic control over Dewey and forces him to commit some of the Whitechapel murders alongside him (Dewey's first name is John, and Jack is a nickname for John; thus, the deadly duo's title "Jack the Ripper"). The story goes on to describe Westinghouse's growing hypnotic power over Dewey's will. Ripperologists may find the first part of this novel somewhat tiresome because it deals with solving a bank robbery, and because it is written in a predictable 19th-century writing style, but those who read the story through to the end will not be disappointed.

The second story in this book is a short tale, anonymously published shortly after the murder of Mary Jane Kelly in November 1888. The story appeared in two American newspapers—the *Indianapolis Journal* and the *Chicago Tribune*—the version reprinted in this volume appeared on the front page of the *Indianapolis Journal* (Sunday Journal) on November 24, 1888, and carried the title, "The Whitechapel Horrors: A Conjectural Story Relating the Facts Concerning Four of the Murders. They Were Committed by an American While in a Condition of Hypnotism–Weird and Thrilling Story of Unconscious Crime." The story supposedly appeared first in the British newspaper the *Pall Mall Gazette*, and it purports to be written by a New Yorker named Charles Kowlder, but a search of the archives of the *Pall Mall Gazette* failed to produce any such article, nor could any reference to a Charles Kowlder be found in searches on the Internet and in several newspaper and journal databases. The tale itself is told by Charles Kowlder, who goes to London for business reasons, but ends up staying there to recuperate from a nervous/mental disorder. During his convalescence, Kowlder becomes captivated by the Whitechapel murder cases, and upon reading the gruesome details of the killings in the daily London newspapers, he gets a strong sensation of déjà vu—and for good reason, since he is the perpetrator of the atrocities. Overall, the story is an interesting one of self-hypnosis leading a person to commit a crime.

Foreword

Explaining the Ripper

Rebecca Frost

The question surrounding Jack the Ripper since the Autumn of Terror is not just one of "whodunit," but *why* someone would do it. Since the introduction of criminal profiling into popular understanding in the late 1980s and early 1990s, explanations for serial killing have become accessible and almost mundane. From Clarice Starling and Hannibal Lecter to numerous police procedural shows and movies since, we might not entirely have a grasp on "who" a serial killer is, but the "why" has become more or less explicable.

The Ripper murders received such widespread attention for their brutality. Newspapers covered the crimes in as much detail as possible, competing for business and even making up information when facts were not readily available. It was indeed possible for readers to become obsessed with the unfolding crimes, as happens here in *The Whitechapel Horrors*. What contemporary readers and reporters lacked was an understanding of serial killing and its causes.

In both of these tales, the "why" part of the serial killing question has been answered with "hypnotism." The main character – the man writing his confession – did not commit the murders of his own free will, and did not even commit all of the murders generally attributed to the Ripper. In each case, the American man who discovers himself to be guilty pens his story immediately prior to his death in order to give the world the "why" it so desperately wanted before accepting his deserved fate.

While twenty-first century readers might balk at the idea of a man being hypnotized to murder when he would otherwise not commit such crimes, each story is also one of obsession. In *The Whitechapel Mystery*, our American confessor finds himself fascinated by a man who claims deep knowledge of hypnotism and can induce hypnotic states in others merely by looking at them. Former detective John Dewey cannot bring himself to stay away from the mysteriously powerful Dr. Westinghouse. He keeps tracking down the other man in spite of all warnings and common sense, and finds himself involved in Westinghouse's personal mission of revenge as a result of his fascination.

In *The Whitechapel Horrors*, another man – also an American, and also from New York – fixates not on a person but on the case of the murdered Polly Nichols. Rather than needing the outside influence of a Dr. Westinghouse in order to invoke a hypnotic state before embarking on a murder spree, Charles Kowlder engages unwittingly in self-hypnosis perhaps brought on by the condition that sent him to visit a physician at the beginning of the story. Kowlder's is perhaps the more unsettling tale because he did not need outside influence in order to hypnotize himself into murder. He did it all himself, and all without realizing.

Each story draws facts from the actual murders attributed to Jack the Ripper, although the details are at times confused, and each has at least a nod to the theory that the Ripper must have been a physician. They are able to play up the tension and fears surrounding the murders, especially since they were published so quickly after the death of Mary Jane Kelly. The concern that the Ripper might not have been finished would still have held strong, although each narrative includes the more or less comforting fact that the man who has confessed is now dead and no further murders will be committed.

While these tales might seem quaint and vintage in many aspects to twenty-first century readers, they still draw many parallels to crime fiction and true crime told today. Dr. Westinghouse has more than a bit of Charles Manson in him, including the threat that a charismatic, charming man can convince otherwise innocent people to commit murder for his own stated cause. Detective John Dewey's strange attracting to Dr. Westinghouse shares similarities with the relationship developed between Will Graham and Hannibal Lecter in the 2013-2015 television series *Hannibal*. Even though the authors – or perhaps only author – of these texts did not have the benefit of the FBI's criminal profile of a serial murderer, the explanations given still share a large number of elements with current belief about serial killers and their motives.

While no serial killer today would face a courtroom and claim to have been hypnotized into committing murder, neither did the subjects of either of these narratives. Dewey knew his death was approaching, aided by Dr. Westinghouse's incredible power, and welcomed it, rushing to finish writing his confession before the appointed hour. Kowlder took matters into his own hands, informing anyone who found his manuscript that he was now beyond the reach of the law. In neither case does the argument of hypnotism get put on trial. Dewey's confession is further framed by the comments of the physician who attended his death, a man who expresses great doubt at the truth of the story he then presents to the reader. Each tale struggles in its own way with fully convincing the reader that the "why" is hypnotism, but the man who tells it clearly believes in his own unintentional guilt.

Those who study the Ripper murders will find factual stumbling blocks in these stories beyond the idea of hypnotism as MO, but overall, the narratives presented here are not as old-fashioned as might be expected. Even with all the forensic and psychological knowledge that has been accrued in the 130 years since, we still struggle to explain *why* a man might feel compelled to commit such murders. At least each of these murderers was able to regain a sense of self in the end and opt for death rather than continuing on his dark path.

The Whitechapel Mystery;
A Psychological Problem
("Jack the Ripper")
by Dr. N.T. Oliver

The Whitechapel Mystery.

THE STATEMENT OF DR. LUCAS

I.

I suppose it would be much better if I were to leave unsaid what I am about to say. There is too much said altogether in this world. Everyone you meet, everyone you know, keeps it up. Chatter, chatter, chatter, like a lot of paroquets or parrots. Jones tells Brown, he in turn communicates to Robinson, and soon the city, town, or hamlet is ringing with the news, scandal, or whatever it may chance to be.

I suppose it is the way of the world. Curiosity and cupidity rule mankind, and womankind as well—the former passion relating more especially to those of the gentler sex; at least so everyone says; but *I* have seen *some* men equally as curious as the weakest woman, and gossip exists among those of the sterner sex just as much as among the ladies. Not exactly on the same order, perhaps, but it exists, just the same. For instance—here I, Dr. W.F. Lucas, a man sixty years of age, well known, considered a good physician—known to be a very successful one—must needs make known to the public certain facts which have come to my knowledge in the course of my practice quite recently, in fact, within the past few weeks. It would be infinitely better if I were to leave these things untold, as I have before stated; better for many reasons. One (and the greatest), that I may be making myself a laughing-stock for those who read. Some, who will say, "These are the ravings of a madman." Perhaps they are. I will not deny it, for I do not know. At any rate, I shall bring before the attention of the public a problem which they will find it worth their while to try and solve, if only for the satisfaction it will bring their minds. Another reason—few will believe that the statements I am about to make are true. They are so improbable; so entirely at variance with the laws of nature and common sense that the majority of the world will shrug their shoulders and say, "Impossible!" "Nonsense!" etc., etc. Well, as I said before, it may be. I simply give to mankind what has been given to me. Believe it, if you see fit; doubt it, if you choose; accredit it to a mind diseased, if you will. *But, solve it—if you can.* To come to my story.

As I have before stated, my name is W.F. Lucas, and the title "M.D." has been attached to my name for nearly forty years. Of late years this title has been supplemented by those of "LL. D." and "D.D.S.," for I have added dentistry to my practice, finding it necessary in the small town where I have seen fit to settle. I also possess a diploma of law. My practice is large. I am somewhat conceited as to my ability, and really think I understand my profession as well as the majority of my confrère; in fact, better than most of them. I have been a hard student, and have taken great interest in this (to my mind) the noblest calling on the face of the earth—the art of relieving suffering humanity of pain and distress; the science of cheating Death of his victims, if only for a short time—experimental, if you wish it, but a glorious work just the same.

I am often called out late at night. I have given obstetrics a favorite place in my studies, and I am often in great demand. The human race must be kept in existence, and it seem as if Dame Nature usually chooses the darkness of night for this, the grandest and most necessary of her works. So when my door-bell suddenly gave forth in clamorous tones the fact that someone (evidently an impatient one) wished to see me one night, at about the hour when grave-yards are supposed to yawn, I naturally came to the conclusion that the population of our town was about to be increased by the advent of one more soul, perhaps more than one, for such things occasionally happen, you know. So I jumped from my bed as quickly as possible, considering my age, and went to the front window to see where and by whom I was wanted. I have a lamp burning on the gate-post in front of my residence, upon the glass side of which my name is painted. In the light of this lamp I saw a child, evidently about twelve years of age, standing upon my doorstep, and just preparing to give the bell-knob another jerk as I raised the window.

"Well; what is it?" I inquired.

"Are you Dr. Lucas?" came the question.

"Yes. What do you want?"

"Come with me, please sir. You are wanted right away, and please come quick."

"Who is sick?" I asked; "your mother?" thinking I might need my instruments.

"No; not mother. Somebody else; a stranger man. Come quick, or you may be too late."

The evident anxiety displayed by the child caused me to hurry in dressing, and, seizing my medicine-case, I hurried downstairs without waking my wife, who was slumbering soundly. I carefully secured the front door behind me, and was soon hurrying down the street behind my youthful guide.

Naturally I asked a few questions of the child (a girl) as I walked along, but received but little satisfaction, she evidently not knowing much about the patient I was hurrying to try and save.

This much, however, I did learn. About two weeks before, a stranger had come to the house of her parents. He was not well, to judge from his appearance, and had not left the house since he had entered it, confining himself to his room entirely. He seemed greatly worried about something, and had done a great deal of writing during the past ten days, sitting up until a late hour nearly every night to do so. She knew this by peeping through the key-hole.

"Commencing young," was the thought that flashed through my mind, as the girl informed me of the source of her information. She went on to say that he had been taken violently ill only that morning, but had positively refused to have a physician called in until an hour before she had come for me. Her father had sent her upon the errand.

"And why did you come to *my* house?" I asked her.

"I have heard of you being such a good man," she replied, "and I thought you would be the best one to bring."

Feeling flattered at the child's reply (for we are all likely to feel gratification at an expression of faith in our particular ability), I said, "You did wisely. I will do all that lies in my power to help the sick man."

Very little more was said on our way to her house. She walked rapidly, for a child, and, being no longer a young man, I had all I could do to keep pace with her.

After a sharp walk of about twenty minutes, the girl stopped before a modest frame house, on the outskirts of the town.

"I live here," she said; "follow me," and opening the door (which was not locked), she led the way into the house.

The hall was dark, there being no light whatever, and, the girl leaving me, I waited impatiently the coming of someone to show me to my patient. In a short time I detected the faint glimmer of a light at the head of the stairs which led to the floor above, at the foot of which I had been standing. Then came a gruff whisper:

"This way," it said; and I quietly and quickly ascended the stairs. At the head I saw a burly, heavily-bearded man, in dishabille, shading the light of the lamp from his eyes with his hand.

"I am Dr. Lucas," I said.

"I know it; my gal has just told me. I hear you are a great doctor, but you'll not do any good this time." Then, with a heavy step, he conducted me to the door of a room in the front part of the house facing the street. Before opening the door he stopped, and, turning to me, said:

"The man you are going to see is distantly related to me, and is going to die. There is no hope for him; I know it. I sent for you to help him die easily; to try and relieve his mind, if you can, so he can meet death in proper shape. If you hear anything strange, don't feel alarmed. He has a good deal on his mind; and, another thing, don't contradict him in anything." And without waiting for me to make any reply he opened the door of the room, and the next moment I stood by the bedside of my patient.

"The doctor, Phil," announced the man with the light. A sudden convulsion of the bed-clothing, and my patient sat erect, his eyes fixed upon mine, his breath coming quickly through his parted lips. "The doctor," he repeated. 'Well, what can you do?"

Somewhat bewildered at the suddenness of the question, I answered, in confusion, something to the effect that I would do the best I could for him, as soon as I could diagnose his case and understand it a little. A faint smile swept over his haggard face.

"Understand my case," he muttered grimly. "No living being can understand *my* case. Can you give a man his mind again? Can you wrest from one man that which rightfully belongs to another, and give it back to him again?" he spoke, excitedly.

"Don't exert yourself," I said, calmly. "A case of mania," I said to myself, placing my finger upon the throbbing pulse of the sick man. He seemed to read my thoughts.

"You think I am insane," he said. "You look upon me as one crazed; you are wrong. I am not crazy; would to God I were. Then I would not know—could not remember. No, it is not that; my brain is in its proper state; *but another—a devil in human form—controls it!*" and with a groan he fell back upon the pillow.

I saw that he was very weak; his pulse denoted a high state of fever; so I made no reply. I opened my medicine-case and administered a powerful narcotic, which acted as if by magic upon the nerves of the patient. He became calm, so calm and quiet, in fact, that I concluded he had gone to sleep. I arose from my chair, and was giving my companion minute instructions as to the proper time of administering the medicine, when, to my surprise, the sick man opened his eyes, and in a weak tone said:

"I am not sleeping; I shall never sleep again, save in the sleep of death, and the sooner that comes the better. Your physic has soothed my mind. I can think more intelligently, but that is all you can do. I wish to speak to you privately; I must speak to someone, and soon, for in the morning I shall be dead. Leave us alone, Bob; I will send for you when I come to die."

The bearded man spoke some cheering words, but the sick man only smiled incredulously, and waved his thin hand toward the door. My companion sighed, and, taking his lamp, left us alone. The faint light of a night-lamp dimly illuminated the room. The door had no sooner closed behind him than my patient turned his eyes upon me.

"You are an able physician?" he said, interrogatively.

"I am so considered," I replied, modestly.

"You understand your profession, I believe, for you have given me a medicine which does me good. I have been sick for some time; not sick enough to give up; I could not, would not, do that, for I had work to do—a task to complete—before I could give in to the fatal malady which is killing me. But I have been suffering with an ailment which will cause doubt in your mind, and it has made me, once a strong, powerful man, but little more than a child. I dreaded to see a physician; I disliked the idea of being ridiculed—doubted, even in the mind of a medical man." Here he paused, while I waited for him to continue. Suddenly he asked the question—"*Do you believe a man can be in two places at one and the same time?*"

This question asked me at any other time or place would have created profound amusement and ridicule on my part, but a look at the man who asked it quelled any appearance of such a thought on my face, although it caused me to laugh inwardly. The sick man was watching me, and eagerly awaiting my answer, so I said:

"I can hardly believe such a thing possible, save in dreams. There are some people who claim to be clairvoyants, controlled by the spirits of the dead, whose bodies are in one place, their minds in another."

"No! not that. Do you believe any man can exist in two places at the same time; act, commit deeds exactly opposite to each other, at the same hour?"

"I do not believe any such nonsense," I replied, firmly, now convinced that my patient was laboring under the influence of delirium.

"I thought not; I could not expect any man of sense to credit such a thing. *Yet, it is true!*"

I gave a start; but, remembering my promise to my bearded friend, I made no immediate reply, merely nodding my head. I felt that my patient must, indeed, be mad to make such a statement. Finally, I said, "If you could give me some little explanation as to the meaning of your words, I could more thoroughly understand you."

"What is the hour?" inquired the patient.

I glanced at my watch. "It wants five minutes to two," I answered.

"I have not the time," he said. "At three o'clock I die. Ah! You shake your head; you think it impossible that anyone should know the hour of their death. It *does* seem incredible, but it is true. *He* wills it that I shall die at three. You will see that it will be so. But if I can not explain to you by words, I can in another way. Open the top drawer of the bureau yonder, and bring me the contents."

I arose, and went to the bureau, or, more properly, chest of drawers, for the piece of furniture was one of those high, old-fashioned affairs from which the modern bureau and dressing-case is the outcome. I opened the top drawer as he had requested, and found the sole contents to be a square packet, neatly tied with strong twine. I removed the packet and brought it to him. He took it from my hands.

"This is what has kept me alive so far," he said. "This will explain to you the meaning of my strange words. Take it."

I remembered the words of the child who had conducted me to the house. She had spoken about the stranger being engaged in writing for ten days back; this must be the result of his labors. I took the packet, feeling rather curious as to its contents. He spoke again:

"When I am dead you can open that packet and read what is written therein. It will startle you; will cause you surprise and doubt; but, remember, *it is true*. I am a dying man, doctor. I have not quite an hour to live. I have been spared to give the world the strange history contained in that parcel you hold in your hand; but I finished it this morning, and now I must die."

"But why do you give it to me?" I said.

"You are a man of science; you may be able to account for many of the remarkable circumstances recorded in my last work on earth. I give it to you so that the world can know, can understand, some things which are now unknown to them. I know I can trust you; I feel that you will give the matter your attention." I thanked him for his confidence in me, a stranger, and said no more. The minutes flew rapidly by; my patient lay quiet before me. I found myself dozing off into sleep.

At this moment the sick man arose in bed, and his face caused a sickening feeling of horror to creep through my frame.

It was demonical!

The large eyes stared at me with a fiendish expression; the long black hair seemed to rise from his head; his hands clutched at something before him; from the parted lips issued a light froth. I was startled for the moment, and drew back in fear, but the next, I sprang toward the bed. I endeavored to press the man back upon the pillow. Useless! He possessed the strength of a demon. He threw me aside and leaped from the bed.

"It is you, is it?" he shrieked at some invisible thing, apparently in the corner of the room. "You! *You!* You! You are here! I knew you would come. I felt that you could not let me die in peace. You smile—*curse you!* That quiet, almost heavenly smile. You—a devil—a fiend, an incarnate demon! You smile—ah! I shall soon be free. Keep away from me! Keep away!!"

His shrieks were appalling; his ravings alarmed me. I stepped hastily toward the door.

One, two, three, chimed a neighboring clock.

"One, two, three!" shrieked the madman. "Thank God; I am free at last."

And with a convulsive upheaval of the chest, a wild cry, an irradiation of the haggard face, he fell upon the floor. I hastened to his side. I lifted the lifeless arm. I placed my ear to his heart.

No sound—

No feeling—

He was quite dead!

II.

As I look back upon the events of that night I inwardly shudder. My flesh seems to creep; my hair seems to feel a peculiar tendency to stand on end. I have often wondered that I did not fly down the stairs to the outer door and hurry to my home. But I did not. I felt a natural feeling of horror, it is true, but I did not leave my patient. He did not require my services any longer, poor fellow, but I lingered by his side.

The sound of his shrieks had awakened the members of the family, and they now came into the room, fearfully, cautiously, as if fearing some wild beast was lurking to spring out upon them and destroy them.

He who had been called "Bob," my friend with the gruff voice and heavy beard was the first to enter; the other members of the thoroughly-frightened family followed him.

"Well," he exclaimed.

"It is all over," I answered quietly, pointing to the inanimate form upon the floor; "he is dead."

"Dead," repeated the children and woman (probably the mother) in an awe whisper.

Then they shrank back. They shared the feeling of horror for the dead that nearly all mankind possesses. The man, however, had no such feeling. He walked over to the corpse, and lifted the pulseless wrist.

"Right," he muttered; "dead at last. A good thing, too."

I turned to him, with a sharp reproof upon my lips. He prevented me from giving utterance to it by saying:

"If you knew how much he has suffered during the past two weeks, you would agree with me that death was a blessing to him."

I remembered the last words of him, who now lay quiet and still upon the coarse rag carpet of the room, and withheld my reproach.

"We will place him on the bed," I said.

The man assented, and, lifting the helpless form, we laid it on the bed. It was nearly four o'clock when I took my departure from the house. I knew there was no further need of my services there, so I picked up the packet confided to me by the dead man, and, promising to send a certificate for burial in the morning early, I hurried home, my brain busy with diverse thoughts, which only a perusal of the manuscript (which I clutched tightly by the twine that bound it) could dispel. I felt in my mind that the man who lay dead in the frame house behind me was possessed of a peculiar mania, one of the *most* peculiar I had ever heard of. One thing puzzled me greatly, and that was, when he made the strange declaration, which the parcel would explain, his eyes were perfectly calm. He spoke eagerly, but not deliriously. To all appearances he was sane at that moment, although his actions at the moment of dissolution bordered on frenzied madness.

I thought these things over seriously on my way home, and came to the conclusion that I would read the contents of the packet carefully and see how the statement made by the deceased could be explained in any way.

It was just beginning to show signs of dawn in the eastern horizon as I entered my front gate. Blowing out the lamp at the entrance, I inserted my night-key in the lock of the door, and ascended the stairs to my room. My better half (God bless her) was still sleeping soundly, and, with difficulty overcoming the temptation to untie the string that bound the packet and read its contents before sleeping, I disrobed and got into bed.

My last thought before sinking into a heavy slumber was on the packet, and I determined that my patients must wait on the morrow until I had digested the contents of the dead man's last work.

It was nearly ten o'clock when I aroused from my slumbers. I found my wife sitting by my bedside, with a look of anxiety on her usually placid face.

"I am so glad you have awakened," she said, with a sigh of relief.

"Why, what's the matter?" I asked, sitting up in bed and yawning.

"Oh! You have been saying some of the most horrible things in your sleep. Calling out for someone to take something from you; you alarmed me."

I laughed. I had probably been dreaming of my patient of the early morning. I arose, and, after a good bath, felt all right.

A man of sixty can not stand the amount of labor that one-half his years can. I usually find I awake with a severe headache when I have had my sleep broken into by night-callers. I will be obliged to give up my night practice soon—I am getting too old to stand it. This particular morning, however, I felt brisk, and free from any uncomfortable or painful sensations. I ate a good breakfast of new-laid eggs, oatmeal, and fresh milk. I keep my own chickens and a cow, and their products are my principal living. I don't believe in over-loading the stomach with heavy food, particularly in the morning. I have often told my patients if they would be more attentive to their diet, they would suffer less from sickness. The majority of ills arise from an illy-used stomach and liver. But enough of this prating. I ate my breakfast, and then went to my front door, for two reasons—first, to see if there were any calls upon the slate; second, to study the state of the thermometer. I found one very urgent call. My wife should have awakened me, and got me off to attend to it. But my wife spoils me; she thinks my rest more important than all the sickness of my numerous patients combined.

When I spoke to her about the call upon the slate, she said it must have been left there very early. She had not heard the door-bell, had not seen the slate, very likely. She seldom interferes in my business. Would that there were more women like her. I quickly donned my heavy overcoat (for the thermometer indicated 10 degrees about zero), and pulling my fur cap over my ears, I started off to attend to the case which seemed so urgent. The youngest child of one of my best-paying patients had been taken suddenly ill. I arrived just in time; thirty minutes later, my visit would have been useless. As it was, my medicine produced a reactive effect, and when I left the bedside of the helpless little one I was gratified to see a change for the better. I hurried along on my rounds, carrying hope, good cheer, and relief from pain to those who watched for my coming with eager hearts.

Ah! a noble calling is that of the conscientious physician. I reached home at twenty minutes past one, and found my lunch set out upon my office table. I dispatched it hurriedly, not a wise thing to do; we should eat slowly—a hurried meal impairs digestion; but I was all eagerness to peruse the manuscript. I cut the twine, and picked up the first sheet of the closely-written paper, but I was destined to disappointment, for I had scarcely read the opening lines when a ring at the door-bell announced a visitor. A man from the country; I must go to his wife at once. He had brought his horse and buggy. With a sigh, I placed the paper upon the desk, and, taking my instruments, was soon ready to accompany the farmer. A case of obstetrics; he was about to have his already large family increased.

The case kept me busy until dark, and it was just ten o'clock as the smiling father left me at my door. He was the richer by one beautiful baby girl.

I found my wife awaiting me in my office. I informed her that I would not retire for a few hours. She scolded me soundly.

"You need rest," she said.

So I did. My wife was right. She is nearly always right; but my whole mind was wrapped up in the pile of matter which lay upon the desk before me. I was anxious to read it; so I sent her to bed, and, trimming my study lamp, arranging the shade so that the light would not affect my eyes, I began to read. The hours passed by unheeding. I could not have put that strange history down until I had read it all to have saved me. The hands of the clock pointed to quarter past two, when, with a sigh, I laid aside the last page of the manuscript. I sat for some minutes bewildered, dumbfounded. I could not credit what I had read. I aroused myself at last and wearily went to my room—to bed, but not to sleep. For two hours I pitched and tossed, unable to close my eyes or to compose myself to slumber. At last I drifted away. My dreams were of the astounding revelations which I had perused. I awoke at eight o'clock unrefreshed, weary in body and mind.

I had read the explanation, but was still unsatisfied. I made up my mind to give to the world that which had been intrusted to me, and so I publish this history.

As I said before, put whatever construction upon the matter you see fit, *but solve it if you can.*

I give it to you just as it was given to me—unaltered, unabridged. It may be the ravings of a madman, but if true, will explain the greatest mystery of modern times. I must confess that I do not understand it. Perchance someone who reads may be able to explain it. *Do so! Try it!*

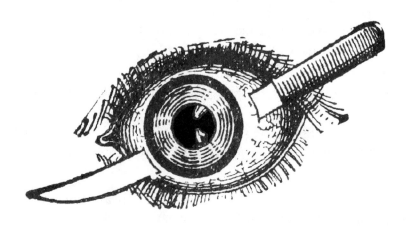

THE STORY

I.

I have ten days, three hours, and twenty minutes to live! How strange that looks upon the paper before me as I write it. I laugh as I finish. Laugh, not through merriment, not from natural lightness of the heart, but because it will be a joyful release to me when that blest time comes.

Strange that a man should feel a delicious sensation of joy at the thought of the coming of his last hour. Strange? Yes; in any ordinary human being—in any one of the thousands who live in the world as it is, as it used to be to me. But I am not as these. The world is not to me as to them. I am not like any creature who draws the breath of life. God would not permit any other to be as I am, to suffer as I have.

I have a short time to live. There is much to do; I must be about it. I must write what I dare not say. I must give to the world the strangest history it has ever heard.

There is a dog howling in the neighborhood. I go to the window and raise the blind. A bright, moonlight night. How peaceful all nature seems—quiet, at rest. Ah! the dog is a large, black one; he is looking up at my window, and howls. He knows that a death will occur soon. He knows I have but ten days, three hours, and twenty minutes to live. He has been howling every night since I came here; he will howl every night until I am free. I must write my history. As I sit and review the past, my brain grows clearer, the horrible memories seem less horrible. My heart still beats with a dull, heavy throb, but the pain there is not so great. It will soon cease to beat.

Yes; I grow calmer. I feel that I can relate my terrible story without wandering. I shall write it just as it happened. I shall divide off the last months of my life, and relate the incidents, as the author divides off his novel into chapters. Each month shall be divided by weeks, the weeks by days, and, in this way, all shall be told. There is a certain amount of pleasure to me in this. It will occupy my time. It will hurry on the days that must elapse between the present and eternity—eternal rest. God speed it!

II.

FIRST MONTH.

MARCH 5, 1888.

My name is John Philip Dewey. Originally intended by my parents for the ministry, I found, after a year's stay at a prominent theological seminary, that I was not suited for the holy work, and so turned my attention to something else.

After five years' dabbling in every business, and losing time and money in nearly all, I finally found a profession that suited me. I became a detective. I was considered a good one; very few cases intrusted to me proved failures; very few criminals slipped through my fingers. As the bloodhound, I seemed to be the possessor of an unfailing scent, a something that led me straight and undeviating upon the track of crime. I became famous in time, and was appointed upon the force of secret workers of the great city of New York. I arrived at headquarters at a quarter past eleven upon the morning of the 5th of March. I found the chief busily engaged in perusing an extra edition of the *World*; so engrossed, in fact, that he did not notice my entrance. The sound of my voice wishing him "Good morning," aroused him.

"Just the man I wanted," he cried, in a voice slightly tremulous from excitement.

"Glad I came, then," I answered.

"Come here, Dewey," he exclaimed.

I advanced to his side.

"Read that," thrusting the paper into my hands.

I read where his finger indicated. This is what I read (I have the clipping before me as I write):

"A Bold, Daring, Inexplicable Robbery!"

I smiled at the free use of adjectives in the heading and proceeded.

"One of the most daring robberies of years occurred here last night, by which the Sixth National Bank is loser to the extent of $60,000.00. The strange part of the affair is the fact that the safe shows no signs of having been tampered with. There is no evidence of force having been used to open the doors of either the building or the vaults from which the money was abstracted. The janitor was found in a heavy stupor from which it was difficult to arouse him, and, when brought to his senses, was unable to give any satisfactory explanation. It would have been impossible for him to have taken the money, as he does not know the combination, the secret of which is intrusted only to the cashier, and is known only to the president, beside. Mr. Gordon (the cashier) was much distressed when the robbery was discovered. He had been by the bedside of his sick mother all the previous night, which fact the physician who is her attendant testified. Here is a chance for some one of the many smart detectives we hear so much about and see so little of."

I read the article through twice, and then handed the paper to the chief.

"Well; what do you think of it?" he inquired.

"I have not begun to think, yet," I answered coolly.

"Do so; I may want to use you on this case."

"When you decide to use me, then I will put on my thinking cap."

The chief frowned slightly. He evidently considered me trifling. The truth of the matter was, I did not know what to think.

"Come, Dewey," he spoke sharply; "give me your candid opinion of this affair. You are the shrewdest man I have on the force, and I would like you to express your ideas. I would like to show these sarcastic 'penny-a-liners' that the detective force *can* be seen occasionally."

The article had nettled my chief somewhat—that is, the concluding portion. I began to run over the affair in my mind.

"Doors not forced; safe not tampered with; combination known only to cashier and president." I spoke my thoughts aloud.

"Yes; yes."

I sat down before the chief.

"The robbery has taken place; someone has committed it. In order to do so they must first have obtained entrance to the building."

"Very evident," my chief spoke, sarcastically. I noticed it.

"If the doors were not forced the thief must have entered some other way."

"There is not a sign of violent entry at any point."

"The paper does not state that."

"I have had a man there already."

"If you have appointed a man, why not leave the case in his hands?" I spoke as I felt, a little nettled.

"I have not appointed anyone, Dewey. I merely sent Rogers up to look over the place. This is a case for *you*—not for him, or anyone else."

"Then the best thing for me to do is to go to the bank and look over it myself. I may be able to express an opinion better after I have been upon the scene."

"That is what I intended to have you do. I only wished to ask your opinion before sending you."

I made no answer; merely rose, and prepared to commence my investigation.

"Then you put this case in my hands?" I asked, buttoning up my overcoat.

"Surely. Report to me at three, and let me know what you have discovered." I bowed. My chief had some peculiarities. He used superfluous language occasionally. I might have been off ten minutes sooner, but for his delay in unnecessary questioning.

That ten minutes would have saved me much trouble. I filled my well-colored meerschaum as I hurried down Broadway. I can always think better when my pipe is well lighted and smoking easily. I had a walk of fifteen minutes before me, and I reviewed the circumstances of the robbery in my mind as I walked along.

I had very little idea about the matter as yet. Most men would have held some suspicions as to the honesty of the cashier, but I did not allow any such thought to enter my head. I seldom take things for what they seem to be; I investigate—one great reason for my various successes, I think. I soon arrived at the bank—a massive building of granite, the upper stories being let out for offices. The business of the bank was done upon the first floor, which was reached by a flight of wide stone steps. The vaults for safe deposit were in the basement, the safe for moneys for immediate use upon the floor of the bank proper. I knew all this, as I had been in the building many times previous to this visit. I walked up the stone steps and into the bank. I found every employé at his particular place; the appearance of none of their faces would lead anyone to believe that anything out of the common order of things had happened so recently. I missed the calm, intellectual face of Gordon, the cashier, however; he was not at his window. I knew Gordon by sight, understood his character pretty well; a decent young fellow, who loved his old mother with the fondness of a young husband. I stepped up to his window; the assistant cashier filled the position.

"Is Mr. Gordon about?" I inquired.

"In the president's room," was the answer.

"Can he be seen?"

"I think not."

"My business is urgent."

"Can't I attend to it?"

"No."

"You had better call again, then. I know he will not be at leisure for some time," and the assistant cashier turned to his book.

I turned also—from the window. I allowed my eyes to glance about the place. I wished to get a thorough idea of the "lay" of the interior. I saw that the walls were of granite, there being no window or aperture of any kind on either side. No possible way for any burglar, no matter how skillful, to force an entrance into this stronghold of wealth, without taking much time and leaving some trace behind him. I carefully sauntered toward the rear of the large apartment. I had a pretty general idea of the location of the president's private office, and wished to find it without asking any questions or creating any suspicion in the minds of the numerous clerks and attachés as to the nature of my business. I took my time, as I wished to examine the interior carefully before appearing before the ruler of this domain. I reached the rear of the building without discovering anything, and saw before me a heavy door of walnut with the words "President's Office" engraved upon a brass plate attached to one of the panels. I rapped—no answer. I rapped again, louder this time. The door opened and I saw George Gordon in the opening. His face looked haggard and careworn, not guilty. His eyes appeared as one who had lost sleep. I presented my card before he had a chance to say a word.

"J. P. Dewey," he read.

"What do you wish?" he asked.

"To see you," I answered.

"I am very busily engaged; can't you make it convenient to call again?"

"I am a detective," I said, simply. He gave another quick glance at my card.

"I have heard of you," he said, quickly. "You are celebrated. Yes, you can see me; you are just the man I want to see."

My chief had made use of words to the same effect an hour before. I followed Mr. Gordon into the room. I found myself in the presence of the directors of the bank, so I afterward found them to be. A dozen well-dressed, elderly gentlemen, each with an expression of anxiety upon his well-bred face.

"Mr. Dewey, a detective," announced Gordon.

"Ah! You were sent here by Inspector Byrnes?" exclaimed one of them; the others looked at me, expectantly.

"You are right, sir," I answered this one, bowing to them all. Gordon pushed forward a chair, which I took; he then took his position opposite me.

"What do you think of this affair?" inquired the gentleman who had spoken before.

"I have come for information that will create thought," I answered.

"You have read the newspaper accounts?"

"Yes."

"They are reliable."

"That may be; but they do not explain."

"Nor can we. Is it not your business to try and explain matters of this nature?"

I thought I detected a slight tinge of sarcasm in the inquiry. I bowed.

"And I propose to try and explain it just as soon as I am privileged to begin," I answered.

"Well sir; you have the privilege—begin."

"Then I must ask that I can be alone for ten minutes with the president."

The directors looked from one to the other, then one of them remarked:

"We are all interested in this matter."

"Do you *all* know anything about it?" I asked sharply.

"No."

"Nor do I," spoke he who had first spoken—the president I now knew him to be.

"Do you all understand the combination of the safe or vault which has been robbed?" I next asked, without noticing the president's remark.

"No."

"Then I must speak to the president, alone."

Gordon arose and opened the door leading to an adjoining room, and the dignified directors filed out one by one, leaving me alone with the head official.

"Now, sir, that we are alone, what is it?" asked the president, stiffly.

I felt nettled at his evident pomposity and determined to bring him off his high horse.

"You lost $60,000.00 last night, I believe?"

"The entire city knows *that* by this time."

"Very likely. Do you wish to recover it, or have thief apprehended?"

"Most assuredly."

"Then oblige me by forgetting for the time being that you are the president of the Sixth National Bank, and become a man of common sense, who is willing to be questioned and advised by one who understands his business, and is willing to assist you."

"I do not understand you."

"Evidently, or you would not adopt a stiff-necked policy in dealing with me. I wished to question you privately for a good and sufficient reason, or I should not have asked that privilege. I wish my plans known only to you and myself when I have formed them. So oblige me by giving me your attention and answering my questions."

The face of my companion flushed under my sharp words. I saw that he did not like them very well, but they had the effect that I desired, for he became less dignified.

"I will answer your questions," he said.

"Good. I understand that the combination of the burglarized safe (if you can call it such) is known only to yourself and Mr. Gordon?"

"That is correct."

"You are positive of this?"

"Absolutely."

"Could the safe have been opened by a skillful removal of the outer knob and its connecting bolts, and then replaced?"

I asked this question knowing full well that such a thing was impossible, as it would leave a trace, but I wished to get at his ideas, and so I asked it.

"Certainly not," he replied energetically. "You have not seen the safe?"

"No."

"I will show it to you."

Just what I wanted, so I followed him. He led the way to the massive receptacle of wealth. I examined it carefully. No sign of forcible entry. The safe had been opened by someone who understood the combination.

"What do you think of it, now?" asked the president, as we were again seated in the private office.

"That the safe was opened by someone who was familiar with the combination," I said positively.

"Then you think Gordon the guilty one?" he cried in a suppressed tone.

"I did not say so."

"You surely don't imagine *me* the robber?" he gasped in astonishment.

I smiled.

"I did not say so," I repeated.

"Damn it, man; you are mysterious," cried the president, excitedly rising from his chair.

"Sit down, sir," I said calmly.

He did so. I continued:

"I do not consider you guilty of stealing your own money, neither do I wish to say that young Gordon has appropriated the funds. One thing is certain. Someone has taken it, and that one did not force open the doors of the bank, nor the safe. Now it comes to a focus. If there are but two men who know the combination, it looks as if one of those two men had opened the safe and taken the cash."

"It would certainly appear so. Some of the directors even think so."

"Oh, they do, eh?"

"Yes."

"How long has George Gordon been in your employ?"

"Ten years."

"Always proven faithful?"

"Always."

"Not wild, dissipated, women, or anything of the kind?"

"A perfectly moral young man to my positive knowledge. He lives home with his mother, and is a good son."

"You are sure of this?"

"Absolutely."

"Your janitor and watchman?"

"Is as honest as the sun; besides, he could not have possibly taken the money."

"Would it have been possible for anyone to have entered the building without being seen by him?"

"No; unless he had been drugged."

"I understand that he was found in a stupor, from which it was difficult to arouse him?"

"Yes; and has not recovered fully yet."

"Who discovered him?"

"One of the clerks whose business calls him here earlier than the rest. He found the main entrance doors fast locked at seven o'clock in the morning. This created much surprise in his mind, as the doors are usually open at six to admit the cleaners, who were even then patiently awaiting admission. Gordon does not live a great distance from the bank, and, knowing that he had a key, the clerk went to his house. Gordon seemed much surprised to hear that the building was not yet opened, and gave Patterson (the clerk) his key, saying he would be over as soon as he had eaten his breakfast. Patterson hurried back, and, opening the doors, found Jewett, the janitor, lying in a stupor upon the floor. He first thought him dead, but his heavy breathing denoted that he was only sleeping, but so soundly that it was only after a vigorous shaking and the application of ammonia to his nostrils that he came to his senses. He was carried to his room in the building and has been nearly unconscious since."

"Have you been able to get anything out of him?"

"Very little. Gordon, upon his arrival, sent for a physician, who claimed that he had been drugged. He administered a preparation that kept him conscious for twenty minutes, and while so we questioned him."

"Had the robbery been discovered at the time you questioned him?"

"Yes. Gordon's first act, upon reaching the bank, was to open the safe, and he at once detected the robbery and telephoned me."

"Why did he go to the safe at once? Did he expect to find it rifled?"

"The janitor's strange condition caused a feeling of alarm, and he opened the safe."

"How could it have been possible to drug the janitor?"

"I can not say. It is a mysterious affair from beginning to end."

"Decidedly so," I answered.

I must confess I felt mystified. I could not bring myself to believe Gordon guilty, although I must say it looked very much against him.

I sat silent for at least five minutes. I was thinking deeply.

"Well, what is your idea?" I heard the president ask, anxiously.

"I would like to see Mr. Gordon privately," I stated, without replying to his question.

"You are through with me, then?"

"For the present, yes."

"You did not answer me. What is your idea?"

"I have formed no opinion, as yet. I may be able to do so before I leave the building. If I do, I will inform you."

The official arose and bowed.

"I will send Gordon to you," he said, and left the room, going into the one where George Gordon had ushered the directors some time before.

In a moment Gordon made his appearance. He walked slowly, like one suffering, to the centre of the room and threw himself heavily in the arm chair recently occupied by the president.

I made no remark for several minutes; I wanted him to begin. As he did not do so, I said:

"This is a very mysterious affair, Mr. Gordon."

"It is to me," he replied. "Some of those worthy gentlemen in the room yonder do not seem to think so, however."

I recalled the president's words.

"They think you know something about it, eh?"

"Yes," with a sigh. I saw that he felt badly.

"I do not think you guilty, Gordon," I said. He looked up quickly.

"You do not?"

"No. I must say that things look very much against you. An ordinary person would say at once that the case was simple enough; that there could not be much doubt about the matter. As but two of you, the president and yourself, knew the combination, and it is evident that the safe was properly unlocked by one who understood it, they would declare that you must be the guilty one, as the higher official could certainly have had no reason for stealing his own money. You can see how the matter appears."

"But I can prove that I was by my mother's side all night."

"So I read in the extra of the *World*. But could not the money have been taken before you left the bank? He rose from his chair.

"I never thought of that. But no; the president was by my side as I secured the safe."

"I do not say that I think this was done," I remarked; "but in order that we can get at this matter, suppose you relate to me the full particulars of last night. State where you went after leaving the bank; who you had any conversation with—in fact, do not omit anything, no matter how trivial it may appear to you."

"I will do as you ask; it is simple enough. I secured the safe at about half-past four yesterday afternoon, and left the building in company with Mr. Lippincott, the president. We parted at the corner, he going into a restaurant upon the corner, I hurrying home to my mother. I found her suffering greatly, and immediately sent for our family physician, who arrived at about seven."

Here he stopped for a moment. I waited for him to resume.

"Well?" I remarked, interrogatively. He recovered himself; he had been thinking.

"Excuse me," he murmured. "My mind has been wandering all day. Loss of rest it must be."

"Very likely."

"To proceed. The doctor arrived about seven. He looked grave as he glanced at my mother's face and felt her pulse. 'Is it dangerous, doctor?' I inquired. 'So much so that I shall remain here all night,' he said. This, of course, alarmed me, and I refused to take my rest, although the doctor promised me that he would call me if he needed me, and urged me to retire. I refused to do so, however, and sat, silent and oppressed, by her bedside all night, the doctor keeping me company until five this morning."

"The doctor was with you all this time?"

"Yes."

"And you did not sleep at all?" A flush came to the weary face of Gordon.

"Well, I must confess. I *did* sleep a short time."

"Why did you keep this back?" For the first time he hesitated, and seemed annoyed.

"It is such a peculiar matter that I did not care to mention it."

"Peculiar? The fact of your sleeping peculiar? Why? Come, tell me all."

I spoke in a tone of amazement. He hesitated a moment, and then said:

"As you wish it, I will, although it can not have any bearing upon the subject. As I before stated, the doctor seemed anxious for me to take my natural rest. 'You will have a hard day before you to-morrow, and you will need your sleep,' he said. As I still refused, he shrugged his shoulders, and desisted from his endeavors in my behalf. Shortly after one o'clock my mother fell into a doze. She seemed to be much easier. 'Your mother sets you a good example,' the doctor whispered; 'you can take a nap while she sleeps.' I agreed to do so, and stretched myself out upon a lounge in the room adjoining. But I could not sleep, and told the doctor so. 'I will help you,' he said, with a smile; and, coming to my side, he placed his hand upon my head. In a short time I felt a tingling sensation. I heard a low voice, saying, 'Sleep! Sleep!' and I knew no more until I was awakened by the doctor, and found it nearly four o'clock. I arose from the lounge; my head felt strange, my body felt unrefreshed and fatigued; my sleep had not done me much good. I told the doctor so. He smiled, and said, 'You were probably worrying in your mind while you slept.' My mother still slumbered, and at five the doctor left the house."

I did not speak for some time; I was thinking. Finally, I said:

"Then the doctor soothed you to sleep?"

"Something of the kind."

"And you were ashamed to tell me?"

"Yes; it seemed to me to be so weak on my part."

"Who is your family physician?"

"Dr. Westinghouse."

"Westinghouse?" I repeated the name. It had a familiar sound. "I think I have heard the name before. I can not place it."

"He is celebrated from a course of lectures he gave some time since, on 'Mind and Matter.'"

"Oh, yes!"

I remembered the man. I had never seen him, but he had created a furore in the city by his lectures. I sat for some time thinking deeply on what Gordon had told me. A wonderful power this physician must have possessed to soothe another into slumber to last until he saw fit to arouse him. A terrible power if used for the wrong.

"And this is all?" I said, finally.

"All, up to the time when young Patterson called for my key to open the bank; and I came, opened the safe, and discovered the robbery."

"I understand that you sent for a physician to attend to the janitor upon your arrival?"

"Yes."

"Was Jewett unconscious when you arrived?"

"Nearly so."

"What did the physician say regarding him?"

"That he had been drugged."

"Can I see Jewett?"

"I think so. But you will not be able to get much satisfaction from him."

"He has made some explanation, I hear?"

"He simply says that he was passing by the door which opens into the street, when he felt a strange sensation, as if someone was taking possession of his senses, so he describes it. He tried to open the door, when he lost consciousness, and knew no more until brought to by the use of ammonia."

"Well, that beats anything I ever heard of." I cried; and, to tell the truth, it astounded me. I determined to see the janitor, and conducted by Gordon, I soon stood by his bed.

A strong, hardy man I saw him to be. Apparently sleeping, I stood watching him for some time. I could see the muscles of the face change as I watched. An expression of fear—of horror—came to the coarse lips and dark, swarthy face; and he suddenly sat erect, opening his eyes as he did so. Glancing about the room as if in search of something, he caught sight of me, and with a sigh, fell back upon the bed.

"Jewett," I said, sternly. The eyes opened again. "I must speak to you," I continued.

"No, No," came in a hoarse whisper from between the parted lips.

"But it is necessary," I cried. "I am a detective; I must hear what you have to say."

"Nothing; nothing," he moaned, tossing restlessly.

I bethought me of my pocket flask. I usually carry some good brandy in case of an emergency. I placed it to his lips; he drank eagerly, and I could see it revived him. He lay still for a few minutes after drinking, and then whispered—

"You are a detective?"

"Yes."

"You want me to tell you what I know?"

"Yes; I am waiting."

"Have you not heard from others?'

"Yes; I have been told what you said this morning."

"That is all I have to say. I don't know any more."

I turned away, somewhat disappointed. The man saw it.

"Listen," he whispered; I *can* tell you something else, but you won't believe it."

I hastily sat down by his side; I could hear the eager breathing of Gordon behind me.

"Tell me, anyhow," I cried. "You don't know whether I will believe it or not."

"*I know how I lost my senses.*"

I started to my feet. He knew how he had been thrown into the death-like stupor in which he was found! How could this be possible?

"Tell me, then," I cried, trying to control myself. In a husky whisper came the words—

"*I was mesmerized!*"

I felt now more surprised than ever. I even felt an inclination to laugh. I could not believe it possible for a man to be mesmerized through a heavy oaken door; but I asked—

"How do you know this?"

"I have been mesmerized before, two or three times."

"Who by?"

It was Gordon who now spoke, his voice sounding unreal. The janitor looked up in his face and replied:

"Oh, it is you, Mr. Gordon. I did not see you. You know, don't you? I told you about it. Don't you remember?"

The husky voice seemed to sound clearer as he spoke to his superior.

"What do you know about it?" I demanded in a quick tone.

Again the face of Gordon flushed.

"Not much," he faltered. "I believe I do recall the fact of Jewett telling me something about going to a meeting or entertainment somewhere, and becoming influenced by a professor of psychology."

"Yes, I told you," cried Jewett.

"What was the professor's name, Jewett?" I demanded.

"Dr. Westinghouse!"

If a bomb had fallen and burst before me I could not have felt greater surprise. I now understood why the face of the cashier became flushed and his manner ashamed. Dr. Westinghouse had mesmerized him to sleep the night before, and he felt sorely ashamed of the fact; so much so, in fact, that any mention of it caused the blush of shame to crimson his cheeks. So Dr. Westinghouse gave exhibitions of mesmerism; he could control the strong and mighty as well as the weak. I was going to speak to Jewett again, when I observed that he had relapsed into his heavy slumber once more. So with a sign to Gordon to follow me I descended the flight of stairs that led to the lower portion of the building. As we reached the foot of the stairs I turned to the cashier and laid my hand on his shoulder.

"I am going, Mr. Gordon," I said. "If Mr. Lippincott should inquire about me, or my questions and investigations, give him an evasive answer. I don't want him to know what Jewett has said. I don't even want him to know that I saw Jewett. This case is a very strange one, but I have a peculiar idea, an unprecedented suspicion, that I know the person who has robbed this bank. Keep your tongue between your teeth (you will not be arrested; I will look out for that), and you will hear of something that will startle you before long."

With these words I hastily left the building. Going to a drug store near by I looked through a directory. I found the name I was in search of, and, calling a cab, was soon on my way to upper Fifth Avenue. We stopped before a fine residence of brown stone. I ascended the steps, rang the bell, and waited the coming of someone to answer the summons. A Negro in livery came to the door.

"Is Dr. Westinghouse at leisure?" I asked.

"De doctah has jist gone out, sah," replied the servant.

"Confound it," I muttered. "Do you know when he will return?" I next asked.

"He didn't say, sah."

"Did he say where he was going?"

"No, sah."

I felt vexed. I wanted to see this man with the wonderful power.

"How long has he been gone?" I next asked.

"'Bout ten minutes, sah."

I descended the steps. Ten minutes! If my chief had not detained me at headquarters this morning I should have seen Dr. Westinghouse! I felt much put out, and had not recovered my good humor when I reached home. I did not report to my chief at three. I sent a messenger boy with a sealed message. It read as follows:

"On the track. Nothing positive. Will report in the morning. DEWEY."

March 6, 1888.

I found Inspector Byrnes awaiting me with considerable impatience the next morning.

"Why didn't you report as I directed?" he asked abruptly as I entered his private office.

"It was past three when I had concluded my investigation, and I was worn out."

"Hum; well, what success?"

"My message was intended to convey to you the progress I was making," I answered.

"It simply says, 'On the track. Nothing positive.' What do you mean by that?"

He was excited.

"I will give you my theory, if you will give me time," I answered calmly.

"Well."

"I examined the safe, building, and every point. I found the safe had been opened in the regular way; the thief had entered by the front door, opening it with the key, for there was no sign of violent entry.'

"Rogers made the same discovery in thirty minutes."

I did not notice the interruption, but continued:

"I interviewed the president, the cashier, and the janitor."

"Ah; good."

"And came to the conclusion that none of them are guilty."

"What, none of them? Then who in the devil was it?"

In a calm tone I related all that I had been told—the cashier's statement, the action of the janitor. I saw my chief growing more and more interested as I proceeded. When I had finished he simply whistled.

"Decidedly mysterious," he cried. "Savors of the black arts. I have heard of this Westinghouse. A good physician; has a large practice; supposed to be very religious."

"I called at his house to hear his side of the story. He was not in. I shall go again this morning. I want to see him more than any of the others, *for I think he knows more about the affair than any of the others.*"

I saw that my words had produced an effect upon the inspector, for his brows were knit in thought.

"It may be," he said thoughtfully. "I have put this case in your hands. Work out your theory. Of course, all this business about mesmerism, hypnotism, and so on, is rather out of the common order of things, but there may be something in it; so go ahead."

I left the office, and in five minutes was on my way to the palatial residence of Dr. Westinghouse. The same servant answered my summons.

"De doctah is not in, sah," he replied in answer to my question.

"Not in?" I was surprised. "He must be kept busy, not to be in his office at this hour."

"He has not come back, sah."

I controlled my features with an effort.

"Not returned?"

I was going to ask another question, when I perceived the letter carrier ascending the steps. He handed two letters to the servant, and so quickly that I could not catch a glimpse of the address; but the man enlightened me unconsciously, for he glanced over the super-scription and muttered as if to himself:

"For Missus Van Buren. Dat's de doctah's handwriting, too."

A letter from the doctor! So he must be absent upon an important case, that he must needs take the trouble to write, instead of coming himself. I resolved upon a bold step.

"Is Mrs. Van Buren at home?" I asked.

"Yes, sah; she's at home."

"Take my card and tell her I should like to see her."

My card simply bore my name, so that no one could possibly understand my business. The man took the card and ushered me into the reception-room. As I entered the door I saw that the office of Dr. Westinghouse was immediately opposite the reception-room. A small silver plate, with his name engraved upon it, gave me my information. The servant left me alone in the reception-room, and ascended the stairs leading to the floor above to carry my card to Mrs. Van Buren, and also to deliver his letters, I suppose. He returned in a short time.

"Missus Van Buren will see you in a quarter of an hour," he announced, and then left me.

I heard the sound of his footsteps as he proceeded to the rear of the house, and after I was sure he was gone I softly opened the door and looked out into the hall. Fifteen minutes would elapse before I could see Mrs. Van Buren; the doctor's office was within a few feet of me; I felt an interest in this most peculiar man, so I softly crossed the hall and tried the doctor's door. It gave readily to my touch, and the next moment I was in the room. A large, comfortably-furnished apartment I found it to be. Several large bookcases held the doctor's medical library; a large secretary with glass doors in the top contained a miscellaneous collection of bottles—medicines of a variety of kinds; but what impressed me the most was the signs of disorder and confusion that showed themselves plainly. Drawers pulled out and contents in disorder; a pile of torn papers upon the hearth; a cuspidor overturned; chairs out of position. I was about to look into this more closely when I heard the sound of footsteps, so I quickly recrossed the hall and was gazing complacently at a fine painting of a handsome woman over the mantel-piece, when the door opened and admitted a lady—the original of the painting, I knew at once—only more matured.

"I have not the honor of your acquaintance, madam," I said, bowing respectfully; "and doubtless my visit has awakened some surprise in your mind. The fact is, I have called twice to see Dr. Westinghouse, and have found him absent upon both occasions. The servant seemed to be ignorant of any knowledge regarding his probable return, and I determined to speak to you, thinking perhaps you could give me some information," and I waited for her answer.

The lady looked at me with surprise plainly delineated upon her countenance.

"Really, I am not cognizant of the doctor's movements," she said. "He does not make me his confidant. He is an old friend of my deceased husband, and for that reason I rent him my drawing-room for office purposes. He sometimes eats his meals here; occasionally sleeps in his office; but aside from that I know nothing."

I felt that the woman was deceiving me, for what purpose I could not imagine. I knew that she had just received a letter from the doctor, and so must know his whereabouts. I hardly knew what course to pursue. I could not well tell her that I thought she was lying. I could not say why I wished to know; so with a respectful bow, I expressed my disappointment and prepared to take my departure, beaten for the while, but determined to yet find out what I wished to know. As I walked toward the door I remarked in a careless tone:

"The doctor and I have been friends for years. He has been attending my wife for some months. I regret that I shall be obliged to secure the services of another physician. Oh, by the way, did not your servant deliver a letter to you a short time ago?"

My first words had so completely taken the woman off her guard that, as I abruptly asked the question, she colored and clutched at the pocket of her elegant morning wrapper.

"Ah! she has the letter in that pocket," flashed through my mind. I made up my mind to have that letter if possible. Mrs. Van Buren had recovered herself.

"Yes, I received a letter," she replied, haughtily; "but it hardly concerns you, a stranger. I might say that it is a piece of impudence on your part to ask me such a question."

"Pardon me, madam," I replied, bowing humbly. "I saw the envelope as the carrier handed it to the servant, and I thought the handwriting resembled that of Dr. Westinghouse."

The lady drew herself haughtily erect. Her eyes flashed as she turned them upon me.

"Your insinuation is cowardly, sir. You forget that I am a lady. I told you I knew nothing of Dr. Westinghouse's movements. I should not have said so if I had received a letter from him. Go!"

She threw open the door and stood by it. The pocket in which I felt sure the letter was deposited was an open one, rather deeper than the ordinary run of pockets on morning wrappers. I observed it was on the side of the garment nearest the door. I bowed respectfully and humbly as I made my way toward the door, and, as I passed through, stumbled over a tiger-skin rug which lay before it. As I recovered myself I placed my right hand in my inside coat pocket, as if to express my regrets, and apologized for my awkwardness, but in reality to hide my prize, *for I had the letter.*

The lady cast a look of haughty disdain upon me as I walked toward the front door, and rang for the servant to show me out. In a few minutes I was in the street, and five minutes later, was reading the letter in a beer saloon not far distant.

The woman had lied. This is what I read:

"PHILADELPHIA, March 5, 1888.

"DEAR BESS: As my departure was so unexpected, you may feel alarmed at my continued absence. I shall not return. There is no necessity for it, as I have another and a better opening for my talents on the other side. I leave to-morrow per American Line. *Send my trunk and the case of instruments in the bottom drawer of the bureau to the Palace Hotel, Westminster, London.* I overlooked it in the hurry of my departure.

"Don't worry. You will hear from me soon.

"Yours,

"West------

"P.S.—Keep my whereabouts a secret."

The full name was not signed, but the servant's words, together with the woman's denial, assured me, and I literally flew to headquarters.

"The bird has flown," I gasped, as I rushed into the inspector's private office.

"What do you mean?" he cried. I laid the letter before him. He read it.

"I don't quite understand you yet," he said.

I turned in disgust.

"Don't you see that Westinghouse has skipped? Can't you understand that he is the robber, and has got away with the boodle," I cried.

"By G—d! it looks like it, don't it? And Byrnes turned pale.

"It is it," I muttered.

"Go after him," said the chief laconically.

"That's the only thing to do," I responded; and I grasped a paper and turned to the shipping news. "See! The *Assyrian Monarch* sails to-morrow. I'll take it. I'll be in London as quickly as the worthy doctor." I felt and spoke excitedly.

The inspector was pacing the floor. He stopped and spoke:

"You are right," he said. "This man is a slick one; we must capture him. What caused you to spot him as the man?" he asked curiously.

"Sit down, and I'll give you my complete theory, which I shall also strengthen before I sail. I was greatly puzzled when I read the account of the robbery, much more so when I looked over the bank. I heard Gordon's statement, and when he spoke of the doctor soothing him into sleep, it flashed into my mind at once that he had hypnotized him, and *that as Gordon was under the mesmeric influence of Westinghouse*, that he could be controlled absolutely by the man, *even to committing murder if commanded to do so*. I have seen these mesmeric exhibitions, and have often felt that way concerning them. I said nothing of my thoughts to Gordon, and went to Jewett, the janitor. When I heard what he had to say, I came to this conclusion: that Westinghouse had known that Gordon had a key of the bank in his possession; that there was also a large sum of money in the office safe that night; *that he mesmerized the cashier, and, while under his control, took him to the bank, forced him to open the door, then got the janitor also under the influence, forced Gordon to open the safe, put the money in his clothing, and returned to the house.* Many things go to prove that this theory is correct. First, the building has not been tampered with; the safe is found in tact. Second, Gordon speaks of feeling tired, worn-out, when he recovers—he has had hard work to do. Third, the janitor, Jewett, is not entirely free from the influence when I see him. He has been mesmerized before; he knows the sensation. Fourth, Dr. Westinghouse is known to be a mesmerist—a wonderful man in that respect, and was with Gordon that night. Fifth, he suddenly leaves a comfortable home, a large practice, without a moment's notice or preparation. He writes that he is going to Europe. He has the $60,000.00 safe in the bottom of his valise. It is as plain as A, B, C."

"By Jove! you're right, Dewey, and if you capture him you'll have your fortune made. This is the greatest case I have had come under my experience. Go; make your preparations to take an ocean voyage, my boy, and report in the morning for final instructions, cipher for telegrams, etc.," and shaking my hand heartily, he turned to attend to his multitudinous duties.

As I reached the door he called me back.

"You said you were going to strengthen your theory. How?"

"I shall call upon Mrs. Gordon, the mother of the cashier, in the morning. She is very ill, I know, but she may be able to inform me whether the doctor or her son left the house at all upon the night or morning of the robbery."

"Ah, yes; I see." And he again turned away.

I went to my lodgings, packed two large valises—one with clothing, the other with various articles of disguise. I never could tolerate a trunk. I wouldn't be bothered with one; they are as much care as an infant. I had everything ready soon, and then sat down to smoke and outline a plan of action. I studied over the various facts of the case until my pipe was exhausted, and with the thought uppermost in my mind, to call upon the mother of Gordon, the cashier, the first thing in the morning, I turned in. I slept soundly.

MARCH 7, 1888

At twenty minutes past nine on the morning of March 7, I walked up the front steps of the comfortable little residence of West Eighth Street, occupied by George Gordon and his mother, and rang the bell. I had purposely waited until the son had left the house.

A neat Irish girl came to the door.

"How is Mrs. Gordon this morning?" I inquired.

"Very wake, sur; but much bettur."

"Can she be seen? Old friend of the family," I added, as I saw the girl hesitate.

"Wait a minit; Oi'll see, sur," she replied, and hurried away.

"Mrs. Gordon says she'll see ye, sur," she announced upon her return.

I followed the daughter of Erin up one flight, to the chamber of the invalid. It was rather dark as I entered, and it took some little time for my eyes to become accustomed to the dim light, but I began to see more clearly in a few minutes, and when I did, saw that the girl was speaking in a whisper to a pale lady, who occupied the bed on the side of the apartment nearest the street.

"You wish to see me, sir?" came in a faint tone from the sick woman.

I stepped forward, hat in hand.

"Only wish to ask a question," I said.

"Ellen informed me that you were an old friend of the family" she said, weakly. "I do not remember your face."

"I am a friend of your son," I remarked, coming nearer to the bed.

"Oh, then you are welcome. Ellen, a chair."

The chair was brought. I drew it up to the side of the bed, and motioned for the girl to retire.

"I wish to speak privately," I said, as I saw a look of inquiry in the eyes of Mrs. Gordon.

The girl left the room. I hesitated a moment; I hardly knew how to begin. I was not sure that the sick one knew of the robbery; finally I said, "You have been quite ill?"

"Very."

"I heard that the doctor was obliged to remain with you all of the night of the fourth."

"Nearly all night," she answered. "He came twice."

Ah, this was a little different from Gordon's statement.

"I understood he remained all night," I remarked.

"I was so ill, that George called him in at an early hour. Both he and my son sat with me until about one o'clock, and then my boy took some rest in the room which opens from this, and the doctor left me. He returned again at about four."

"Are you sure of this?"

"Why, yes. I was perfectly conscious."

"Are you sure that your son did not leave the house with the doctor?"

I spoke eagerly. She observed it.

"Why do you wish to know this?" she asked.

"I hesitated. I did not care about giving my true reason. I could not think of any other for the instant. At last I said:

"Oh, I did not know but what your son had gone out for a breath of fresh air, or had gone to the door with the doctor."

She turned wearily in the bed.

"I hardly think he could have done so, as he was sleeping."

True, but in a sleep which could be controlled by the author of it. I did not say this, but it came to my mind. I glanced about the room; I saw the door opening to an adjacent one.

"That is the room where your son slept?" I asked.

"I can not remember. Please excuse me, sir, but I feel very weak, and it seems to me that your questions are of a strange nature."

I arose to my feet.

"Pardon me madam," I cried; "only idle curiosity. I came to question you upon another subject, but I can see you are fatigued. I will call again.'

She made no reply. I could see it was an effort for her to speak. I knew what I wished to, and so thought it useless to annoy her further. I left the room.

The girl was waiting outside. As I walked down the stairs, I casually inquired:

"Has the doctor been here this morning?" I asked the question simply for something to say. The answer surprised me.

"Not this mornin', sir. *He called at tin o'clock last night.*"

I nearly fell down stairs.

"Dr. Westinghouse?" I cried sharply.

"Yis. Sure, we has no other."

I stood for a moment at the foot of the stairs, dumbfounded. Had I not read a letter from him, in which he stated he was about to set sail from Philadelphia for London the day before? How could he possibly have done so and be in New York at the same time?

The only reasonable solution that came to me was that he had changed his mind and had returned to New York—rather a foolhardy thing. So much the better. I will have him right in my hands, I muttered.

"Is he coming to-day?" I asked the girl.

"Sure, I don't know, sur," she replied.

I saw there was nothing to be got from her; so I left the house and hurried to the bank, thinking that I could get an explanation from Gordon.

I found him at his window.

"Has Dr. Westinghouse been at your house since the night of the robbery?" I asked him in a low whisper, without any appearance of eagerness.

"Yes; he called last night, for the last time, he said, as he was going to take a trip to California for his health, and would not be back for several months."

Ah! he had been there sure enough; was probably in the city yet. I told Gordon I expected to be absent myself for some time, and instructed him to report anything new to headquarters, and then bade him good-bye. I proceeded to headquarters, reported to the chief what I had discovered, and sent Rogers to the office of the doctor to see if he was at home. I did not care to go myself, for fear of being recognized.

In an hour Rogers returned.

The doctor was not at home; had been absent several days.

I felt puzzled.

Why had he come to New York? Surely not to visit Mrs. Gordon especially. Perhaps Rogers had been deceived; they might have lied to him at the residence of Mrs. Van Buren. There must have been *some* urgent reason for the doctor's presence in the city.

What was it?

I determined to go to the house myself. I was close pressed for time, if I had to take the ocean voyage; I had not secured my passage nor completed my arrangements; but I thought it best to run the risk of capturing the wily doctor in the city, rather than make any uncertain jumps across the "big pond." I told the chief my thoughts; he agreed with me. So I arranged a clever disguise, and sallied forth.

I did not go to the house at once; I watched it from the outside. Nothing suspicious. So I boldly walked to the front door for the third time, and, simulating great anxiety, pulled the bell violently. I was made up for a genteel, middle-aged man.

"For God's sake, tell the doctor I must see him at once," I cried, as the negro opened the door. I even tried to force my way in. The servant pushed me back.

"De doctah ain't in; don't be shovin' dat way."

"But my wife—she is dangerously ill. He was to have called this morning," I persisted.

"He ain't in," repeated the man.

"He was at my house last night," I said, for a feeler, "and promised to be back this morning."

"Do you reside at 240 West Fourth Street?" inquired a voice in the hall.

I recognized Mrs. Van Buren. She came to the door. I saw she had a card in her hand. An inspiration—"Yes, yes!" I answered, not knowing why.

"The doctor will call at your house at 2 o'clock. He has been gone for several hours, visiting his patients, and he left word with me that in case of anything urgent he would be at that address at 2. He mentioned the fact of having been there last night; also one other place."

I thanked her, and descended the steps with a feeling of triumph in my heart. I congratulated myself that I had acted as I did. I returned to headquarters and related my experience to the inspector.

"You see, there is something crooked," I said. "The woman knows all about it, and lied to Rogers to shield the doctor. I acted my part of the grief-stricken husband so well that she gave herself away. I will be at 240 West Fourth Street at 2."

I looked at my watch. It was nearly 1. So removing my disguise, I went to a restaurant near by, had some lunch, and, well satisfied with myself, made my way to the address given me by the woman. It wanted ten minutes of 2 as I reached the corner of Tenth Street and West Fourth.

I wanted to be punctual; so I stepped into the saloon upon the corner, called for a glass of beer, sat down at one of the tables in the place, and drank it leisurely. At precisely 2 I rang the bell at No. 240. A little, dried-up old woman appeared at one of the front windows.

"What do you want?" she demanded.

"Is Dr. Westinghouse here?" I asked.

A change came over her face. Why, I was puzzled to explain. An expression of satisfaction, it seemed to be. She left the window and came to the door.

"He is not here yet," she said. "But we expect him every minute. Did you wish to see him?"

I informed her that I did. I did not say *how* eagerly I desired to gaze upon his face.

"Well, you kin come in and wait if you want to. He'll be here byme-by."

I followed her into the house and was ushered into the parlor. A dingy, dark-looking place. My hostess seemed desirous of making my waiting pleasant, for she took the trouble to unfasten the front windows so as to admit the light and reveal to my gaze the interior of the room more distinctly. She gave me a complete history of her family, showed me all the portraits in a dirty album, mentioned the fact that a remarkably plain young woman, in a stiff looking black dress, whose portrait adorned the wall, was her "darter," who was sick upstairs, and in this way filled in a half-hour.

I grew impatient.

"The doctor is late," I ventured to say.

A smile broke through the wrinkles of her face. I could not see anything amusing in my remark.

"Yes, kinder late," she said; then, with an apology, saying she would be obliged to leave me for awhile, she left me. I breathed a sigh of intense relief. I was glad to get rid of her.

I waited for thirty minutes longer, and was growing decidedly impatient, when I was relieved by hearing the door open behind me. I was staring at a badly executed crayon of a large man with small eyes and flowing side-whiskers, upon the easel in the corner, so my back was toward the door. I turned, and uttered a cry of astonishment; for before me, with an illy-concealed smile of triumph upon her lips, stood *Mrs. Van Buren*!

She advanced to the center of the room, dropped gracefully into an easy chair which stood by the center-table, and motioned me to a chair. I remained standing.

"You did not expect to see me?" she questioned.

"Hardly."

"I thought not. Sit down. I have quite a little to say to you. You will grow fatigued."

She spoke easily, carelessly, like one who holds a winning hand. I could not comprehend her, although my brain was busy. I concluded to hear what she had to say. So I took the chair she motioned me to, and sat down.

"I know you are amazed to see me here instead of Dr. Westinghouse, Mr. Dewey. Shall I say that I am not at all surprised to see you?"

"Well," I muttered.

"I knew you were coming. I provided entertainment for you until I could find time to have this conversation. An hour ago it would have been premature, but now, it is just the time. You are a very smart detective, Mr. Dewey. I have heard of you frequently. Your astonishing skill and peculiar aptitude for disguise has often appealed to my admiration. It is something to defeat you. I feel a thrill of pleasure as I think of it."

Defeat! I sprang to my feet. I stood before her.

"Explain yourself, woman," I demanded.

"Now, don't become ungentlemanly; remember, I am a lady, and a poor, weak woman. You are a *great, strong* man, whose very name makes criminals shudder." She spoke mockingly.

"What does this mean?" I cried. "Where is Dr. Westinghouse?" I trembled with eagerness and passion. She looked up at me and smiled.

"You are like a parrot," she said. "You have done nothing but ask that question for the past two days. I wonder if you really wish to see the doctor. How is your poor, sick wife?" Again that mocking laugh.

I now understood that she had known me despite my disguise of the morning, and had sent me to this place to throw me off the track. I made up my mind that the proper course for me to pursue under the circumstances, would be to hear what she had to say. I felt decidedly humiliated; I determined to appear more so, for she might in the flush of triumph let drop something of importance. So I hung my head, as if in shame. She observed it, for she said:

"You may well hang your head, for you have cause to feel ashamed. You made a grave mistake when you stole that letter from my pocket yesterday, for when I discovered its loss my suspicions became aroused. I sent a faithful servant to inquire for one J. P. Dewey, at police headquarters. I learned of your fame through what he heard. I determined to beat you. I have succeeded in doing so; for while you, decoyed me, have been waiting to see Dr. Westinghouse, whom you wish to see *so* badly, he has left the city and the country, and is even now beyond your reach."

I turned red with anger. I began to understand. The woman had telegraphed, or in some way conveyed to the man that I was upon his track. He had not sailed from Philadelphia as intended, but had come to New York under cover of night, knowing that he would be safe, as I thought him already at sea; had probably called upon Mrs. Gordon in order to inform her son of his departure so he could get another physician, and had very likely been in his own house when I called. But the woman had slightly over-reached herself. She had said he had left the country as well as the city; if I could find out *how*, it might not be so bad after all. I acted boldly.

"So you have kept me here while the worthy doctor has made his preparations and got on board ship. You are a smart woman. You have kept yourself posted as to the movements of the ocean steamers. You knew the *Assyrian Monarch* sailed at 3, and you have delayed me, so he could get away on board of her."

"Precisely!" she cried, rising and facing me exultantly.

I gave a cry of satisfaction. She had admitted that he had gone upon the *Assyrian Monarch*; I felt rejoiced. My cry puzzled her; she looked at me inquiringly.

"You are a smart woman," I cried sarcastically. "Very smart. You have told me just what I wished to know. You did not remember that we have in the police department of New York City, a steam launch that can easily overtake the steamer before she reaches Sandy Hook. It is but a little past 3. I can be on my way in thirty minutes. Dr. Westinghouse is on board the *Assyrian Monarch*. He is going to England; I will accompany him."

I started for the door, throwing the woman from me as she endeavored to delay me. I reached the hall; I heard her voice behind me.

"Fool," she cried, panting with rage. "Go! You will never capture Dr. Westinghouse. You do not know with whom you are dealing. Go to England; you will not be successful. You will see; you will remember my words."

I did not stop to hear any more. I threw open the door and ran down the street. I luckily found a coupé before the beer saloon upon the corner. The driver said he was engaged by a party for whom he was even then waiting. I showed him my badge; he agreed to serve me as soon as he could inform his fare of the state of affairs. He entered the saloon, but returned in a few minutes. I ordered him to drive to my lodgings. I secured my valises, hurried to headquarters, got an order for the use of the launch, and in thirty minutes from the time I left Mrs. Van Buren was at the Battery, ready to pursue the steamship which had sailed an hour before. Here I met my first set-back. The police boat was not at her moorings. I found, upon inquiry, that she had gone up the river a short time before. I felt bewildered for a moment, but only for a moment. It suddenly came to me that there were plenty of fast tugs on the river which could make as good time as the launch. I knew the mighty steamer, while under the pilot's hands, would go slow, so I thought I could overtake her if I could get under way soon. I drove to Peck Slip. Luck was on my side, for I found there one of the very fastest tugs which ply in New York Harbor. I soon made a bargain with the captain, and in ten minutes was nearing the Statue of Liberty. Sitting upon the prow of the little snorting tug I reproached myself for showing my hand to Mrs. Van Buren. I need not have told her my plans, but I felt so elated at the time that I could not help it. I felt sure that she would cable my man to Liverpool, but I thought I would have him just as I wanted him before that point was reached, and did not give myself much uneasiness upon that score.

It soon began to grow dusk. Before it grew quite dark we sighted the long, dark hull of the steamer, and in twenty minutes were along-side—none too soon, either, for she was preparing to discharge her pilot. I saw the captain, gave a satisfactory explanation—sickness on the other side, etc.—and was assigned a comfortable cabin.

I slept that night upon the same steamer which carried my intend-ed prey. He knew it not. I had only thoughts of exultation in connec-tion with it. If I had only been privileged to look into the future—if I had only known. Better that the good ship had gone to the bottom, consigning me to a watery grave, rather than I should have been carried in safety to that which followed!

MARCH 10.

The first three days of an ocean voyage are not usually pleasant ones. Nearly everyone on board, except the old timers, are more or less given to seasickness and consequent seclusion. I was not troubled that way myself, but I was about the only passenger on board who was not prostrated. I did not miss a meal. I did not see my man until the morning of the tenth, when I met him for the first time at the breakfast-table. The captain introduced us. I was traveling under the cognomen of John Hardmann. I knew the doctor at once from the description which had been given me by Gordon upon the occasion of my first interview. I failed to chronicle this fact before, but as we were going to Jewett's room I casually asked the cashier what kind of a looking man the doctor was, and he described him minutely. I did not enter into conversation with my man. I ate my meal silently, and observed him stealthily. A peculiar-looking man was the professor, as I shall now call him; a man once seen, never forgotten. Tall, measuring about six feet, with a clean-shaven face, a massive head, adorned with a luxuriant growth of jet-black hair, so black, in fact, that it created the impression in my mind that it was unnatural, but I afterward discovered that he used no dye. Eyebrows heavy and bushy, forehead very high and broad, hands and feet large but well formed, features bold but attractive. His lips, when parted in a smile, disclosed an even, white set of teeth, and that smile, I can not describe it—so gentle, so winning—it drew one's soul directly to the man; and his eyes—those wondrous organs—they were large and soulful; an expression of kindliness, almost love, shone forth from their depths. I looked upon him as if bound by a spell. I could not bring myself to believe that he was the criminal I was pursuing, the daring thief I was bent upon bringing to justice. I finished my meal and went on deck; I felt ashamed of myself; I was carried in sympathy to this man. I was attracted to him.

I filled my pipe and lighted it. As I puffed away the last words of Mrs. Van Buren came to me. "You do not know who you are dealing with. You will not be successful."

I gave a mighty start. *This* was the secret of the man's power; *this* is what she meant—the soulful eyes, the winning smile. I shrugged my shoulders; I was myself again. He would find that *I* would not be taken in by any such nonsense. *I* would prove impervious to his power. That little word *I*, how often we use it; how much we set store by it.

I was walking slowly along the deck.

"I think we will have a pleasant passage," sounded a gentle voice behind me. I turned. Professor Weichsler.

"Yes; it looks like it now," I answered.

"Yet storms come suddenly; sometimes without warning. The brightest day sometimes precedes the darkest, most terrific storms."

"Yes; often."

His voice was like the gentle murmur of the sea upon the shore. I could not reply to him, even upon this most commonplace subject. He changed the subject.

"Traveling for business or pleasure?"

"Business."

"Ah! So am I. Business and pleasure combined. I am taking my niece to show her the wonders of Europe, as well as to arrange some matters of commercial interest."

His niece! I started. This was something I did not expect—a girl in the matter.

"I am a German, as probably you may have inferred from my name," he continued. "I shall visit 'Das Vaterland' before I return."

"Then you calculate to return?" I asked.

"Surely; my home is in America. I am wedded to my adopted country."

"You speak very good English for a German," I ventured to say.

He smiled—that gentle, winning smile.

"Why not?" he said. "I am an educated man. I have lived in the United States for thirty years; I am but forty. So you see I was quite young when I came to the country. We learn our first language when we are infants, in four or five years, merely from hearing others talk it. A German infant would speak English even if the parents could not speak one word, simply by being surrounded by English-speaking people. So, in thirty years, a person could even forget their native tongue, and learn that spoken by those around them. You can comprehend?"

I bowed. His explanation was rather uncalled for, especially at such length; but I found by a closer acquaintance that he took great care to explain at length any subject he chanced to drift into.

We talked upon various topics until the hour for luncheon; then, with a heavenly smile, he apologized and left me. I stared after him as he disappeared from sight. I never met a man I liked better, but I determined not to let that feeling control me. I must do my duty. We did not meet again until tea, but I found the majority of the passengers at the table at dinner, and amused myself studying their very expressive faces. They had all been violently affected with the sickness attendant upon a first voyage, and their faces were an amusing study, as they gathered around the table for the first time since eating their dinner while in New York Bay.

I found the place on my right filled by a young man, probably not over five and twenty, who talked very loudly, affected loud costumes, ditto ties; in fact, rather forcible in every respect. Like many others in this world, he knew it all. Every subject broached he broke into. He knew that Sullivan would get worsted in his battle with Smith; he knew that Maxwell would be convicted; in fact, he was positively certain of everything happening as he said. A decided nuisance I found him to be. Opposite me sat a pale, dignified gentleman, a minister I judged him to be from his appearance. A vulgarly-dressed man taking his large family of vulgarly-dressed children to the continent, accompanied by his wife and an intimate friend of the family, filled the balance of the seats upon the opposite side. A number of tourists, commercial men, and the usual run of voyagers, completed the list.

I did not interest myself much in either their conversation or their appearance, after my first curious survey. I finished dinner and left the cabin. At tea I met the professor, or doctor, again. He bowed politely, I might say, even ceremoniously, from his seat near the head of the table, and did not notice me again during the meal. We were all gathered in the saloon that night, each endeavoring to amuse his or her individual self before retiring. We were not well enough acquainted as yet to provide entertainment for each other.

The eldest daughter of the vulgarly-dressed man I had met at the dinner-table, was carelessly strumming on the upright piano; her father and the intimate friend of the family were discussing the markets as they were quoted when they left New York.

My neighbor of the loud voice and costume was buried in a number of the *Century*, while the sedate gentleman in black was engaged in perusing the *Christian Era*. Suddenly the young man threw down the *Century* and exclaimed in a tone of disgust:

"What blamed nonsense! Seems to me people are gittin' more superstitious and cranky every years."

As this outburst was not addressed to me, I held my tongue; the vulgar-looking man took it up, however.

"By G—d, you're right," he cried, "never seen nothin' like it."

"I've just bin readin' some of the darndest nonsense in the *Century* that I ever heard of," asserted he of the loud tie.

"What was it?" and the vulgar man leaned forward eagerly, while his daughter allowed the piano to rest for the time.

"Oh, a lot of stuff about some feller readin' a man's mind, people hidin' things and him findin' 'em. It says he could take any man from the audience and tell him just what he thought. I'd like to see that done." This in a strong tone of unbelief and ridicule.

"All fake," asserted the other.

"Of course," averred the intimate friend. "I suppose you've heard about this mesmerism business?" he continued, addressing the company at large.

"Yah!" snorted the young man. "Don't believe it. Nobody could mesmerize me. A feller tried it once, but he had to give it up; I was too much for him."

"I don't believe sich things," and the vulgar man pursed up his lips and tried to look very knowing.

"You do not understand them," remarked a quiet voice at the entrance.

The entire party turned to see who had made the remark. I recognized the voice; it was Professor Weichsler.

He came toward the group, a smile upon his face. The man who had expressed his incredulity turned slightly red.

"No; nor nobody else," he muttered.

"There you are wrong, my friend;" and the smile upon the professor's face grew more genial and kindly. "You must not think for a single moment that because some things in science are dark to your intellect, they must be so to the balance of the world. You must bear in mind that the opinions of one man do not constitute the thoughts of the millions of the world, nor do they rule it. You do not believe in mind-reading, mesmerism, and kindred scientific experiments because you do not understand them. Others do; myself among the rest."

The father of the family made no reply. He could not; but the young man who had started the subject leaned back in his chair and said in a very positive tone: "Well, I don't believe in it, either;" and picked up his book, as if that settled the argument.

"*You* are not *capable* of understanding these things," said the professor, quietly, somewhat contemptuously.

The young lady tittered, the gentleman in black smiled, the young man turned fiery red.

"I guess I know about as much as the most people," he asserted angrily.

"Perhaps;" and the professor turned the full force of his radiant smile upon the young man. "But *most* people, as you state it, don't know very much about these things."

The preacher laid aside his paper.

"Do you really believe in this so-called mesmerism?" he asked politely, addressing the professor.

The professor turned quickly. "Allow me to answer your question, sir, by asking you one. Were you hungry before you ate your dinner?"

"Decidedly."

"Were you in the same condition after you had finished the meal?"

"Certainly not."

"Do you believe that the meal satisfied the cravings of your appetite?"

"Yes."

"Why do you believe it?"

"For the reason that I had proof of the state of my condition after disposing of the meal."

"Then I will answer you. I believe in mesmerism. Why? Because I have proof of its power."

"That may be; but others have not that same proof. Upon what grounds do you take your stand as to its power?"

"Grounds?" The professor's eyes grew larger, almost luminous. "Would you really like to understand this wonderful science? Would you lay aside narrow-minded prejudice and look upon the matter unbiased by bigotry and opinion? If so, I will explain. *You*, sir, are capable of comprehending these things. Will you *allow* your mind to do so?"

He flashed those wondrous eyes full upon the minister. That gentleman slightly colored, but answered calmly:

"If you can explain to me in a consistent manner the theory of this most unreasonable, to me *unnatural*, science, as you term it, I will willingly believe."

"Good;" the genial smile again. "Mankind is peculiarly, wonderfully constructed. The student of anatomy, physiology, and so forth, will explain to you that man is composed of so many parts—bone, muscle, and so on. Life is created and kept in existence by the proper action of heart, liver, stomach, and other organs. Very good. The student of psychology divides man, living man, into two parts, which, for convenience, he terms mind and matter. It is the power of the mind which keeps the entire physical force of man in operation. Proof? While the mind is active man does not rest; he moves, lives, thinks, puts his thoughts to practical use; suffers pain, sorrow, or joy; mind it is that does this. Man sleeps; the mind is dormant. He knows nothing; sorrow, pain, joy, all emotion is done away with. Subdue the mind and we do not suffer. The use of anaesthetics in the practice of medicine is well known. Why are they used? To produce unconsciousness, to control the active power of the mind. Pain is felt in the *mind*. Does it exist there? No. Does rheumatism of the knee-joint affect the brain? No; the disease is in the *matter*, the *mind* but records it, conveys it to the sufferer. If we but control that recording power, we do not suffer, do not know.

"We take from a man suffering from deep sorrow his mind; he becomes insane, as you term it. He forgets his sorrow, because the recording power is no more. Mind rules matter. Remove any portion of that matter, the mind lives on; remove that mind, and matter becomes more or less helpless, and finally ceases to exist. You have heard of the power of imagination. What is it? Nothing more, nothing less, than an example of the controlling power of mind over matter, and that power is so great that fearful consequences have been known to ensue from its effect.

"For illustration: Some years ago a criminal was sentenced to be hanged. Certain physicians wished to exemplify the theory I have spoken of, and obtained permission to experiment upon the fellow. He was led into a room half darkened; was told that he was to be bled to death; his eyes were bandaged; he was stretched out and fastened to a bench. One of the party slightly pricked the skin at the wrist with a needle, and another allowed lukewarm water to trickle over the wrist and drop into a basin below. From time to time, one or the other would make some remark calculated to make the man believe that they were watching the flow of blood, and in a short time the fellow died. What killed him? The power of mind over matter."

Here the professor stopped. The minister smiled.

"All that you have said I agree with. I know that these things are true. I am willing to admit the power of mind over matter, as it exists in the *same body*; but can the *mind* of one man control the *mind* and *matter* of another?"

"I am coming to that. You have heard of John L. Sullivan?"

"Yes."

"He is physically stronger than you."

"I admit it."

"In a test of strength he could probably overpower you."

"Yes."

"Very well. Some men are mentally stronger than others. If John L. Sullivan were to strike you a heavy blow upon the head, you would fall senseless. You would lose the power of both mind and matter for the time being, his physical 'matter' being greater than your own."

"It is not on the same footing."

"Why not? Listen. You are a minister of the Gospel, I take it, from your dress."

"I am, sir."

"You preach to save souls."

"Yes."

"Have you ever converted any?"

"Surely, sir, this has nothing to do with the subject."

"Ah, but it has. I have attended religious revivals. I have listened to the impassioned pleadings of good men like yourself. I have seen hard, worldly men rise from their seats and come to the front to be prayed for. Why did they do it?"

"The Spirit of God spoke to their souls."

"Admitted; but the power of mind of the exhorter over that of the penitent produced the effect."

"I can not agree with you."

"Narrow minded, eh? Well, another illustration: I do not say that the hand of the Almighty is not shown in these things, but did you ever hear of Moody and Sankey?"

"Yes."

"Did you ever know of any other laborers in the good cause who were rewarded with such good results?"

"They have been fortunate."

"I have seen some preachers—good souls, earnest Christians—who have preached and prayed, preached and prayed, and yet the power of the Almighty has not shown itself to reward their efforts. I have seen another preacher take the place of this one and do good work for salvation. Why is this? The power of one man's mind is greater than that of the other. It is not only so in this particular instance, but is shown throughout all nature, both in man and the lower animals. Some men are better salesmen than others; some men are more convincing talkers than others. Mind and matter, sir; mind and matter is the cause and effect."

"But you have not yet explained the power of mesmerism to my satisfaction. I will agree with you in what you have said. I understand the fact that some men are stronger mentally than others, but this power of causing one to do as you say, while unconscious, I do not yet comprehend."

The professor wiped his forehead.

"I can only explain that theoretically. Its causes I have instructed you in; it is nothing but that. But why those causes actually produce the effects they do no man can clearly define. You have heard of somnambulism; you have read of men and women who have actually, while in an unconscious state, arisen from bed and performed household duties, gone upon the street, and many other things?"

"Yes."

"The subject of mesmerism is really in a state somewhat similar, only he performs the bidding of the operator rather than the unconscious action of the somnambulist. Ideas become associated in our minds by habits and otherwise, and one being awakened brings on another, thus forming a train thought. This is *internal* suggestion.

But impressions from without originate and modify these trains, constituting *external* suggestion. While awake the *will* interferes with and directs these trains of thought, selecting some ideas to be dwelt upon, and comparing them with others and with present impressions. A comparative inactivity of this selecting and comparing faculty, leaving the flow of ideas to its spontaneous activity, produces the state of mind known as *reverie* or *abstraction*. In dreaming and somnambulism, the will and judgment seem completely suspended, and under its internal suggestions the mind becomes a mere automaton, while external suggestions, if they act at all, act as upon a machine. These are well-known facts of the human constitution, and independent of mesmerism, though their bearing upon it is obvious. I claim that while the subject is in the state of reverie or abstraction I have mentioned, that any outside impression brought to bear upon his mind will find ready lodgment there, and he will act upon it without actually being conscious of having done so."

The black-robed gentleman made no reply to this line of argument for some time; finally he said:

"I begin to grasp your meaning. In order to mesmerize an individual the mind of the subject must be in a semi-comatose condition."

"To a certain extent, although I have seen some people susceptible to the influence without any preliminary condition. I have seen some that I could control merely by a pass of the hand, a glance of the eye. That is animal magnetism, so called. I can only liken this power to that of the cat upon the bird, a snake upon its victim."

"You said a moment ago that you had seen some *you* could control. Are you a mesmerist?"

"I possess that power, sir."

"You do? Why, then, not give us an exhibition of this power. Your explanation has interested me greatly. If I were to see an illustration of the facts, I believe I should be a convert."

The professor smile; the soulful eyes swept the apartment; the even, white teeth glittered in the light of the lamp.

"You wish to see my power demonstrated," he said slowly. "You shall. But not to-night; it is already quite late. I am exhausted. But to-morrow night, at an early hour, you shall see; you shall know." Again that survey of the saloon with those beautiful eyes; again that peculiar smile. "Good-night, gentlemen."

He was gone.

An involuntary sigh broke from me; I could not help it. As for the vulgar man and his daughter, they arose and left the saloon without a word, followed in a short time by the "loud" young man. I looked at the preacher; he answered my look.

"A wonderful man," he vouchsafed.

"A strange being," I remarked.

I turned in early. I tried to sleep; impossible. The smile of Dr. Westinghouse (or Professor Weichsler) haunted me. I finally dropped off into a troubled slumber. Those bright, beautiful eyes shone into mine, into my very soul. I seemed to hear the musical ringing voice:

"You are mine!" it seemed to say. "Body and soul. Mine! Mine!"

Through the long night, ringing, chiming, like silver bells.

"Mine! mine!"

March 11,

I awoke with a heavy feeling at my heart. I had not rested well. I laid awhile thinking of all I had heard the night before, of the dreams that had haunted my slumbers, laid and thought until I began to feel decidedly unpleasant; then with an effort, a strong exercise of will, I jumped out of my berth and dressed. I went upon deck.

It was a beautiful morning. The sun was shining upon the broad expanse of water brilliantly, joyously. The fresh air and brightness of the morning drove my doleful thoughts away, and when the voice of the steward, announcing the morning meal, was heard, I hurried to my place and ate heartily. The professor was not at the table; neither was the young man who had made himself so conspicuous the previous night.

After breakfast I took possession of a deck-chair, and ensconced myself in a place where I would not be likely to be interrupted, and gave myself up to smoke and thought. My thoughts were of the man I was upon the steamer to watch, to capture. I came to the conclusion that he had done a very unwise thing in entering into argument upon the pet hobby of a man well known by that same hobby in New York, viz., Dr. Westinghouse. When I came to arrest him upon the charge of robbery, all this would go to prove the identity of the man; whereas, if he had not exploded his ideas, I might have had some little trouble in proving that Professor Weichsler and Dr. Westinghouse were one and the same. I congratulated myself that such was the state of affairs, however, and felt well satisfied so far.

The day passed without my meeting with the man. His niece I had not yet seen at all; he kept her secluded.

I avoided the other passengers; they did not interest me in the least. I was eager for night to come; I felt an impatience to witness the exhibition of mesmeric power to be given by the professor.

Darkness came at last. The news of the rare entertainment had spread, and the saloon was filled with passengers, officers of the steamer, and all who could gain admittance at an early hour.

The professor had not yet made his appearance when I entered. I took a seat near the minister, who, I could see, was eager to witness the exhibition of power he had but little faith in. Everyone was silent; even the loquacious individual of the loud cravats held his peace.

Soon I detected a slight stir near the door, and the professor entered.

A quick glance about the well-filled apartment, and then he said:

"To-night I shall illustrate to you all the wonderful power of mind over matter. What I shall do is not the result of jugglery nor magic; it is a higher order of science, the proof that one man's mind can control the mind and body of another. I shall experiment upon any here present who are willing to be operated upon. I shall not take advantage of anyone, nor hold them up to ridicule. I would also say, that it is claimed by some that all people can not be mesmerized. I claim that *anyone can* be mesmerized if he will, and the operator has sufficient power to control him.

"My first experiment will be to show you the power of so-called animal magnetism. I shall select a subject from among you, and you will see that I will control him merely by fixing my eyes upon him."

A death-like stillness; not one objected. They seemed as if bound by a spell. Slowly the large, luminous eyes roved the saloon, first gentle in their look, then piercing, powerful, penetrating; seeming as if ready to pierce the soul, to penetrate to the innermost recesses of the heart.

At last they stopped. Their unflinching, unvarying gaze was fixed upon someone. I followed their line of vision and saw that the object was the young man who had proclaimed so bombastically the night before that *he* could not be controlled. I saw him shrink back in his chair, as if to escape from the terrible eyes. I saw his own optics suddenly become fixed and staring; then he rose, as in a trance, and slowly approached the professor.

"Go!" commanded the operator, turning his eyes toward the door. The subject obeyed, crossing the saloon, opening the door, and leaving the apartment.

"Return!" he cried, and the man re-entered. Then, by simply closing his wonderful eyes, the professor broke the spell; for the subject, standing in the center of the apartment, came to himself with a start, turned very red, and, muttering something under this breath, returned to his chair.

A deep sigh broke from all. We had been spell-bound during the experiment. The professor smiled.

"That is what is termed animal magnetism. Now I will repeat the same experiment upon others."

He did so, and failed in no case. The influence of those beautiful, yet terrible, eyes could not be resisted.

"Now for mesmerism as it is usually produced."

He glanced around the room until his eye rested upon the eager face of the vulgar man with the large family. "You, sir;" he said quickly. The man nodded his head. "Look at me, sir." The man's eyes were riveted upon his face.

A few rapid passes, a pressing of the thumb of the right hand between the eyes, and the subject slept.

"While in this condition an arm, a leg, or both, could be amputated; the subject is insensible to pain. I shall bring him to, and prove to you that my mind controls his."

A clapping of the hands close to the ear of the subject and he recovered with a start.

"What is your name?" demanded the professor.

"Henry Balk," in an uncertain tone.

"No, sir; your name is Joshua Whitcombe."

"Yes; Joshua Whitcombe," acquiesced the subject.

"You are a fine singer."

"Yes; very fine."

"You are now upon the stage of the Academy of Music; sing for the large audience you see before you."

In a cracked, broken voice, Balk began to sing; in the midst of it the professor brought him to.

He rubbed his eyes, and then seemed to realize that he had made a fool of himself, for he flushed angrily and said:

"I will see that you don't make anything out of this, sir. You had no business—"

"Silence! You can not speak."

He said no more; he had lost the use of his tongue. I sat amazed. I could hardly credit the evidence of my senses.

A few more experiments, some laughable, some serious, and the wonderful man turned to the man of God.

"Are you satisfied now, sir?"

"Fully," answered the minister. "I believe that mesmerism is a fact." Then slowly and curiously, "Do you think me susceptible to the influence?"

"Look at me." The eyes of the preacher rested calmly upon those of the operator.

I could see that he had determined to resist the power of the other, and he saw it, too, for I saw his eyes dilate and contract; I saw a look as of a demon come to them; saw the tall form begin to undulate and sway from side to side; saw that he was laboring under some great emotion. Then the long arms stretched forth, the large white hands began to make rapid passes, weird signs, and movements in the air, and suddenly, with a moan, the minister fell back upon his chair, unconscious.

A smile, sardonic, in place of the usual genial one, came to the face of the other.

"He tried to resist me," he muttered. "None can do that. He over-rated his strength of will. Arouse!" he commanded. With a feeble gasp the minister opened his eyes. "You are all right," said the professor, and his genial smile beamed upon his victim. "You see you *were* susceptible, sir," he added. The man of God looked up with a frightened look upon his face.

"Yes," he muttered. "Yes; God save me from ever being subjected to that ordeal again. Your power is something horrible. I do not envy you, sir. Good-night." He rose and walked toward the door like one in a dream; he pushed it open, and we heard the sound of his receding footsteps. The professor turned to the assemblage, his eyes flashing, his appearance wild and thrilling.

"You see!" he cried. "He was of the most skeptical—now he believes. He knows; he has felt. But one thing more. I will give you further proof. Watch yonder door."

We turned our eyes toward the designated point. The man, who now looked almost demoniac, began those wild, weird gestures; they gradually increased in rapidity. He began to talk in a low tone. I caught the words.

"I control your spirit—even at a distance. You can not withstand my power. You can not rebel against my will. Come. Come. COME!"

This last he cried aloud. Awed, breathless, we waited; and then the door opened and a beautiful creature, robed entirely in white, entered with a faltering, uncertain step. Her hair, of a bright golden color, fell in masses to her waist. Her eyes, of deep blue, were open, but there was no speculation in their liquid depths. She advanced to the man, or demon, who held her mind in his grip.

"I have come," came in a soft murmur from her lips; "I am here."

"Yes, Ethel, you have come, my bright flower. You are here; look into the future, child; tell me, what do you see?"

A far-away look in the eyes, then a murmur:

"Danger! Danger for you! One near you; one you can see—look!"

A rapid twirl, and the eyes of the professor scanned the room—upon one, then another, until they rested upon mine. Then that beaming smile—the even, white teeth.

"You! I heard him say.

I saw the eyes dilate, and became unconscious. Then the most delicious sensations came to me. I was being carried by unseen hands to a rose-colored cloud in the distance. Heavenly music, melodious voices sounded in my ears. Beautiful women—ravishing houris—peopled the space before me. I trembled with delight. I stretched out my arms to grasp one. Then all became dark. Fire flashed above and below me. I heard a hissing as of many snakes. Then a voice cried, "Beware!" and I recovered consciousness. I was in my chair. The balance of the company were staring at me with bewildered eyes.

The professor smiled upon me. "I see *you* are also susceptible to the influence, Mr. Hardmann. Allow me to introduce you to my niece, Miss Ethel." The girl stepped forward and gently inclined her golden head. She was herself now, no trace of her former state being visible, save a wearied look in the eyes.

The professor took her hand. "I sincerely hope you have enjoyed my little entertainment," he said. "I have endeavored to please you. You can speak now"—this to Mr. Balk. "Good-night. Sleep well, Mr. Hardmann; may your dreams be blissful."

He was gone.

The company slowly filed out. Balk said not one word of complaint; he was probably thankful to be able to have the use of his tongue at all. I went to my cabin in a dreamy, uncertain way. I turned in.

"Lost—body and soul!" A voice from my heart kept repeating this until I slept; slept only to dream, to dream of a golden-haired girl with blue yes; a girl with a face like an angel. To dream of a tall form, with a massive head, surmounted with jet-black hair; a face of wondrous strength, and eyes that burned into my soul; a voice that cried "Beware!"—the face, the voice of Professor Weichsler.

March 20.

On the morning of the 20th we slowly steamed up the River Mersey. We were at our journey's end. Our passage had been a long one, thirteen days; an unlucky passage the sailors said. After the night of the mesmeric exhibition, which had so impressed us all, the weather, which had been so delightful, suddenly changed; we were tossed upon the angry waters in storm; we broke a shaft and were delayed for days.

"The devil is on board," the superstitious sailors muttered. They had heard of the exhibition, and it had a bad effect upon them; but the sun came out again, the damage was repaired, and the mighty vessel reached her destination in safety five days overdue.

I did not feel like myself for some days after my experience in mesmerism. My head ached; my brain seemed incapable of thought. I felt singularly depressed, but the feeling gradually passed away, and, thinking of it in the course of a few days, I was inclined to believe it the effect of a mind overwrought by the effect of the surroundings the night of the demonstration rather than the power of Professor Weichsler. I really gave the man credit for remarkable power, as shown in his control over the number of subjects he had experimented upon that night; but the illustration in which the fair-haired girl had figured so conspicuously I was inclined to look upon as prearranged. I could not bring myself to believe that anyone could look into the future and fortell any particular thing; neither could I believe that the mind of any man possessed the power of controlling one not within the scope of vision or the sound of voice. My dealings with the man of mystery were of a limited nature after that; when we met, always the genial smile, a pleasant word—nothing more.

The girl I saw but once after that night.

As I have stated, it was early morning as we steamed up the Mersey. I knew that in a short time our vessel would be safely moored, and we would part, perhaps never to meet again. I had my traveling-bags in readiness to go on shore at once, and was prepared to follow my man until I considered the time propitious to reveal to him the business that brought me to the shores of Britain.

I found the professor on deck, accompanied by his niece, as I made my appearance. He turned toward me as I approached and smiled, a peculiarly significant smile, it seemed to me; but it was but momentarily, for the next instant he put out his hand and said cheerily:

"Good-morning, Mr. Hardmann. You see the sun shines on us upon the first day of our arrival at our destination. A good omen, Mr. Hardmann."

I made some remark, something to the effect that it seemed so, and leaned against the rail. The man's presence affected me strangely; I could not account for it. In an hour we landed. I found my man was not encumbered with superfluous baggage, a small trunk and two hand-bags being all. We went ashore at the same time, and he selected a Hackman from among the clamoring crowd, carefully assisting the girl to a seat.

"What hotel, sir?" inquired the Hackman.

He mentioned a first-class one.

"Where are you going to stop?" he suddenly inquired, turning to me.

"I was thinking of going to the one you have just directed your man to drive to."

"So? Well, jump in; there's plenty of room; we will go together."

I climbed into the vehicle; he followed me and we were driven away.

He was very voluble as the vehicle rolled over the stones, calling my attention to the many objects of interest to be seen in the streets. I said but little, merely answering "yes," or "no," as occasion required, when he addressed a direct question to me. The young girl was also very quiet. She seemed melancholy.

We reached the hotel, were assigned rooms, and ordered dinner. I kept to my room the greater portion of the day, for the reason that the professor also kept his. He seemed to be well satisfied with himself; even jubilant. "Glad to have put the ocean between the scene of his crime and himself," I thought.

I had not as yet cabled the fact of my arrival, and was thinking about doing so; was even preparing to go out for that purpose, when the door opened and the professor entered.

"Excuse me for not rapping," he apologized. "I did not think. I came to invite you to my apartment; you must be lonely. Come."

I determined to send my dispatch in the morning. So rising, I followed him. I never saw him more jovial, more entertaining. For two hours we sat smoking and chatting. He had a box of very fine cigars, and I enjoy a good cigar. I was thinking to myself, "How his manner will change when he finds out who I am," when he suddenly stopped in the midst of an amusing recital of some personal experience, and looked me in the face.

"I did not tell you I had received a cablegram from New York?"

He asked a question. I controlled my features, and answered:

"No! News from home?"

He took a large wallet from the inside pocket of his coat, and carefully removed therefrom a paper.

"Yes; news from home," he said slowly; "read it," and he handed me the message. I took it, my mind busy with a variety of emotions. What was he driving at? I opened the paper and read:

"To Professor Weichsler, on board *Assyrian Monarch*:

"Be watchful. Look out for J. P. Dewey. You must be careful.

Bess."

I gave a start. I could not have helped it if I had been put to death the next minute. What on earth had possessed him to give *me* this dispatch to read? I felt his eyes upon me. I looked up. He was calmly smoking, but his eyes were reading my heart. I handed back the message. He replaced it in the wallet.

"I received this, this morning, on shipboard. A messenger came out on the pilot's boat."

"Some trouble?" I asked, in an unconcerned manner.

He laughed unpleasantly.

"No; not much. What do you think of it?"

I did not reply for the moment; at last I said:

"Why, I don't know anything about it. Why should I think?"

He rose from his chair; he paced the floor for a short time; he walked to the mantel and leaned upon it.

"Do you know J. P. Dewey?" he inquired.

"I have heard of him."

"Ah, a detective?"

"Yes."

"Considered a good one?"

"I believe so."

"Don't you *know* so?"

"Well, I may say, yes."

"I thought so." Silence for a second. "You see I am warned to look out for him."

"Yes; the message says something to that effect."

Silence again. I leaned back in my chair and blew clouds of smoke to the ceiling. He left the mantel and once more resumed his former position in the chair opposite me.

"You have probably heard of Dr. Westinghouse?"

The question came so suddenly, it was so unexpected, that I started slightly again. I was bewildered. What was coming?

"Yes; I have heard of him," I answered.

"Ah, you have. He is supposed to be a good physician?"

"Yes; I believe so."

"Rather eccentric, some people say, eh?"

"I really do not know."

"Don't, eh? Well, he is; I know him."

I looked him in the face.

"Do you?" I remarked steadily.

"Yes. *I am Dr. Westinghouse.*"

I arose to my feet. What did the man mean? What was he driving at? I stared at him across the table. I did not know what to say.

"Yes. I am Dr. Westinghouse," he repeated, "*and you are J.P. Dewey.*"

I fell back in my chair again. Where had this man obtained his information? He did not give me a chance to make a denial; no chance to say anything, in fact, for he spoke again, quickly, half in a whisper, his cigar held in his right hand, emitting a cloud of blue smoke that arose forming a halo about his head.

"You are the man that I am warned to look out for; such are the words of the cablegram. Why am I warned against you? Because you are dangerous. Why are you dangerous? Because you are on my track to bring me to justice. Will you be successful? No. Why? Because you are but a plaything in my hands. Keep your seat; don't rise. I can render you powerless in a second. I can make you a jibbering idiot, a raving maniac, a dumb imbecile in a moment. Keep your seat! I have known you since the first day I met you on the steamer. I *knew* you were on the steamer five seconds after you had climbed on board. How did I know? I was standing on deck when you came; you did not see me, but I saw you. I know your face of old; I have known you for years. Now, J. P. Dewey—smart man, shrewd detective—you came on board the *Assyrian Monarch* in search of Dr. Westinghouse. You have found him. You came to track him to earth as an escaping criminal, as a thief. You have tracked him—or, rather, he has allowed himself to be tracked. You are probably even now conjecturing the easiest and best manner of taking him in charge and confining him in durance vile. *You will not do so!* I have a mission to fulfill upon this side of the water. I could not allow you to interfere with my plans. I leave for London in a few minutes. You can see by glancing over your shoulder at the clock on the mantel that it wants but five minutes to 9. My train leaves at 9.20; it will take me fifteen minutes to reach the station. My niece is already there; she has been instructed to await my coming. I shall go to London, but you will remain here in Liverpool. You will be found in your room in an insensible condition; the physician will say you have had an apoplectic stroke. You will recover; but a fortnight will elapse before you are able to follow me. *My work will have then begun!* You can follow then if you desire, but you will find yourself powerless to injure me."

Like one in a dream, I had sat and listened to all he had said. Several times I had been on the point of springing upon him and putting my strength against his, but his eyes were upon me, they held me powerless, I could not stir. As he finished, I exerted every effort and sprang upon my feet. He smiled, not angrily, not sardonically, but rather pityingly. The expression of his eyes changed to one of tenderness. I never saw a more divine expression upon the face of man.

"Poor fool!" he murmured gently. "You do not know."

I stood transfixed. I could feel my senses leaving me. I could see those wonderful eyes fixed upon me. Then, in a dimly conscious state, I saw him raise his hand—that strong, white hand. I saw him make a sudden pass toward me; a feeling of having been struck a heavy blow, and I became unconscious.

SECOND MONTH.

APRIL 1.

I opened my eyes with an effort. I could not see for a moment. I felt weak; my limbs refused to act; my hand felt heavy as I essayed to lift it. As my eyes grew accustomed to the semi-darkness I perceived that I was in my own room, and that the shades were lowered, shutting out the sun. I turned with an effort, and saw that I was not alone. A man, a stranger, sat in a chair near the door. He saw my movement and came toward me.

"You are conscious, sir?" he whispered.

"Yes," I answered, feebly.

My voice was so weak that its tone filled me with vague surprise.

"What am I doing here?" I asked.

"You have been very ill, sir; we thought you would die."

I could not understand; I could not comprehend the fact of my weakness, my exceeding illness. I racked my brain until at last the truth began to creep into my befogged memory. I remembered the night in the doctor's room; his words, his actions.

"What has been the nature of my illness?" I whispered.

"A stroke of apoplexy, the doctors pronounced it. They have exerted every effort to bring you around, sir."

"Who are you?"

"A nurse, sir, from the hospital."

I lay quiet for awhile; then I asked:

"How long have I been ill?"

"Nearly a fortnight, sir."

Unconscious for two weeks! I could not credit it.

"What day of the month is this?" I asked.

"April first, sir."

"It was true. I had been sick for two weeks. Twelve days blotted out of my life! A helpless, almost lifeless, body; a thing possessed of no reason—for a fortnight. What a hellish power was that possessed by Dr. Westinghouse? Would I be able to combat this man, to conquer this power, to bring him to justice? My heart sank as I realized what a struggle it must be. I doubted my ability to make it victorious for myself. Still, I would try; I would follow him; I would bring him to earth if possible. But how long must it be before I could pursue him? I felt so weak, so helpless.

"When will the doctor be here again?"

"Very soon, sir."

The nurse placed a glass containing some liquid on a stand near my bed.

"What is that?" I asked.

"A cooling drink, sir."

"Give me some of it."

He carefully put it to my lips. I drank eagerly and felt refreshed. My mouth had been parched and dry. I turned over on my side and fell asleep. I was awakened by the sound of voices in the room.

"He is conscious," I heard the nurse say.

"Sensible?" another voice inquired.

"Yes."

"Good. Some hopes now."

I moved so I could command a view of the apartment. I saw that the newcomer was a gray-haired gentleman with a kindly face. He saw my eyes fixed upon him, and approached the bed.

"You are better, sir," he said kindly.

"Yes."

"I am thankful to hear that. We will have you out in a few days now that you have recovered consciousness."

He talked with me awhile, took my temperature, felt my pulse, nodded his head as if satisfied, and, giving some instructions to the attendant, left me.

I felt hungry, and was provided with some light, digestible food. My nurse was attentive and methodical; my medicines were given me regularly, and toward night I felt strong in mind, though still weak in body.

I slept well that night.

APRIL 2.

I awoke feeling strong; I actually thought I could rise and go about my business. I glanced about the room; the attendant was absent. I slowly crept out of bed. Yes, my limbs supported me, although I felt rather strange. I determined to dress; found my clothing in a closet on the opposite side of the room; took a hearty drink of some iced liquor on the stand by my bed, and felt good.

I was sitting in a rocking-chair near the stove as the man entered the room. He turned pale.

"You must not get up, sir," he cried; "you are not strong enough yet."

"Nonsense," I replied. "I feel all right. Go and bring me some breakfast and I'll surprise you."

The faithful fellow remonstrated, but I laughed at him; so he finally obeyed me, brought me my breakfast, and, feeling much better after eating it, I ventured to fill my old friend, my meerschaum; and much to the alarm, I might say consternation, of the nurse, I enjoyed a smoke.

"You are tempting Providence, sir," insisted the man.

"I will take the chances," I retorted.

I was still smoking when the doctor entered the room. He (good man) threw up both hands in horror.

"Are you trying to kill yourself?" he cried, coming quickly toward me.

"No, doctor; I want to live too much to do that."

"But you will, sir; what a foolhardy thing to do. You have no business to be out of bed. You should remain quiet for a week at the very least."

I laughed at the old man's concern.

"I feel all right this morning, doctor, and although I appreciate *your* feelings, still I know my *own* better. Feel my pulse; you will find it steady and strong. Look at my eye; you will see no sign of mania there."

He placed his practiced finger upon my right wrist, and his face showed extreme surprise.

"You are right," he exclaimed. "I never saw such a change in a man in this short time in all my experience. It is wonderful."

"I suppose I shall be able to get away from here soon, then?"

"Not for a week, sir; don't think of such a thing."

I said nothing, but my mind was made up. I had determined to leave Liverpool that night. The doctor left some medicine, a tonic, and, advising me not to overtax my strength, left me. I kept to my room until about 4 o'clock in the afternoon, and then, sending my attendant upon some trifling errand, I descended the stairs to the street. I wanted to try my strength. I found I could walk without difficulty, and, congratulating myself, I slowly returned to my apartment.

The clocks in the neighborhood were striking six when I nearly threw my nurse into a fit by inquiring the exact leaving time of the next train for London.

"You don't mean to say you are thinking of going to London, sir?"

"That is just what I am going to do," I answered, amused at the fellow's consternation.

"The doctor won't allow it, sir."

"He can't very well help it, my man."

"But I can; you must not think of such a thing."

"Now, my good fellow, don't try to oppose me. I must be in London to-morrow morning. I feel strong and able to go, or I should not attempt it. You go and get me a hansom; accompany me to the doctor's residence; I will settle my bill both with you and him, and shall bear with me the remembrance of your exceeding kindness through this, my most severe spell of sickness. First, bring me my tea; and then go find me a hansom."

The man remonstrated, even with tears in his eyes; but I was firm in my resolution, and he finally obeyed me. I settled my hotel bill, and at 7 o'clock was in the hansom on my way to the doctor's.

I need not mention the effect of my appearance upon the good man. Suffice it to say that he condemned my action, prophesied a relapse, etc., etc., and wound up by accepting a liberal fee and wishing me God speed.

At 9.20 I left Liverpool behind me. Six hours later I was in the great metropolis of England—smoky, foggy, dirty London.

I procured a hansom and was driven to my hotel, feeling well, a little weak, but strong in mind; strong in my determination to conquer him who had caused me all my suffering.

APRIL 3.

I had eaten breakfast and was standing before my hotel the morning of the third. Nearly opposite me was that magnificent pile, Westminster Abbey, whose fame has lived in history for centuries, and can never die. I felt that delicious sensation which sometimes comes to a man when the day is fine, when he has eaten a good meal, and is provided with ample funds. I heard the newsvenders crying their wares, and distinguished the word "murder."

As any well-informed individual knows, the venders of newspapers are very liable to exaggerate, and a slight quarrel, a manslaughter, is converted into "a horrible murder." Not but what manslaughter is sufficiently horrible, but it does not carry with it that curiosity-arousing effect that the one simple word *murder* is capable of producing.

I felt not one atom of curiosity regarding the theme of the paper sellers. I probably would not have purchased one at all had not the conversation of two men, who had been reading one of the morning papers, and who halted a few feet from me, riveted my attention.

"The most 'orrible thing I 'ave 'eard of in my life," said one—a portly gentleman with red side whiskers.

"And she was actually cut to pieces?" inquired the other.

"Butchered," asserted he of the whiskers.

"My, my! what are we a comin' to," and they passed on.

I felt curious now. I called a man who was loaded down with papers, and who was selling them with great rapidity, and secured a copy of the *Times*. I found the front columns literally bristling with startling headlines, announcing the most horrible murder of a low woman of the town, one Emma Elizabeth Smith. The murder had been committed in the early morning, in an outlying section of the great metropolis, known as Whitechapel. I read the well-written account with interest. There was not a great deal of information regarding the affair, as but few facts were known—the paper being already in press when the body was discovered—but the few facts recorded were of a sufficiently horrible nature to cause me, hardened as I was to crime in its worst phases, accustomed to the most loathsome details, to shudder. I forgot for the time my mission; all thoughts of Dr. Westinghouse left my mind. I felt attracted toward this most foul and fiendish assassination. The paper stated that the throat had been cut and the body ripped open, several parts having been taken away entirely. I determined to visit the scene of the murder, and in ten minutes was on my way to Whitechapel.

Arriving upon the scene, I found a large crowd of coarse-looking men and women gathered upon the corners and crowding about the spot where the unfortunate woman had been found.

In low tones they were discussing the event. From fragments of conversation I learned that the woman had been of the very lowest type of humanity, but the horrible manner in which she had met her death caused a great feeling of pity, even among her low associates. One woman, coarse and blear-eyed with her hair plastered down over her forehead, her skirts dirty and ragged, moaned:

"Pore Hemma; we never was good friends, but Hi forgives 'er hall she hever done me. She's 'as gone now. Ho, hain't it 'orrible to think has 'ow she died."

I felt a strange feeling of morbid curiosity to gaze upon the remains of the victim. A sturdy policeman guarded the spot where she had been found. He was stationed there to keep the crowd in order—a needless precaution. I approached him.

"Where is the body?" I inquired.

"Hat the morgue," he answered.

"Is it possible to see it?"

"No."

"I am a detective."

He looked at me sharply.

"Go hand enquire hat the place," he muttered.

I left him. As I was proceeding to the Houndsditch Mortuary, where the body had been taken, I saw two men engaged in earnest conversation upon the corner.

"The work of a butcher," said one.

"No," asserted the other positively; "not the work of a butcher. I have assisted in the dissection of many bodies. I never saw a cleaner, neater job in my life; the parts are removed as skillfully as though I had done it myself. I was attendant upon the inquest; I saw the work. The assassin understands the use of the dissecting knife, depend on it."

I stepped up to them. "Excuse me, gentlemen," I said, respectfully, "I have overheard a portion of your conversation; I am interested in this horrible affair, and would like information. You, sir, say you were at the inquest. You think the assassin a skillful worker, not a bungler?"

"That is my opinion, sir."

"Has any probable cause for the murder been discovered?"

"None whatever. Of course, all women of her type have their enemies among their associates, but to my mind the deed was not committed in a mere fit of jealous rage by a discarded lover and an enraged companion; it was done coolly, premeditatedly. The assassin took ample time to complete his work, as the condition of the body would amply convince anyone. He knew what he wished to do, and did it."

"Can the remains be seen?"

"Not unless you are a physician or an officer of the law."

"I am an American detective. I have taken a great interest in the affair."

"Probably you will be allowed to view the body. I will accompany you; I am physician."

I thanked him and walked with him to the mortuary. His companion went in another direction.

We soon arrived at the place where the body of the murdered woman lay, guarded by two grim officers of the law. We found a crowd gathered about the door and had some little difficulty in forcing our way through. At last we stood before the marble slab, where, under a dirty sheet, lay all of the mortal portion of what had once been Emma Elizabeth Smith. We were not alone. Several reporters busily writing the horrifying particulars for the afternoon papers; two men in plain clothes whom I afterward found to be detectives; the two officers in uniform; a group of physicians discussing the facts, were gathered around the slab. My companion spoke a few words to one of the physicians, who, after casting a sharp glance in my direction, nodded an assent, and gave some instructions to one of the policemen.

He, obeying instructions, removed the sheet, and I recoiled as I beheld the frightful sight before my eyes. Never had I been brought to face such an evidence of fiendish crime. I turned sick at my stomach. My companion pointed out to me the facts upon which his theories were founded, mentioning each disgusting feature in a calm, business-like tone; then the covering was replaced. I longed for the open air, and, thanking my companion, left the place.

From some unaccountable reason I felt a strange desire to ferret out the mystery of this woman's murder. I had other work to do, but felt in my heart that I would be successful in unearthing this most despicable assassin and still devote some time to finding Dr. Westinghouse. I determined to go at once to Scotland Yard, the celebrated headquarters of the London detective force. I would lay my case before the head of the mighty machinery of law-enforcing power of this great city, and offer my services in discovering the cowardly murderer in return for such assistance as might be rendered me. It was long after midday when I entered the large and decidedly gloomy office of Sir Charles Warren, the chief. He was at liberty, and, after glancing over my letters of introduction given me by Inspector Byrnes previous to my departure from New York, asked me, in a slightly lofty, but still kindly tone, what he could do for me.

"As my papers will show, sir, I am engaged upon a secret service for my country; for the City of New York."

"Yes; I understand that."

"I am a stranger here in your great city; am entirely unacquainted. I may have need of the services of your force."

"Call upon them at any time, sir; you will find them ever ready to assist you."

I thanked him.

"One thing, however, I would ask," I continued. "If you will oblige me with written authority which will instruct any officer on your force to render me aid, it will be productive of more prompt attention than if it came from an entire stranger. I may need such authority."

"That can be easily arranged, sir. It shall be as you wish."

A few words to his secretary, and I was the possessor of unlimited power to command.

"A mysterious tragedy, this Whitechapel affair," I remarked.

His brow knitted.

"Very," he said slowly. "I have sent some men to investigate."

"I have been upon the ground," I said.

He turned to me eagerly.

"What is your opinion?" he cried.

"Really; I have not formed one as yet. One thing, however, I do think;" and I told him what I had heard the physician state, omitting the fact, however, that it came from him.

"You think, then, that the murder was premeditated?"

"Yes."

"Who could have had such a feeling against this poor creature as to so barbarously destroy her and then mutilate her dead body?"

"That I would endeavor to find out, if the case was in my hands," I replied, cautiously.

"You are interested in this affair?" inquired Sir Charles.

"Very much."

"Why not work on it?"

"I was going to propose it."

"Good. I will be pleased to have you undertake it."

I could see he was gratified at my evident desire to ferret out the mystery, and left the office armed with full authority to act in any way I thought best, instructed in the various signals in use by members of the force, also secret ciphers to use in dispatches.

One thing Sir Charles explained to me before I left. The rules of the detective force stipulated that each officer must report once in every twenty-four hours the progress he had made in that time, and wait for orders before proceeding.

I tried to explain to the head of the department that this rule was a very bad one, as a smart criminal would succeed in making good his escape while the officer was waiting for orders. I saw that Sir Charles did not take my explanation in the same spirit in which it was offered. He frowned slightly and said:

"We are obliged to be governed by the state of the report of each officer detailed, and issue our orders according to the amount of success he has met with. We prefer to use our own judgment in these matters in preference to that of our inferiors."

"But do you not think that the man, being upon the ground, is sometimes better able to judge than you?"

"His report gives us the state of affairs and we can best decide what to do. Our force is large; if we were to allow each man to use his own discretion one might conflict with another, and so do more harm than good. There must be a system in these things."

I agreed with him in that and did not argue further, although I condemned his system. "Too much red tape," was the thought that entered my mind.

At parting he said:

"I will not insist upon your rendering a report in the same way. I give you the privilege of working for the discovery of this vile wretch, whoever he may be, in any way you see fit. Your chief speaks of you in the highest terms of praise. I think I can place unlimited confidence in your judgment."

I left the headquarters of the London secret service considerably elated. I vowed to unearth the Whitechapel murderer. If I could have torn aside the veil of the future how much misery, how much unparalleled horror, I would have saved myself. Tongue can never tell, pen can never write, what I was called upon to pass through. These pages, as I glance over them, seem to me but a terrible nightmare. I would fain stop where I am; but the balance must be told, and so I press on with throbbing temples, with a dull pain at my heart, to the end. It is not far distant.

APRIL 10.

The days and nights intervening between the third and tenth of this second month of my remarkable experiences were passed by me in frequenting the dens of crime and debasing iniquity with which Whitechapel abounds.

I was carefully disguised as a rough-looking sailor, and so had no difficulty in gaining admittance to any of the low dives and public houses in the section.

My inquiries were necessarily conducted with great caution. I had formed the acquaintance of a number of the murdered woman's low female associates, but learned nothing from them that would throw any light upon the assassin. By a liberal expenditure of money I soon stood hand in glove with all of the proprietors of the dens where the woman has passed most of her time; and was looked upon by them as one of themselves—brutal, heartless, a wretch who would not hesitate at any crime, or allow himself to be troubled with any compunction of conscience after committing it.

I adopted this plan thinking it the most likely to produce results; but aside from becoming posted as to the woman's past degrading history, I learned but little.

Among the facts which I did discover was the probable hour the woman had met her death. She had been drinking in a public house kept by one "Joe the Boozer," until 2 a.m. the 3d of April. She had been accompanied by a female associate, and had been considerably under the influence of liquor. She had parted from her companion, and gone in the direction of her lodgings alone. When next seen she was dead.

I inquired as to the possibility of a lover being connected with the affair.

"Noa. She hed no 'Charley,'" the low-browed dispenser of liquid fire answered with a leer.

The circumstances were enveloped in a shroud of mystery, and I was beginning to form the conclusion that the murderer would remain undiscovered. It was nearly midnight of the 10th instant. I was sitting at a beer-stained table in the hostelry of "Joe the Boozer." A light, drizzling rain was falling outside, converting the dust of the streets of dirty Whitechapel into black mud. The room was well filled with roughs, pickpockets, denizens of the pave, and their prey. A pint mug of beer stood upon the table before me, from which I pretended to drink from time to time. I was thinking deeply, so engrossed in fact, that I did not notice the coming and going of the *habitué* of the place. A voice behind me recalled me to my senses.

"A dirty hole," it said. "Isn't there a clean place near here where we can have a mug of ale and talk?"

Another voice answered:

"Joe has some private rooms upstairs; we can go there."

"Speak to him."

I heard the sound of a moving chair, as if someone had risen from a table and pushed his chair back. I cautiously looked around. I could not have explained why; perhaps I was surprised to hear a complaining voice among the frequenters of the dirty place. Most of them were accustomed to filth. Perhaps there was something familiar in the tone. At any rate, I looked around; I saw a commonly dressed man, shading his face with one hand, sitting at the table immediately in my rear. I did not recognize him as anyone I had seen before in the locality. I could not see his face. I looked toward the bar and saw him who was his companion speaking to Joe. As I looked I saw the proprietor shake his head, and the next moment the man returned to the table.

"The upstairs rooms are all occupied," he said. "Joe does a big business at this time of night. Suppose we go some other place."

The other acquiesced and rose from the table. The next moment they left the place.

There was nothing particularly suspicious about the actions of these men. One had but expressed a desire to drink his beer in quiet and cleanliness; only said he would like a place to have a quiet talk; but I felt strangely curious to see where they went, to hear some fragments of their "quiet talk." I arose quickly and paid my score.

"Goin'?" queried Joe.

"Yes. I'm tired and sleepy to-night," I answered.

"Bin up late a good deal lately."

"Yes."

I left the public house; the two men were a few paces before me. One tall, the other short in stature. The tall figure struck me as being familiar. I could not place it at the time, however.

They walked two blocks and entered another den kept by a woman who rejoiced in the nomen, given her by her customers, of "Big Nosed Kate;" a befitting title, her nasal organ being by far the largest I had ever seen. I had been there several times, and was acquainted. The room was well filled with men and women, smoke from a number of pipes also helping to fill the space near the ceiling.

Kate was standing behind the bar, while her assistant, a young man who affected corduroy and much bear grease, was showing the men I had followed to a room which was unoccupied just beside the door that opened into this room. I affected intoxication, as I wished to be left alone and listen to what was going on around me; and people will speak more freely before a drunken person than they will before a sober one. I ordered some ale from the assistant barkeeper, and after drinking some of it, leaned back with my head against the partition, which position brought my ear near the key-hole of the door. The partition was a thin one. I could hear much of what was taking place in the room, but heard nothing to reward me for my trouble; evidently the parties I had followed only wished a "quiet talk" upon ordinary topics.

I heard one man remark, "Then you think it a paying scheme?"

The other replied: "Yes; I have every reason to think so."

As I had not heard anything said previous to this about any scheme, I was at a loss to understand the meaning of the question and answer. Presently the word "murder" caught my ear. A rumbling, unintelligible hum, as of something preceding it, reached me, but the one word was all I understood. Then I heard:

"Some difficulty in finding the assassin."

"They will never find him," came next in a positive tone.

"The London police are shrewd."

"Bah; they are a set of old fogies."

"Do you think so?"

I did not hear the answer; probably the party addressed did not reply. A silence.

"What is your feeling in the matter?" came next.

"I think it a good thing." The voice now sounded more distinctly.

"What—the murder?" The questioner seemed surprised.

"Yes; a good thing that the character disposed of is out of the way."

"Well, she was a despicable creature, but to my mind the circumstances of her untimely end are horrible."

I heard the sound of a chair moving, and then clear and bell like came the words:

"You, like the rest of mankind, are impressed with the, to your mind, horrible facts of the case. You do not stop to consider that the death of this woman is a blessing to herself and the community. God put her on earth, pure perhaps, fitted for the noble work of life; endowed with power to assist in making the world profitable to herself, beautiful to others. He made her a woman—a being to comfort man and be his helpmate. How did she use the gifts of the Almighty? How had she fulfilled her mission upon earth? By debasing her mortal body, by sacrificing her immortal soul, by using the power born in her, to lure men to their destruction, by making use of God's gifts to prey upon man. Not only this, for by the force of example, by her hellish teachings, others of her sex are led astray, and the streets are filled with the young, the innocent, on the road to destruction.

"There are hundreds like her, but the eye of the All-seeing Power is upon them—it was upon her. The emissary of the Almighty was sent to remove her, to warn others of her kind of the terrible punishment which is in store for them. That life which she made such poor use of was taken from her; that which had been given her to benefit the world, to glorify herself, and which she turned to hellish profit, was removed. It has come to her. *God may see fit to visit it upon others.*"

The rising and falling of the clear voice struck upon my heart. I felt a strange thrilling of my very soul. I had heard that voice, now sounding muffled and partly indistinct, caused by the intervening partition. Oh, if I could only see into the room! I tried the door; it was unlocked; I resolved to enter the room, and take advantage of my assumed state of intoxication to excuse the intrusion. I opened the door. I entered, and the next moment was in darkness, for as quick as thought a hand had reached forth and extinguished the gas. Before I could recover myself I was thrown violently to one side. My head struck the projecting edge of a table and I became unconscious. I was aroused by feeling some cold substance thrown in my face. It was water, administered without stint by the proprietress of the establishment.

"So you've cum around, 'ave ye? What were you a doin' in 'ere?"

I looked around the room; the men who had occupied it were gone. I mumbled something about looking for the front door and rose to my feet. My head hurt me. I put my hand to it and found it bleeding. It had been cut by coming in contact with the sharp edge of the table. I settled for the ale I had ordered and staggered into the street. I puzzled my aching brain for the solution of the voice I had heard. Ah! it came to me like a flash—*Dr. Westinghouse*. Strange that I had not remembered it at once. My head must be getting bad that I should not be able to immediately place that voice. I sighed. My brain was not as clear as formerly.

THIRD MONTH

MAY I.

During the weeks that followed I made but little progress. My head troubled me greatly. I was often taken in the street with peculiar sensations of giddiness; once I even fell. I dreaded the idea of going to see a physician; I did not want to make myself believe that I required the services of one. I had been unwise in getting up from my bed and coming to London against the wishes of my physician. I had been working hard since my arrival, getting but little sleep, agitating my brain too severely. I was now paying the penalty of my rashness. I at last grew so bad that I was compelled to see a doctor. He looked grave as I related to him my feelings.

"Is it serious, doctor?" I inquired.

"It may become so, unless you are very careful," he replied.

He advised absolute rest, and wrote a prescription. I disliked the idea of giving up my investigations, but concluded that it was better to do so rather than lose the use of my mind entirely, probably life as well. So I secured comfortable lodgings (I had left the hotel long ago) and gave myself up to rest and recuperation.

My physician even recommended the advisability of refraining from reading. I had eagerly perused all the papers during the first few days of my enforced rest, and the doctor had found me literally up to my eyes in one upon the occasion of a visit. So I stopped the papers, but I questioned my servant daily as to the topics of the day, and knew that the murderer had not been found.

I had not made up my mind to give up the search; I was only too eager to be out and at it again. I daily grew better. My brain began to feel active again; my memory, which had been sadly impaired, grew more retentive, and I felt that I could once more pursue my investigations without difficulty or detriment to myself.

The sun shone more brightly than I ever remember of having seen it before as I walked down stairs and out upon the street upon the first of May—May-day—a holiday throughout all England. I sniffed the fresh air as eagerly as the released prisoner who has been languishing within the walls of a dungeon. I walked quickly and lightly, exhilarated by the bright sunshine, the chirping sparrows, the fresh air. I felt like a new man, and rejoiced in the beauty of nature, as seen in the parks as I passed through them.

I sat down upon a bench. I had not read a paper in over a week. I determined to indulge in the luxury, and, hailing a boy, I purchased one, and was soon oblivious to my surroundings. I read the political topics of the day; Gladstone's speech, the Irish question, all eagerly. I waded through the advertisements, secretly wondering if each one of the many advertisers succeeded in gathering in filthy lucre from the strength of his efforts. I had nearly finished the large paper, had probably been reading two hours, when an editorial struck my eye. I seldom read editorials; the facts as recorded are sufficient for me without reading the editor's opinions. But this one was headed in such a way as to attract my attention. The line was as follows: "The Age of Credulity;" and the article went on to speak of the many people who were daily taken in by the so-called powers of spiritualism, clairvoyancy, mind-reading, mesmerism, etc. The writer boldly asserted that the effects produced were governed entirely from the effects of superstition and imagination. "Clothe any of the most ordinary of our daily vocations in a cloak of mystery and the morbid appetite of the public will find something decidedly out of the common in that which, if revealed to them in its true light, would awaken no interest whatever." He further likened the exhibitions of the professors of these sciences to those of the sleight-of-hand performer—strange if you do not understand them; ridiculously simple when you have a knowledge as to the means used to produce the effects.

"At the present time there is a bold humbug creating a furore in a section of our metropolis. We visited his exhibition a few nights since. We saw several well-trained subjects perform a number of ordinary antics upon the stage. The 'Professor' (?) claimed that they were not conscious of their actions; that each and every one was controlled by his mesmeric power. The large audience applauded him to the echo. They were delighted—highly pleased that they were being humbugged, although they would have indignantly denied any such thing if accused of the fact. Verily, the people like to be humbugged, and Professor Weichsler is making a harvest of golden shekels from the credulity of the public."

Professor Weichsler—Dr. Westinghouse.

"He is bold, at any rate," I thought, as I unconsciously folded the newspaper and put it in my pocket. Operating here in London right under my very nose. He certainly must have known that I was here. I marveled at the man's audacity. I admired his boldness.

"I shall take in your exhibition, doctor," I muttered, as I returned to my lodgings. I found a dispatch awaiting me.

"It was left here some little time after you had gone, sir," my servant informed me.

I had kept my chief posted as to my whereabouts, although I had not reported for ten days past.

I opened the dispatch.

"Arrest Westinghouse. Hold him until papers arrive. Authentic proofs. BYRNES."

My heart gave a leap in my breast.

I had full authority now, authority upon which I could act.

I first thought I would go and capture my man at once, but after some thought, put it off until the next day. My exercise of the morning had made me nervous. I needed all my strength when I met this man, so I did not go out again that day, and retired early.

MAY 8 TO 15.

It was a good thing for me that I did not attempt to act upon the instructions received upon the 1st instant, for I would have met with a sad mishap, I am afraid. About midnight I awoke with a strange feeling in my head again. I had staid in the park too long, and had caught some cold. I was confined to my room for a week, obeying the doctor's orders, although I felt well enough to get out in two days.

Ah! this head of mine. It was beginning to give me much trouble. My doctor informed me that I would probably have fallen in the street, if I had gone out that night. I was glad that I did not make the attempt.

My servant had found out the full particulars in connection with Professor Weichsler's entertainment, and at 7 p.m., on the night of the 8th instant, I sallied forth; all right now; no danger of relapse. I walked the distance from my lodgings to the hall of the exhibition.

It was probably a mile, but I stood in need of exercise, and had plenty of time at my disposal, as the performance did not begin until 8. I walked slowly, enjoying the air and a fine cigar. The streets were alive with people; flower-sellers, match-vendors, hawkers of notions, filled the air with their cries. The theatres were not far off, and as I passed some of them I could see the throngs of people pouring into their doors.

All in search of amusement. It set me to thinking. What is life? One long struggle for food, raiment, amusement—nothing more. I was deep in philosophizing when I was suddenly brought up with a short stop by a long line of people who stretched out over the sidewalk into the street even, and whom I could not pass without crossing to the other side. I looked up at the building they were entering and saw that I had reached the hall where Professor Weichsler was holding forth.

What a tremendous crowd there was endeavoring to gain admission, "eager to be humbugged." I smiled as I recalled the article in the paper. I fell in line; I hastened to do so for fear I would be debarred from obtaining entrance at all.

I had come that night, not for the purpose of arresting my man there, but rather to spot him, to shadow him, and find out his place of residence, and then on the quiet I would bring him up with a short haul. I feared his influence over me, and to guard against that I proposed to arrange with an officer to be near when I needed him.

In fifteen minutes I was in the hall, long before the curtain went up. It was literally jammed with a crowd of sweltering humanity. As the time approached, some of these grew impatient and began to have recourse to the various devices employed by the hoodlum element to create discord—stamping, clapping of hands, shrill whistles, and like annoying and unnecessary practices. The curtain arose, and a tall form dressed in black appeared.

"Silence!"

The word proceeded from the lips of the tall figure, and the house was as still as death.

I sat with my eyes riveted upon the man. It was he—Dr. Westing-house.

I dimly heard and understood the opening address. I knew he was explaining his theory. I felt that same peculiar sensation which had come upon me the night on board the steamer. I vainly essayed to arouse myself, but found it almost impossible.

An Irishman sat next to me. He probably observed that I was affected, and said in a whisper:

"I think ye're affected by the heat; take a drink," and handed me his flask. I drank several gulps of whisky, and braced up. I thanked the fellow, and fixed my attention upon the stage. The professor was asking for subjects, and had no difficulty in getting all he desired, the semi-circle of chairs arranged upon the platform soon filled. Then began the manipulations, the experiments in animal magnetism, etc. The entertainment lasted for two hours, and the operator never failed to control his subjects in any particular instance. He dismissed the people who had assisted him and stepped off into the wings amidst a storm of applause. I was about to leave the hall, to go around to watch the stage door, when the Irishman next to me whispered:

"Don't go yet; that's only the first part."

I resumed my seat. There next appeared upon the stage a man more portly and shorter in stature than the professor. I immediately recognized him as the companion of my man the night I saw him in "Big Nosed Kate's" den. The short man explained that the next feature upon the programme would be a series of spiritualistic tests, such as rope-tying, cabinet tests, etc. I sat for thirty minutes, but little interested in what I saw, waiting for the professor to make his appearance again. He did not come. I rose and went into the lobby.

"Does the professor appear again to-night?" I inquired of an usher.

"No; he has gone home. He does mind-reading to-morrow night," answered the fellow.

So, he had got away. I walked home in a bad humor, but I vowed I would not lose sight of him the following night. But I did.

The next night I planted myself near the stage door. I was there when the professor arrived. I remained there until I saw the lights being put out in the hall. I ran around to the front. I perceived an attaché putting out the gas lamp over the door.

"Has the professor gone?" I asked.

"Lor' bless ye, an hour ago, sur. He went out by the front way."

I bit my lip with vexation. I was not fortunate. It seemed that the Fates were against my finding out the professor's lodging place, for I attended the entertainments for a week and in some unaccountable way missed him every night. One night I took another man with me. I watched the stage entrance; he watched the front of the house. We both remained until midnight upon our posts; the professor did not come. I found out the next night that he had remained in the hall all night, practicing some chemical experiments that he was going to produce the following night.

The night of the 15th I was waiting opposite the hall for the appearance of my man. I had been inside until I saw him leave the stage. I had then hurried out and stationed myself opposite the building. I knew that he could not come out without being seen by me, and I had made up my mind to boldly enter the hall and take him in charge, if he did not come out. I did not wish to take this step, but something must be done, and quickly, for my chief was getting impatient, as numerous dispatches testified. Besides, I wanted to proceed upon my Whitechapel investigations. The performance had long since ended. I was getting impatient, when lo! upon the opposite corner I spied my man. He was looking cautiously up and down the street, which was thronged with late theatre parties and others. His survey seemed to satisfy him, for he started up the street at a brisk walk, and I started after him. Along the brilliantly lighted street, elbowing his way through the crowds, hurried the professor, and, keeping my eye constantly upon him, I followed on the opposite side. He suddenly turned down a side street, which was almost deserted, and which was only lighted by a stray lamp here and there. I crossed the street, and keeping in the shadows of the houses still followed him. He walked more slowly, and finally halted immediately beneath a gas lamp. I was not prepared for his sudden stop, and he heard the sound of my footstep as I made one step after his. He came toward me, and I determined to face him rather than show any sign of fear. I boldly advanced. He saw me approaching and stopped, waiting for me to reach him. He stood erect with his arms by his side. I stood before him the next minute.

"Dewey?" He murmured gently.

"Yes, Dewey," I answered.

"What do you wish?"

"You." I replied.

"Ah!" A smile upon his lips; "I live near here, come, I will listen to your desires."

I dreaded to follow him, now that he knew me, but I had a whistle convenient that would summon an officer; I had a revolver. Why should I dread him, or show fear? I had faced danger before. Such danger as this? No, I think not. No man ever possessed the power of Dr. Westinghouse. I overcame my feelings and walked beside him, as he strode along silent and preoccupied. He did not go far—turned the corner at the next street, and let himself into a modest dwelling with a night-key. A light was dimly burning in the hall. I took a careful survey of my surroundings before following him in, so that I would know the place again. He threw open a door to the left and entered. A flood of light swept out into the hall; he had turned up the gas. I glanced around the room. The light came from a double-burner chandelier, suspended from the center of the ceiling, one burner of which was alight. A square table covered with a common red cloth stood immediately beneath it. A few chairs, an old-fashioned clock, a large cupboard with glass doors in the corner, and a map of the City of London, hanging upon the wall, completed the furniture and surroundings. Nothing very cheerful—nothing very fearful. He walked to the cupboard, and, opening the door, took from one of the shelves a square morocco case, about the size of an ordinary hotel register. This he placed upon the table. I felt curious as to the meaning of his action. He made no remark, but opening the case showed me the contents—a full set of shining surgical instruments! A chill ran through me as I gazed upon their polished surface. Why had he shown me them?

"My instruments," he said he smiling, showing his white teeth. I am proud of them; they were presented to me by Professor Lafourche of Paris. I contemplate practicing here; thought you might be interested in such things."

I looked from the case and its contents to the man. He was calmly surveying the bright knives and saws.

"They have seen service," he continued. "You would not think it to look at them."

"No," I murmured involuntarily.

He closed the case, and I breathed easier. He motioned me to a chair and sank into one opposite me.

"So you want me," he began slowly, with an absent air.

"I have tried to find you for some time," I answered.

"I know it." Then quickly looking me in the face: "Why will you not be governed by your former experience? You know you are powerless to combat with me. Have you not had ample proof? Must I give you further demonstration? I know you have been trying to shadow me for the past week; I saw and recognized you in my audience a week ago. I have kept out of your way."

"I thought as much," I answered.

"Did you? Why did you suppose I avoided you?"

"From the fear of conscious guilt."

He smiled gently, kindly.

"No; not that. I will tell you. I do *not* fear you, Dewey; *I like you.* I have never met a man whom I more thoroughly admired than yourself. I knew why you wished to find me; I knew your mission. I kept out of your way because I liked you; because I knew if you found me you would endeavor to do your duty, and I should be forced to protect myself. You know from past experience how well I can do that. I saw you were determined to follow me; so to-night I permitted you to do so. I wished to speak to you; wished to warn you for the second time, need I say, for the last time."

I felt angry, vexed, that this man should talk so to me, knowing that I had the power to arrest and take him back to the United States.

"You can not escape the law," I cried.

He laughed, a laugh of genuine amusement.

"The law," he cried; "what has the law to do with me? Consider; what could you prove against me, even if you should succeed in giving me up to justice? Give this good, sound reasoning from the standpoint of any sensible juror, and you will see that I would be acquitted of any charge. I have read the New York papers since I have been abroad; I know the ridiculous charge which has been brought against me. Do you think any intelligent jury would convict me? No. They say, you declare, that I mesmerized a man, a cashier of a bank, and forced him to deliver to me a sum of money. I also successfully hypnotized another man, the janitor, through a four-inch oaken door. Will any jury convict on such evidence as that?"

"Any who have seen your power demonstrated will believe it possible."

"So? You do me great honor. I tell you it is ridiculous."

"Why, then, did you leave New York at all? Why did you assume a fictitious name?"

A quick change overspread his countenance.

"Not from any fear of being convicted of robbery," he said. "Listen; I told you in Liverpool that I had work to do on this side of the water, a mission to fulfill. To prevent you from interfering with my plans I used my influence over you and delayed you a fortnight in Liverpool. That work is still unfinished. When it is done I shall return to New York. I have begun—I must finish. You need not ask the nature of my undertaking. You would not be any the wiser for so doing. Now, understand me. Let me alone! Dispatch your chief that Dr. Westinghouse can not be found; return to your country. Professor Weichsler will finish his work, and when that is done, then, and not till then, will Dr. Westinghouse be found. Allow me to rest in peace. Watch me as much as you like, if you choose to remain in England, but do not attempt to trouble me! I shall continue to entertain friendly feelings toward you; I may prove a valuable friend if you do as I say, but neglect my warning, attempt to thwart me, and *you shall soon wish that you were dead. REMEMBER.*"

He had risen from his chair while addressing me. His eyes burned and cut me to the heart. His voice, clear and distinct, penetrated to my brain. I tried to speak; my voice failed me. I tried to rise; my limbs refused to act.

While I sat riveted to my chair, he raised his hand and turned off the gas. I was left in total darkness; I heard his voice again.

"You can easily find your way out, by turning half-way around and walking straight before you. The gas is still burning in the hall. Do not attempt to search for me when you recover power of locomotion, for you will not find me. If you come to this place to-morrow, I shall not be here. I have given my last exhibition, so you will have nothing by which to trace me. I shall not leave the city, but for your own good do not try to look me up. Good-night."

In five minutes I found myself able to rise. I did so; I groped my way to the hall. I did not attempt to search the house, but opened the street door and went out into the night.

The street was dark; a gentle wind softly moaned about the corners of the houses. A sudden feeling of fear took possession of me. I ran as if pursued by unseen demons, ran until the lights of the thoroughfare relieved my overwrought nerves.

I took a hansom and was driven home. I do not believe I could have walked there. I could not comprehend the feeling of terror that had taken possession of my heart. I was like a school-boy who has been listening to stories of ghosts until his very shadow appalls him. The words of the man I had been with were words of warning only, but they filled my entire being with nameless dread.

The clock on my mantel chimed 3 before I slept.

FOURTH AND FIFTH MONTHS.

JUNE—JULY.

I did but little during the next two months. But little of an exciting or interesting nature occurred. As cowardly as it may seem, I dreaded to pursue the strange man who had gained such supremacy over me. I feared to disobey his warning. I did what some might censure me for doing; I dispatched Inspector Byrnes to the effect that Dr. Westinghouse had escaped me; that he was no longer in England. I did more; I sent in my resignation. I was not a wealthy man, but I had been saving during my years of active service, and could afford to live without work for some time, at least.

The month of June passed. July, with its burning sun, its dusty streets, followed. I passed my time in reading, theatre going, anything that would serve to pass the time, which lay heavily upon my hands.

I had even lost my interest in the Whitechapel murder. I knew from the papers that the assassin had not been captured; I began to feel that he never would be.

I did not try to find Dr. Westinghouse; I did not hear of him through the medium of the newspapers. He had spoken truly; he had given his last exhibition, and Professor Weichsler had passed out of the knowledge of the thousands who had, night after night, sat open-mouthed, spell-bound, by the awful power demonstrated before their eyes.

Toward the latter part of July the weather grew very warm. My apartments were so close that I could not sleep with any degree of comfort. It was like attempting to rest in a bake-oven. So I often arose, dressed myself, and took long walks through the deserted streets. These walks finally became a pleasure, a second nature. I enjoyed them; my brain seemed more active; my heart felt relieved of that dull feeling of depression which had troubled me so much of late. It was refreshing to linger on the deserted pave and think of all nature at rest; it was invigorating to watch the pale moon sailing majestically through the heavens, shining upon the earth below, on rich and poor alike, on the good and evil indiscriminately.

It was the night of July 30. Two days more and August would be upon me. August, the sixth month of my experiences. I was standing before the Bank of England. Surrounding me on every side were buildings of commerce, insurance, trust companies, and the like. I was leaning against the triad of lamps that stand immediately before the bank, when, without warning, without any previous thought, came an overwhelming desire to again see Dr. Westinghouse. Not to do him harm—I had long since given up any idea of that—but to see him; to look upon his face; to witness that gentle yet awful smile. I stood amazed at myself at this singular desire. Why had it come upon me? I could not say, but my heart was longing. I was as eager to start upon my search, as anxious to hear his voice, as the fond lover separated from the mistress of his heart. I was some distance from my lodgings. It was nearly midnight, but I felt no desire to return, only that uncontrollable feeling that I must see the man again who had been a curse to me. I walked eagerly along the sidewalk. I had no idea where I was going, yet I walked as though I had some objective point in view; walked for an hour, and then stopped. Why I stopped I can not say, but it was as if a hand had been placed upon my shoulder and forced me to halt. I looked about me; I was standing before a large dwelling, which stood a little back from the street. I looked up at the windows of the second floor; there was a light shining forth from one of them; the shade was pulled half way up. Why had I looked up at those windows? I could never tell, but my eyes were unconsciously directed there. I could see someone moving about in the room, but could not distinguish the face. I watched for at least a half-hour; then a form drew near the window. The light shone upon a divine face, framed in a wealth of golden hair. I saw a look of settled melancholy in the beautiful eyes. I was some little distance from the house, probably ten yards, but I seemed to be gifted with preternatural vision. I recognized the face.

It was Ethel—the niece of Dr. Westinghouse. She could not see me, as I was in the shadow, but I saw her distinctly. At this moment, another figure approached the window; a hand was laid upon the young girl's wealth of curls—a large white hand. Another face was at the window, seemingly looking out into the night.

A thrill ran through me. I had found him—Dr. Westinghouse.

SIXTH MONTH.
AUGUST 1 TO 7.

I waited in the shadow until the faces left the window and the disappearance of the light convinced me that I would see them again no more that night. I slowly walked home. I arrived at my lodgings as dawn was breaking in the east. My servant was sleeping, so I did not awaken him, but threw myself, dressed as I was, upon the bed. I slept until 2 in the afternoon. I did not take my nocturnal walk that night. I felt weary, and had no difficulty in sleeping, notwithstanding the fact that I had already slept nearly twelve hours of the day. But the night of the 1st, I felt again that desire to be out in the air. Alone with my thoughts, in the streets, my footsteps involuntarily led me in the direction of the house I had stood before so long two nights before. I seemed to be led there by unseen hands. I saw no one this time, however; but this did not seem to cause any surprise in my mind. It seemed to me that I *must* go to the house, and every night for the next week found me staring at the windows, as if expecting something that never came. The night of August 6th (Shall I ever forget it? Never, until I rest in my grave) I was at my post. It was about 11 o'clock, and the residents of the surrounding houses had not all retired as yet. I did not care to stand still, and I considered it might look suspicious to a chance observer; so I walked slowly from one corner of the block to the other. There was a light in the same window of the doctor's house I had before taken notice of, and also one below. I had never seen a light in the lower portion of the building before. One by one the houses around me became dark, and I concluded that the neighbors had retired; but still the lights shone out of the windows of the house I was watching.

Watching? Yes. What for? I did not know. I could not have explained. As the clock in a church tower not far distant tolled out the hour of 12, I cautiously crept to the window (which was in the basement) where the lower light was burning. The shade was pulled down, but not to the bottom, there being an inch or more unprotected. I fell upon my knees and applied my eye to this portion. I could see the interior of the room. It was furnished as an office—a doctor's office—and sitting at a table in the rear portion of the room, with his massive head resting in his hands, his elbows upon the table, was Dr. Westinghouse. He appeared to be reading, letters they seemed to be. I could not see his face, but observed that his fingers were nervously twitching. Suddenly he arose and turned his face toward the window. I drew back, startled, astounded. That face, usually so calm, so self-possessed, was twitching and working, as if in the most horrible agony. The eyes, so gentle, so powerful, shone as two coals. They seemed horribly strange to me; an expression different from anything I had ever seen in them flashed forth from their depths. His further action seemed out of place, knowing the man as I did, as I had seen him before. He raised his hands above his head and seemed to be praying. Every movement of the lips seemed to indicate it. I watched him, breathless and awed. His prayer finished, he sank upon the chair once more, and buried his face in his folded arms upon the table. When next I saw that face, a great expression of joy rested upon it; it actually shone. The eyes were filled with determination. He rapidly turned to a desk near by and pulled out one of the drawers, removing something from it. I did not see what it was at first, as his back was toward me, but as he turned and carried it to the table, I recognized his burden. *It was the case of surgical instruments!*

What could he be going to do with them? was the question that agitated me. I had not long to wait for an answer, for, throwing open the case, he removed two sharp, polished knives; one, long and with a wide blade, the other shorter and curved. These he secreted in the inside pocket of his coat, and then replacing the case, he put away the letters he had been reading and turned off the gas. I quickly hurried to the street and crouched alongside the steps leading to a mansion next door. None too soon, either, for I had no sooner crouched in my hiding-place than I heard a quick footstep upon the walk, and the next instant the doctor passed me. He walked as if bent upon an errand of life and death. He looked neither to the right nor left, but went straight ahead. I stealthily followed him; he did not convey to me by any sign that he heard me, but hurried on. On through dark streets; through wide thoroughfares; through narrow courts. On for several miles, it seemed to me, and yet he showed no signs of tiring. I began to feel worn out. He was walking so rapidly that I had some difficulty in keeping up with him. The neighborhood we were now coming to was not entirely familiar to me. I could not remember of ever having been there before. Suddenly, on the side of a building, I saw the name of the street we were traversing. It was painted upon a board and read

"Commercial Street." I did not know of any Commercial Street. Ah! the rapid footsteps gradually grow slower. I can hear the quick breathing of the man, although he is a half-block distant. He draws back in the shadow of the building. Why?

A woman is approaching from the opposite direction. I can see that she is neither young nor handsome. Her features are coarse, and her clothing dirty and common. All this I can see by the light of a dingy lamp, suspended over a door, upon which is painted the words: "Lodging, four pence." The woman reels as she walks. She has been drinking. I crouch low in the protecting shadow of a doorway. I am interested in the action of the man I am following. As the woman passes him, he steps out of his hiding-place and speaks to her, I can not hear what he says, but the woman answers in a thick tone.

"Got the tin?"

The reply must have satisfied her, for she says: "All right. 'Ere is as good a ken as enny."

They enter the building and are lost to sight. I ran to the spot recently occupied by the pair, my mind beset with curious thoughts. What can the patrician Dr. Westinghouse want of such a creature as this. I peer into the building; I can not see, neither can I hear. I stand bewildered. How long I stood there I never knew. I was brought to my senses by being jostled by a man evidently in great haste. I turned; Dr. Westinghouse; his face aglow, his clothing disarranged. He saw and recognized me.

"You?" he cried in a low tone "You, Dewey?"

"Yes," I murmured.

"You are following me; you have not profited by my warning. Fool! Why will you destroy yourself?"

This he almost cried.

I assured him I had no motive save curiosity in dogging his footsteps. I meant him no harm. I spoke as one in a dream.

"No harm! Curiosity!" he repeated. "You know where I live?" he suddenly demanded.

"Yes."

"You have been watching me there?"

"Yes."

"Come there to-morrow night at 10. I want you. Some months ago you wanted me. The positions are changed. *I want you.* Peculiar;" and he smiled.

I nodded my head. He smiled again, and left me.

I felt no desire to follow him. I only wished to rest. Every fresh encounter with the man left me weaker in body and mind. Why did I not keep away from him? I could not. As the magnet attracts the needle, so did this man attract me. I was powerless to save myself. The gray light of early dawn was creeping over the city as I turned and crept along the sidewalk. I found a hansom, at last, and was driven home.

The afternoon papers chronicled the foul murder of Martha Tabram. She had been found upon the first-floor landing of the George Yard building, Commercial Street, Spitalfields. The head was nearly severed from the body. There were thirty stab wounds, beside the same horrible mutilation that marked the other assassination. I read the account with a dazed feeling of wonder, my mind filled with diverse thoughts. I put the paper from me and mechanically filled my meerschaum.

I smoked for an hour.

AUGUST 8 TO 31.

All that day and the next my head gave me trouble; no ache, no pain, but a peculiar, swimming, dazed sensation. Loss of rest, very likely. "I must stop this night-walking." I thought; that is, after to-night. I had promised to be at the house of Dr. Westinghouse at 10 to-night, and I would not break my promise. I could not; my heart longed for the hour when I could take my departure. I was punctual. My watch chronicled but a few minutes past the hour as I knocked on the basement door. I did so, as I saw the light burning in the office. I had not long to wait. The door opened and the doctor stood in the opening, his tall figure robed in a long dressing gown, his black hair covered with a skull-cap.

"You are prompt," was all he said, and I followed him into the room.

He motioned me to a chair, and, after carefully pulling down the shades, occupied the one at the table himself. I sat silent, waiting for him to begin. After a lapse of about ten minutes he did so.

"When last we sat together I warned you not to attempt to interfere with my plans. I advised you as to the best course to pursue, among other things, to leave England. I find you still here. I detect you in the very act of watching me. Is it not so?"

"Yes; I *was* watching you."

"You admitted as much when discovered. You said then that only curiosity led you to dog me. Was that true?"

"Yes."

"Nothing else?"

I replied that I had given up my profession. I could have no other reason. He sat deeply thinking for awhile; then suddenly:

"You have neglected my advice. You persist in linking your destiny with mine. I have tried to avoid it, but you have thrust it upon me. *Now it is too late!* I can see it before me. Your soul is linked to mine; you are mine to control. Well, be it so. I need help. You shall render me valuable assistance. Do you know why I told you to come here to-night?"

I answered in the negative.

"You shall know. Twice I have told you that I had a mission to fulfill upon this side of the water. You shall know what it is. You shall hear the story of a soul lost, a life sacrificed; then you will understand all; then you will see."

He spoke rapidly. I waited with beating heart, not for long, for he began almost immediately.

"Twenty years ago there lived in Yonkers, New York, a family by the name of Westinghouse—that is, the mother and the children lived there, the father being dead. The mother, a fragile creature, grieved sorely at her husband's death, and she, too, passed away. There remained now but the children, the boy Louis, the girl Ethel. The boy was deeply interested in his studies, being a student of medicine, and, as he attended college in New York, the sister was left alone a greater portion of the time. The young man loved his sister, a bright young thing of eighteen, and would proudly show her week after week, upon his return to his home, the progress he was making. 'For your sake, dear sister,' he would say. The girl grew weary of living in solitude during her brother's absence, and so a companion was engaged—a beautiful woman of about thirty. She seemed to take great interest in the young girl, and she soon idolized her older companion. The intimacy grew; they became inseparable. The student began to see signs of discontent upon the face of his loved sister. He puzzled his loving heart to find a solution for it, but failed.

"One Saturday night he came home as usual. The house was dark; no loving sister flew out to meet him. The place seemed deserted. With anxious foreboding he opened the door; no sound within! He stepped into the sitting-room—a pretty nest—but the bird had deserted it. His sister was not there. He ran up the stairs calling upon her loved name; no answer. All as silent as the grave. He returned to the sitting-room. 'Why should I feel anxious?' he said to himself. 'She has probably gone to one of the neighbor's.' He solaced his heart with this thought, but not for long, for in turning over some things on the work-table he found a note—a tiny note in his sister's handwriting. He opened it and read; read that she, his pure, innocent sister, had determined to leave her quiet, happy home for one more gorgeous; had gone to exchange her girlish innocence and beauty for gold; had gone to lead a life of sin and shame across the waters of the Atlantic. Her dark-browed, beautiful companion had poured the morsels of enticing baseness into her girlish ears. She knew no better; she was but a true daughter of Eve, and she fell.

"The blow nearly crazed the brother, but his brain stood the test, and in his heart rose but one feeling—that of a terrible revenge. He searched Europe, seeking the beautiful devil who had entered his Eden; seeking his sister, but he was not successful. Five years ago an old hag came to the residence of a certain Dr. Westinghouse, in the City of New York. She brought with her a fair-haired child of twelve and a letter. The letter was from the lost sister. She had sent her child, born in shame, to the brother she had wronged. In the letter she begged his forgiveness, prayed that he would bring up her child in the right path, and said that ere the note reached him she would be dead. The brother accepted the trust. He was famous; his name was known throughout the entire country. He took the child to his heart, and to keep her there *riveted her soul to his*.

"This is *my* story; the story of *my* sister; the story of that golden-haired child who sleeps above us. *She* lives only in me; knows only what I deem best. She is in another world, for, by the strength of my power, I keep her in a paradise. She does not understand the sins of this world; it is best that she should not.

"Now for the end. As the burning eyes of that brother ran over the last words of her who had been his sister, a great feeling came over him—a feeling of undying hatred, of bitter enmity toward all of that class who lead astray the innocent and good; who lure men to their destruction. He quickly counted the years his sister had suffered in crime and degradation. He found them fifteen. Fifteen years blot upon the good name of his family. Fifteen years a creature of shame, and led to it by one experienced in the cursed trade. He raised his hand to heaven and recorded there an oath *that for each year his sister had sinned some vile creature should perish; should give up her life to him, and that the cause of woman's fall should be taken from them*; THUS MARKING THE WORK OF THE AVENGER; *thus striking terror to the hearts of all who engaged in the vile traffic.*

"The years passed on. Although possessing a good practice the brother was not wealthy, and without money it would be impossible to start upon his work of vengeance. So he plotted, and gave way to temptation; he became a thief—you know how; but he put the money to good use, for he came to England, bringing the child with him. He began his mission and TWO YEARS are blotted off the sin-stained record. Two of the vilest of the vile have given up that life which they did not esteem worthy of better use. *Others must follow*—the list is still incomplete. You know all now. Look upon me—*the avenger!* Is not my mission a glorious one?"

I shrank in horror from him; he, the self-confessed fiend of Whitechapel; he, the brutal butcher of Emma Smith and Martha Tabram. My God! and this fiend held me in his power. I dreaded to think of the use he might make of it. I looked up into his face; it was as if glorified. The soulful eyes were raised to the ceiling; his hands were clasped as if in fervent prayer. He suddenly collected his thoughts and walked toward the desk, returning with the case of instruments. I shuddered violently as I remembered when I had last seen them. He opened the case and gazed lovingly at the shining blades.

"You have seen these before," he said gently. "They are my treasures. I told you they were presented to me by Professor Lafourche of Paris. I lied to you then. I never thought I would tell *you* the truth. They were presented to me by my mother and sister upon my birthday, three months before mother died; eight months before sister died, to me. Is it not proper that they should play a part in this work of vengeance? They reflected her smile the day when she gazed upon their polished surface."

Tears stood in his eyes. He put them away, and, looking me in the face, murmured as if his mind was far away:

"I had determined to carry out this work alone, unknown, but I have changed my mind. You have been associated with me since my first step. *You have unconsciously been sent to aid me.* You may shrink from contemplating it, but that will not be for long. You will, in a short time, be only too willing. I see you turn pale; I see you shudder. Ah! Dewey, my friend; you should feel grateful that I am willing to grant you a share in my glory. You came here to-night John Philip Dewey. You are at this moment half my slave, as you still have the power of thought in your inner self. You will not leave here, for in ten minutes *you will be part of my very self; have my thoughts, my desires, live only in me*, as does that sweet child sleeping upstairs. Do not attempt to resist me. *You can not!* YOU CAN NOT!"

Like a wave of overwhelming power came the thought of what he had said in my former interview, the night I had followed him from the hall to his residence: *"You will wish you were dead!"* I grew faint; my stomach felt keen distress; my heart throbbed as if it would burst. I tried to turn my head from him—useless; the face, now shining upon me with all the eagerness of a loving father or brother, held me riveted to my chair. The burning eyes were fixed upon mine. I felt a change taking place in my inner self; felt my lungs expand as if eager to take in something, I knew not what; felt my brain teeming with strange thoughts, wild ideas, and with a loud cry rose to my feet. To my eyes he seemed a beautiful vision. I loved him; I fell upon his breast; I embraced him. I heard his voice murmur "perhaps it is better so, poor fellow." The last expiring effort of myself. The sound of his voice. The next instant I was another being.

As I sit alone, with the subdued light of my lamp shining upon the paper before me, the events of the next few months seem too unreal to be true. I would doubt myself, if I did not know; if it were not all indelibly imprinted upon my memory.

It all seems so horrible now, yet at the time I gloried in it all. I was happy, with a wild ecstatic happiness; I was a child living in my master's smile.

The weeks passed by. We were always together, the doctor and I. We would sit in his study when night had fallen; he would read me the only two letters he had ever received from his sister, the beginning and the ending of her life of shame. He would take out the sharp knives and caress them. I would do the same. We would read the papers and laugh wildly over the accounts of the two murders.

"They will soon have more to record," he would say, and I eagerly waited for the time to come when the city would be convulsed with horror again.

One night he knelt beside his chair and prayed. I sat and watched him, anxious to hear what he would say when he arose to his feet. In an indistinct way I could recall the circumstances that followed the first prayer I had ever seen him indulge in. I hoped this one would result in the same manner. It came. He arose, and, looking me in the eyes, said:

"It is the accepted time; we must be off."

I danced about the room in glee. I remember it all now.

"We must be careful," he said.

I agreed with him. He secreted the knives in his coat. I followed him out of the room into the street. We walked along in the darkness; there was no moon. We drew near the Whitechapel district. The streets were alive with people. I recognized the familiar portions of the town. I remembered the place where the body of Emma Smith had been found; we passed it.

"Number one, there!" he muttered, as we passed the spot.

"We entered a drinking-house. I had been there before. There was a back entrance, opening from a side street. I knew it well. The place was crowded, although it was midnight—probably long past it. We sat down at one of the tables and ordered drink. I gulped down the ale eagerly; my mouth felt dry, my throat parched.

For an hour we lingered. I saw a woman, who had been sitting at one of the tables, get up and go into a back room. He followed her.

He was not gone long. When he returned he was as calm as ever. He gave me some whispered instructions. I rose and went into the back room. Then I saw why he had gone there; I saw his work. *Number three!* The body was lying upon the floor. He had done his work well. I gloated over the helpless, mutilated corpse. I picked it up and hurried into the street. All dark. No one saw me. I carried it as far as I could, and there left it.

He met me on the corner. He quickly wrapped a cloak around me that he had before worn himself. We reached home. I found my clothing covered with blood when the light shone upon me. He had wrapped the cloak around me so it would not be seen by a chance passer-by. He had thought of every detail. In the morning we laughed over the account of the finding of the body of Mary Ann (Polly) Nichols in the street, in Buck's Row, Whitechapel. The paper stated that she had probably been killed somewhere else and her body carried to the place where it was found, as there was little blood discovered where she lay.

The paper was right. I carried the body. There was no blood found on the floor of the room where she had been killed, either, although no one looked for any. The same cloak which covered me had lain beneath her when she fell.

SEPTEMBER.

We did not rest after this. Our work went bravely on to completion. Night after night we walked the streets of Whitechapel, eager for victims, but cautious as well. We must not be captured or the work of vengeance would not be completed. Courtesans smiled upon us; they little knew the feelings in our hearts for them.

At last another came. Unsuspicious, eager to ply her trade, struck down while making her base bargain. Again the victim was found in a drinking den. She could drink oceans of beer. I waited in the street while he managed her inside. It was quite light when they left the place—the light of early morning. She was leaning heavily upon his arm. He gave me a look as he passed me, and I kept out of sight. Up the street, around the corner to Hanbury Street, through a court to the rear of some houses. I watched lest someone should interrupt. I could see them, also noticed the fact that several windows were open in the surrounding houses, but no one saw the deed. The keen knife did its work quickly, elaborately. A great surgeon was Dr. Westinghouse; he understood his work.

He joined me in ten minutes. I noticed that his hands were clean; he never soiled them. As we hurried along the street—now becoming filled with laborers going to their work, women, poorly clad, with small baskets on their arms, going out to purchase their morning meal—he said, with a pleasant smile:

"I think I will puzzle them a little this time. I have left conclusive evidence of the perpetrator; at least, the police will think so."

I did not understand him; I did, upon reading the papers.

A leather apron had been found near the woman's remains. A character known by the sobriquet of "Leather Apron," owing to the fact that he always wore one, was well known in the vicinity. He would probably be arrested.

We read of the talk of forming a vigilance committee, and laughed. They were also thinking of putting on bloodhounds. Bah! Bloodhounds could not track us. Ours was a work of vengeance. We would not be discovered.

"We will rest now for awhile," said my master, "and then change our locality. There are others besides the low creatures of Whitechapel; we must extend our field of operations."

He said this in a thoughtful manner. It was a matter of business to him.

The city was literally upset over this last murder of Annie Sievey, or Chapman, but it did not affect us any. We were happy, even joyful.

Somebody had sent notes to the chief of the vigilance committee; they did not come from us. We did not indulge in any such frivolous amusements. The notes and postal cards were signed "Jack the Ripper." My master smiled his usual smile, as he read the account.

"Good," he murmured; "it will keep them from us. Let me see; *your* name is John; Jack is a nick-name for John. You shall bear the title. *You shall be 'Jack the Ripper.'*"

We both laughed at the title. I felt proud that he should bestow it upon me.

Those were happy days to me. Great God! What a creature I had become. I turn cold as I think of it now. I pray for death to come to efface it from my memory. Happy in the thought of inhuman butchery! Delighted at the sight of blood!"

We rested for a few days. Then he told me one day that he was going away for a short time. I wept; I prayed him not to leave me. He opened the case of instruments, and, selecting a knife therefrom, handed it to me.

"Look about you while I am away. You will find something to occupy your mind. Although I shall be absent in body I shall be with you in spirit. You shall see me; you shall know how I am progressing."

He left me. I did not comprehend the meaning of his words then. *I did afterward!*

That night I walked out alone. I shunned the Whitechapel district. I was in search of fresh fields. My walk brought me to a different part of town. I heard the flow of waters; I was near the river. It was moonlight. How brightly the silver queen of night shone upon the river. I walked along the Thames embankment. I was alone. Suddenly I felt a strange presence. I thought I heard a voice sounding in my ear; a gentle voice whispering. I looked around me; I saw no one. I continued my walk. Ah! Someone is coming! A woman. How my heart beat—throbbing, jumping with joy. A woman, and alone; a vulture of the night! She is near me; she speaks. I hear her proposition; I acquiesce. We are before a pile of abandoned architecture, an unsightly pile, looming up into the night. I persuade her to accompany me to the rear. It is soon over. The knife springs from its hiding-place. She is taken so suddenly that she has no time to cry out. *The work is done. I stand alone on the roadway. JACK THE RIPPER of a verity!* I laugh; I am deserving of the title. Again that feeling of a presence. *Now I see a dim street at the foot of a bridge—not London. The surroundings are unfamiliar. I see a man and a woman. I KNOW THE MAN! It is my master. I know what is to follow. I see the moonlight shining upon a glittering object; the next instant it is buried from sight. He has made excellent progress. I know my master has been successful.* Then I am on the Thames embankment once more. The wind blows cold from the river. I tremble. Is it fear, or am I only affected by the cold? I hurry home; the light is burning in the basement—in the doctor's study. I carefully rid myself of all signs of blood, wash the knife, and go upstairs. I sleep well; I am fatigued. My master is at home when I awake in the morning. He tells me that he has been at Gateshead, in the north, opposite Newcastle-upon-Tyne. He tells me he has been successful. I already knew it. I had been in London in body, Gateshead in spirit. *Two places at the same time!* I make a record of the day. *Sunday, September 23.*

A week passed by. We did not leave the house. We had been doing noble work; we were tired. But I was eager to carry on the mission in which I was permitted to share the glory, and on the night of Sunday the 30th I begged my master to allow me to go out upon the streets again alone. He curbed my impatience for a few hours, but finally consented. We left the house together, but parted before we had gone far.

"I shall watch you," he said, as he left me. "You will feel my presence. Be careful; be sure, but do not assume any risks. I can not afford to lose you."

I knew what he meant by losing me. If I should be caught the stupid officers of the law would not accept the true circumstances of the case, and I would be hanged. I did not wish that; the work was not yet done. I wandered about the streets until past midnight. It was a windy night; the dust arose in clouds to the sky. Some careless persons had left their shutters unfastened, and they were banging to and fro in the wind. I noticed these things as I hurried along. I met a policeman.

"Windy night," he said, as I passed him.

"Yes," I answered. I hugged my knife. He had no idea of what I was seeking. How ignorant he was of my intentions.

I was crossing Berners Street; the wind, coming around the corner with a howl, blew off my hat. I chased it with childish glee; I laughed aloud as I captured it. I heard another laugh sounding like an echo of my own, but it was not. It proceeded from a woman standing upon the sidewalk. A well-built woman, with a red shawl thrown about her shoulders—*a shawl the color of blood!* I walked up to her. She spoke to me. She seemed a pleasant kind of a woman, *but she was a courtesan, and was doomed.*

We walked along the street side by side; we reached a dark place no one was near. Suddenly, with the strength of a fiend, I sprang upon her. The red blood gushed from the wound in her throat. *Her shawl was doubly red now!*

I was about to complete my work. Then the feeling of the presence of my master came over me. *I saw him finishing his work upon the body of a woman in a section which I recognized as Mitre Square. The red blood was on the walk; his hands were dyed with it.* I can see it standing out vividly before me now. I heard his voice.

"Fly," it said; "Fly."

I looked down upon the body, which I had not yet mutilated; I hated to leave it, but the command was positive, and, secreting my knife, I walked back the way I had come. At the corner I passed the policeman; five minutes later he discovered the body of "Hippy-lip Annie," or Elizabeth Stride. I had a narrow escape.

How we laughed when, the next morning, we read of the finding of the two bodies; they were discovered fifteen minutes apart. The papers said "Jack the Ripper" had killed them both. Well, the papers make mistakes sometimes; they had no way of getting at the truth.

EIGHTH MONTH.

OCTOBER.

We were doing nobly. How easy it is to kill, fly into the night, and escape detection. Eight in a few months. Five in four weeks. The body of the woman I had met upon the Thames embankment had been discovered. She was not recognized; no one knew her. A homeless wretch, without friends. The woman my master had disposed of on the night of the 30th was Catherine Eddowes; I marked down the names; I kept a record of them all.

The stupid police of London were moving heaven and earth to find us, but we felt no fear. Too much system, too much "red tape." I had thought so the day when I had seen the chief, Sir Charles Warren. I looked back on the interview and wondered at myself. I was surprised to think that I had felt a desire to bring the murderer to justice. Justice! Why, we were engaged in a deed of justice.

My master thought it best to leave London for awhile. We must be careful now; we had done so much work during the past month that everyone was watching. Even the women themselves were fearful of plying their vocation; so we must let some little time elapse.

We went to Paris, the doctor, Ethel, and I. Gay Paris! But we did not stay there; we did not feel in the mood for work; besides, England was the selected country.

We traveled through Italy, Germany, Austria.

It was the 21st day of October. We were in Monte Carlo, the gambling hell of Europe. The season was at its height; hundreds of gaily-dressed men and women thronged the monster hotels, crowded the gambling palaces, day and night.

My master was growing tired of travel; we were to return to England soon. I was glad to hear it; I was eager to return.

We were standing by a table one night, where a large crowd were gambling; the game was "Rouge et Noir," Red and Black— a famous game. I was interested in the various changes depicted upon the faces of the players, as luck came to them or went against them; eager, anxious, impatient, as the cards turned. Despairing, saddened, sorrowful, as they saw that the turn was against them.

"Such is life," murmured my master, "ever hopeful, until the turn of the card, then despair. But hope springs eternal in the human breast, and mankind will ever play against fate, until the final trump. Some are favored for the time, but in the end, naught but misery, hopeless despair, anguish, death."

He spoke solemnly.

The girl Ethel stood by him, her eyes upon the scene, her heart with him.

Constant association had awakened a strange feeling in my heart for this fair creature; I could not account for it then, but it all came to me afterward. I loved her, but seemed to think it natural that I must be kept away from her; she, to my diseased mind, was a rare flower; I might inhale the fragrance of her presence, but must not touch her with the love of my heart. She was not for me.

We stood side by side; her dress touched my hand; I felt content that she was near me.

Suddenly I heard my master give utterance to a muffled exclamation.

I looked up into his face; it was livid. His lips were parted, and his breath came quickly; his eyes seemed bursting from their sockets.

"What is it?" I whispered.

"Look! See!" he gasped, never turning his eyes; "that woman yonder, the second from the 'croupier.'"

I looked as he directed. I saw a magnificently-dressed lady, of perhaps forty years. Beautiful is hardly the word to describe her. Royal! Yes; that is more like it. Royally beautiful, proud and haughty in her bearing, her hands white and uncovered, her fingers and hair literally blazing with jewels.

"She is divine," I murmured.

"She is a devil," answered my master harshly.

The next instant he had left me. I stood alone by Ethel's side. He had gone.

I turned my eyes from the regal-looking woman at the gaming-table to the golden-haired creature by my side.

"You are beautiful to-night, Ethel," I said.

"Uncle says I am always beautiful," she answered innocently.

"You are! You are!" I cried eagerly.

I was about to say more, when I perceived him returning.

"Come; we will go," he commanded, and we left the place.

"The Countess of Arno," he muttered, as if to himself, upon our way to the hotel. "Of the Inferno would more properly apply to her."

He said no more until we were closeted together in his room. Ethel retired. We were alone. He was very thoughtful, scarcely spoke for a period of thirty minutes. Then a change overspread his countenance; his eyes glowed; he moistened his lips with the tip of his tongue.

"I have it," he cried joyfully.

Then to me, tenderly, kindly, as he ever spoke.

"Jack, Providence has directed our footsteps. We have been sent here. The Almighty has delivered the sacrifice into my hands."

I listened attentively; I felt my blood coursing more quickly through my veins; I did not speak.

"You saw her, Jack—she of the diamonds. Is she not handsome?"

"Divinely beautiful."

"Only skin deep. Her heart is as black as the pit of Erebus. *Jack, she was the cause of my sister's ruin!*"

I nodded vehemently; I awaited his further speech.

"*Jack, she must die!*" Solemnly, like a judge pronouncing sentence. Then quickly, "Not as the others; they are spotless angels in comparison with her. No; not as they perished, but something more horrible; something that will turn her glossy black hair to the color of the Alpine snows; something that will freeze her blood and turn her heart to ice; something that will destroy the body and allow the brain to exist. What shall it be? Think, Jack! Think!"

I thought. I tried to devise some especially cruel thing; some torture known not to man, but my mind was dazed. I could not form any satisfactory plan. I shook my head despairingly.

"I can not think," I lamented.

"It does not matter. I had formed a plan, but wished to see if you could not think of a better one, Jack. She must suffer as no woman ever suffered before; the lines of her face must be drawn and hardened through the intensity of her torture. Ah, I have it all mapped out in my mind. To-morrow will see it put into execution."

We parted for the night. I felt that something rare was about to be presented to me. I could not sleep for thinking of it. I laid awake trying to picture that beautiful royal face disfigured by anguish; the magnificent form writhing in pain. I fell asleep as day was breaking; I slept until nearly noon. My master was not in the hotel when I descended the stairs. I did not look for him; I knew he would summon me when he wanted me. I met him at dinner; he seemed lively, gay, satisfied with himself.

After dinner he took me aside, and gave me my instructions. I was to be in waiting at a certain place with a carriage and horses; a lady would approach me and ask the hour. I was to reply: "The hour is propitious." Then I was to assist her into the carriage, and drive her to a villa, a few miles out of town, which had been vacant for a year. A Frenchman had shot himself there, and the people were superstitious; no one cared to rent it.

"She will not fail?" I inquired.

"No fear. I met her at the gaming-table; I formed her acquaintance easily. I represented myself as a German count. She is willing to fleece me; it is her business, and she thoroughly understands it. No; she will not fail to come."

I felt impatient for the hour to come; it drew near. It all turned out as he had said. I was standing by my horses' heads at the junction of two roads; the night was dark, only the stars were visible. I saw the figure of a woman hurrying toward me. It was she—the Countess of Arno. She asked the question; I answered as instructed, and I was soon driving at a rapid pace toward the deserted villa.

My master met her at the door. His tone, as he addressed her, was one of tenderness—the tenderness of an infatuated lover. Ah, he could be tender. I secreted the carriage and horses in a clump of trees which grew near the house, and then hurried to my post near my master to be ready to render him aid. The doors were locked; the woman was in the power of my master. They were sitting side by side upon a richly upholstered sofa. She, feigning an appearance of passionate love; he, as an ardent lover.

"And you would be true?" he whispered.

"As the stars," she answered.

He clasped her to his bosom. This was my signal. He had instructed me fully what to do at the same time he had spoken of the horses.

I crept toward the unconscious woman. I seized her arms and bent them backward, then strapped them together at the elbows and wrists behind her back, my master rendering me the aid of his powerful arms. The woman struggled and screamed.

With a calm smile he arose. "I must first put a stop to that," he murmured; "I will fix you so you can not scream, although your cries could not be heard; then I will explain to you why you are confined, why I had you brought here."

He turned to the table which stood near the door. I followed him with my eyes; I saw the miserable woman also watching him. She had ceased screaming, and was now only breathing rapidly, her magnificent bust rising and falling quickly—spasmodically.

Upon the table I saw what I had not before observed—*the case of instruments!*

He had opened it, and turning, I saw he held in his hand a long narrow knife.

Before the wretched creature had time to shriek, before I knew what he was about to do, he was upon her, his knees pressing her backward, his hands forcing open her jaws. A rapid action of the wrist, and he held up before my eyes, *her tongue*, the red blood dripping from it to the rich carpet.

He had cut it out at the root. He threw it from him into the burning grate.

"If you were going to leave this place you would probably miss that necessary organ to a woman's happiness; but, as I do not intend that you shall ever leave here, and wish to talk with you without any reply from you, I thought it best to relieve you of it."

He spoke calmly, wiping his knife upon a chamois skin, which he carried in the case for that purpose.

I looked toward the woman; she had fainted.

With deliberation, this man, who possessed a heart of adamant, drew from his pocket a medicine case; he slowly uncorked a tiny vial and allowed a few drops of some liquid to fall into the disfigured mouth.

"That will serve the double purpose of restoration, and keeping her conscious," he observed.

He spoke truly; for, with a gasp, the woman opened her eyes and looked up in his face.

"Of course, you had to indulge in the feminine weakness of fainting," he remarked coolly, as she opened her eyes.

"Now that you can hear and understand me, we will get through with this business. Isabel Ward—look at me!"

He spoke sharply. The large eyes of the woman were slowly raised to his face. Surprise, horror, strangely intermingled with agony, was what I saw there.

"You doubtless are more than surprised to hear that name again. Let me see. You are the Countess of Arno now, so you claim." Then a slight contemptuous laugh.

I sat, eager to hear, to see what was to follow. I felt it was to be something horrible. I rubbed my hands in expectant glee.

"But I shall address you by the name I know best, remember the most vividly. I shall never forget that name; it has been recorded on the tablets of my memory twenty years. A long time, eh? You must be about fifty now; you do not look it. You have taken excellent care of yourself. You would probably live to reach seventy, or perhaps eighty, if I permitted; but I will not permit it!! You have live too long already. You should never have been born; better for hundreds of poor wretches who will outlive you, live to curse you, to make your tortures in Hades more acute from the strength of their curses, their bitter anathemas. Ah! you should shudder! You will have *cause* to do so before long. I see your eyes are studying my face. I see you do not recognize me even yet. Your memory is not so good as mine. You should have cultivated the memory for faces, so you could have recognized mine, so you could have fled from me when we met, and thus escaped my vengeance. Study me well. You do not know me yet? Then I will introduce myself. Isabel Ward, Countess of Arno, Louis Westinghouse. Ha! Ha! I see you draw back in terror now—you know me now."

Through all this speech my master had kept his eyes upon the woman. He had spoken clearly, deliberately, a tinge of sarcasm permeating his demeanor. She made a desperate attempt to turn her head as he spoke his name. Useless. I was holding her.

"You know me now," he continued. "We meet in a strange manner. It is singular that I should see you here, but it was ordained. Remember the words of the Saviour: 'Be sure your sins will find you out.' They have found you out, and I am the emissary of the Almighty sent to punish you. *The wages of sin is death*; not only that—everlasting torture. But, as your soul goes before, I can not have the pleasure of seeing you suffer in torment. I have arranged to prepare you for what is to come in the great hereafter. You shall suffer some before my eyes. I slept not last night. I was planning your punishment. While you are writhing in torture before my eyes, think! Look back over your past, and bring to your memory a golden-haired girl, the innocent, pure sister of the man who stands before you! Recall the agony of a happy home blighted; a man's heart broken; an angelic maiden's life blasted and withered. Then pray. Pray that you may die soon, for your punishment will be more than you can bear, but lighter than you deserve. You have heard. You know what is to follow. *Now, pray.*"

He turned to the case of instruments in a quick, impetuous manner; he selected a few of them, and laid them, shining, glittering, upon the table. Then stepping into the adjoining room, he returned with a pan of sheet iron, about five feet in length; it was apparently new. Then, going to the grate, he seized the fire shovel, and transferred the burning contents to the pan—bright, glowing, red-hot coals. Then he seized a hatchet, and with rapid, powerful blows cut out the upholstered part of the sofa, scattering the horse-hair padding over the floor; soon only the wooden frame remained. The woman lay perfectly still. I could feel the beating of her heart. I could see her eyes following his every movement.

He turned to her; she began to move her lower limbs; they were as yet unconfined. "Tie her limbs," commanded the avenger.

I did so. They were soon tightly strapped together. Then he began to strip the rich, elegant clothing from her form; rending, tearing the glistening silk and precious lace. In five minutes he had finished, and the nude figure of the beautiful woman lay before us. "Lift her, and tie her to the sofa," he commanded. I obeyed him. I secured the unresisting form to the frame-work of the article of furniture. Then I saw what he proposed doing.

With a mighty effort he dragged the bench of torture that he had fashioned over the pan of hot coals, and then stood over the helpless form of his victim, a smile upon his face, his arms folded. A hoarse gurgling in the throat showed how much the woman was suffering. Her dark eyes rolled in the horrible agony she was enduring; beads of sweat stood upon the white brow. She tried to move; useless—I had tied her securely.

He stood and gazed upon her sufferings for a period of ten minutes; then he turned to the table where the instruments lay, and picked up a lancet. Before I could comprehend his action, he had made an incision in the thigh, another in the lower limb. The blood gushed forth, falling into the flames, causing them to leap higher. The sight of blood seemed to overpower his stoical indifference; he grew wild, demoniac. He call the helpless, dying creature by the most opprobrious epithets; he slapped her face, cut off her ears and threw them into the flames; then, with a quick skillful movement, he drew the shining knife across the scorching abdomen. Eager as I was for blood, crazed as I was, I felt horrified. It was over in a moment—the woman was dead. Never had mortal been so cruelly tortured. My pen fails me when I try to record it. My heart turns sick at the loathsome, hideous details.

The head was severed from the trunk; each limb was cut off, and, removing the pan to the cellar, the fire was made stronger and fiercer, and each part was burned. We left the pan in the cellar, and in the early morning returned to Monte Carlo. My master was silent all the way; I was unable to speak.

At 10 o'clock we started for England.

NINTH MONTH.

NOVEMBER.

We were safely and comfortably housed by the end of the week. The weather was not warm; November is a disagreeable month.

My master did not associate with me as much as in the time before we left England. I felt hurt; grieved. I also found that the gentle girl I loved was kept more and more from me. I wondered at it in a dazed way; we had been together so often during the month abroad that I could not comprehend it. My mind was not so active, it seemed to me, as it had been. I found myself muttering strange fancies; I felt sometimes a sad sinking of the heart. The memory of the noble work of vengeance I was assisting in, did not elate me as much as formerly. While in the presence of Dr. Westinghouse, my feelings would return; I was as eager as ever then; but when he left me, I would sink back into my depressed condition. What was coming over me? I even began to feel fearful of being discovered. I never felt that way before. I first felt the change the night I witnessed the horrible tortures of the Countess of Arno; I did not enjoy that rare spectacle as I thought I would.

Several days passed. It was the morning of November 8, a dull foggy morning. My master had left me after eating breakfast; he had gone into the city. I sat, moody and depressed, in his study; I had lit the gas, and the mixture of dull daylight struggling in at the window, and the glare of the gas seemed to make me feel even more despondent.

In the midst of my gloomy thoughts came the quick inspiration that now, as my master was out of the house, I might see the rare treasure he guarded. I might even speak to her. He would not know it. It would satisfy the longing at my heart. I turned out the gas and leaped up the steps, two at a time. I knew her room; it was at the head of the stairs, and faced the street. I tapped gently on the door; no answer.

"Ethel!" I called softly.

Still no reply.

I tried the door. It was unlocked.

With a dull feeling of curiosity as to the apparent heedlessness of him, usually so careful, I entered.

The room was darkened, the shades being pulled down.

I stopped and listened, feeling like a thief, like one treading on forbidden ground.

I heard the soft, regular breathing of one apparently slumbering. It came from the rear portion of the room. I turned and saw in the dim light the face of her I loved.

She slept sweetly, peacefully, unconscious of my presence. I drew near the bed; the gas-burner was beside it; I ignited a sulphur match, and lit it, allowing the soft, mellow radiance to shine full upon her angelic face. Still she did not awaken. I stood and drank in the sight of her fresh, young beauty, exposed to my gaze. I stooped and kissed her crimson lips. She awoke.

"Is it you, uncle?" she murmured dreamily.

"No; it is Jack," I answered.

She opened her eyes to their widest extent.

"You, Jack?" she murmured in mild surprise.

"Yes, Ethel; I thought you might like to see me, I have seen so little of you of late. Your uncle has gone to the city."

She looked at me as if puzzled.

"Yes, I know," she murmured. "Did he give you permission to come?"

"No."

"He will be displeased."

"But you are not, are you? Tell me, you are not angry at me for coming?"

"No, Jack, I am not angry, I am glad to see you—but uncle?"

"He will not know. Ah! I could not help coming to you."

I fell on my knees by the bed.

"I love you so; I love you, dear."

She placed her little hand upon my head.

"Do you, Jack? I love you, Jack; I love you dearly."

She spoke in the same tone she would have used in petting a dog.

"I would take you from here if I could; I would have you all to myself."

I said much more. I can not remember it all; I was wild, overjoyed to be with her alone.

A stern voice brought me to myself.

"Rise!" it said.

I arose, trembling, to my feet. I turned and saw my master. He was gazing sternly, terribly at me.

"So!" he cried harshly, "you love her? You have forgotten yourself. I thought it. It has been fixing itself in my mind for some time. Know you not she is not for love? Her heart is not for the base passion of man. Leave me! To your place! I will see you soon."

Like a whipped cur I clunk down the stairs. I trembled in every limb. In a short time he entered the study. I feared to look at him; I felt guilty of a crime.

"Look at me, Jack," he commanded.

My eyes sought his; they were harsh and cruel. He had never looked at me that way before.

"It is as I feared," he began. "I have noticed your growing affection for Ethel, and for that reason have kept her more secluded. I thought, however, that I could trust you; you have proven to me that the confidence I have had in you was misplaced. Have you not heard her unhappy history? Do you not know that she has no name, no existence, save as I choose to give her? The work of vengeance I am carrying on, is to wipe out her shame. Would you thwart me?"

His breath came in short gasps; his eyes shone like a wild beast's.

I fell on my knees before him.

"Forgive me, master," I cried, "forgive me."

He raised me to my feet; his manner had changed; he was kind and gentle now.

"I will forgive you, Jack; you are but mortal, and she is beautiful. You have been guilty of a breach of confidence, but I will overlook it. We have been idle too long." The voice grew tender. "We should not have lingered here so long; your mind has been allowed to have too much sway—has been dwelling on other ideas save that which it should entertain solely. We must do our work again."

My heart went out to him. I agreed with him with childish fervor. No thought of love now. No sinking at the heart. No despondency.

The day dragged through; night came—welcome night—in which we could work, protected by the darkness.

We wended our way to the old familiar district, but did not frequent any of the places where our former victims had been found. My master felt some fear of our being recognized. Through the dark streets we walked, the fresh air producing a peculiar feeling of elation upon my mind. We separated at the corner of two dark, narrow streets. I did not recognize the place. I thought it looked familiar, but could not place it exactly.

I stood alone. Many people passed me, but I did not move. I was controlled by some new and strange emotion—a feeling as if I had been bound and was about to be set free; that is the only description I can give. Opposite me on the wall I could detect a yellow poster announcing something; what, I could not make out. I walked to it, and in the faint light of a street lamp saw that it was a reward notice—"**£100 reward for the arrest of the Whitechapel murderer**." It stood out in bold black letters. I walked up the street; I found them posted everywhere. The police were determined to find the man; determined to check us in our glorious work.

I returned to my former position. Men and women passed me, many of them entering a large and somewhat pretentious building near me. It was a lodging-house. A policeman observed me. He tapped me on the shoulder. "Move on," he said. I muttered something about going to seek lodging in the building near me. He seemed satisfied and left me alone.

It was past midnight, when I heard the sound of laughter on the street not far off—a woman's voice, then the deeper tones of a man. I stood in the shadow and waited for them to pass me. They drew nearer. I recognized the man, and saw that the woman was much prettier than the majority of females I had seen in the vicinity. They did not pass me, but turned up a narrow court which ran in beside the large lodging-house. As they passed the reward poster the woman pointed to it and said, in a jeering tone:

"A new dodge of the 'bobbies.' The man will give 'imself hup now, to get the reward."

The man laughed heartily; he evidently enjoyed the joke. It was my master.

They entered a low door leading off the court. I crept to the opening. Neither of them were aware of my presence; my master probably thought me far away. I heard the sound of the woman's voice in tones of drunken endearment; from other sounds I knew she was disrobing. Then all was silent for a moment. I listened eagerly. *I next heard a swishing, cutting sound.* I tried the door; it was unfastened; I stood in the room—a narrow, close den; the atmosphere nearly stifled me. My master was at his work. He stopped as I entered, but knew me and continued. I was carried away, for the time, by the fascination of the horrible crime. I was anxious to assist. I drew my knife and fell upon the body; I cut at every part that exposed itself, and then, standing gazing at the horrible remains, my head began to swim. I saw a blur before my eyes; a sharp cracking sensation, and I knew no more.

A feeling of agonizing pain, and I opened my eyes; all was dark about me. I thought I was in my lodging in the heart of the city. But why this pain in my head? I put out my hand; it touched something cold and clammy. I felt for a match, and finding one struck it on the floor; it flickered and burned, throwing a faint light about the place.

I did not recognize it at first. I looked to see what my hand had touched. My blood ran cold; *it was a sightless severed head!*

I cried out in horror; I groped for the door and found it; I ran down the street until my breath failed me. What was I doing in that place, with my hand grasping the ghastly object? I sat down on the steps of a house and racked my brain.

Gradually I began to recall events, my meeting with Dr. Westinghouse on the street the night of August 7, and the interview of the night following, being the first that came. I faintly remembered his words; recalled the fact of the marvelous change that took place in me. Like a dream came the recollection of all that had passed; it did not all come at once, a little at a time. *I realized that I was free from his cursed influence; knew that I was myself again.*

I dragged my weary limbs to my distant lodgings, those I had occupied previous to the night of August 8. I found the room door locked. I hammered upon it. No one came. I had no idea of the date of the month; I did not know then that I had not been there for two months. At last my hand, which I had plunged in my pocket thoughtlessly, came in contact with a bunch of keys. I remembered that there was one upon the bunch that would open the door. I inserted it in the lock and entered the room. It was in darkness. I struck a match and lit the gas. Everything seemed as I had left it. I looked at myself in the mirror connected with my dressing-case. I started back in horror.

I was covered with blood. I quickly stripped off my clothes, and, building a fire in the grate, burned them. Then I carefully washed myself, and turning out the gas and locking the door, I turned into bed, for the first time in two months *MYSELF*. I was awakened at noon by hearing a key inserted in the lock of my door. I felt no disposition to rise, but lazily turned my eyes in the direction of the door. It was my servant. He entered with a careless whistle. He stopped in astonishment, as he saw me in the bed. "I am glad to see you back, sir," he said. "Been out of town? You left rather sudden."

I made some reply, and turned over on my side and slept again. How sweet, how refreshing was that sleep. It invigorated me; it made a new man of me.

I found a nice lunch set out for me when I awoke. My servant was a faithful fellow. I felt grateful to him for his kindness, as I devoured the broiled bird, and ate the nicely-browned toast which accompanied it. He entered while I was eating; had been to the laundry to get my clean linen.

"Morning paper, sir?" he said, handing me the *Times*. "Another murder in Whitechapel; a horrible one this time, worse than any of the rest."

I took the paper and read the account of the murder of Mary Jane Kelly. I asked for, and read the full accounts of every one of them. My first recollections had been vague and indistinct, but it all came to me now. I was "Jack the Ripper." I could recall the tone of Dr. Westinghouse's voice as he gave it to me.

What could I do? I knew I was blameless of any intent to kill. I

Mary Jane Kelly

was under the hellish influence of a demon at the time, but would anyone believe that? I doubted it. Neither could I give up this man to justice without criminating myself. I pondered, horror-stricken, terrified, for an hour, and then my mind was made up. I would leave the country. I would return to America. I had a relative living in a small town in Illinois; I would go to him. I set about packing my valises that night. It was midnight when I had everything in readiness. I was about to retire, when I heard someone trying the door. I, secretly wondering who it could be, walked over to it and opened it. I drew back in surprise.

Dr. Westinghouse!

He smiled, as he saw my preparations for travel.

"So you are going to leave me," he said.

"Forever," I cried. He smiled, and sank into a chair.

"You forget the tie that binds us."

"I forget nothing. It has all come to me; at first but faintly, but now I know all. I am myself again. I am free from your influence."

He waited until I had finished; then he asked: "Where are you going?"

"To the United States."

He seemed surprised, but pleased.

"You would have been wise if you had come to that decision two months ago."

I made no reply.

He rose and paced the floor.

"Dewey, when, upon the night of August 8, I bound you to myself, a deed was done that can never be undone. You are now free to a certain extent, but can never be entirely so. I knew your intentions as quickly as you did yourself. I knew where to find you, as my presence here indicates. I came here because I wished to explain to you this fact, so you would understand in the days to come that you can never escape me. If you were to make mention of anything you know regarding some mysterious crimes which have lately been puzzling and horrifying the world, your tongue would be paralyzed before you had finished, so great is my power over you. This, however, would be ridiculed by any intelligent person, as such things are not clearly understood. I know you believe it, as you have had ample proof. Remember this: I shall not see you again until you come to die; I shall be with you then. The day is not far distant. Away from me, free from my protecting, strengthening power, your overwrought brain will grow weak and incapable; the loss of mind will affect your animal power, and as mind controls matter, the destruction of one will affect the other. You will feel strong and comparatively well as long as that part of my very self lives in you, but as that wears away you will grow weaker and die. *At three o'clock, on the morning of the thirteenth day of January, you will draw your last breath.* Farewell. I shall miss you; I shall be obliged to do my work alone, but it will be done. It is still unfinished."

He was gone.

JANUARY 12—5 a.m.

The first month of a new year. The last month of my life! I know it; I feel it. My kind relative has seen me daily grow weaker; has remonstrated with me for overtaxing my strength by writing. I know I am not able to do it, but it must be done, for to-morrow I die. Only twenty-two hours to live! And yet I would not extend the time. I have nothing to bind me to earth. I would like to gaze upon the face of that angel in the power of a demon again before I die, but I know that is impossible. I kissed her pure lips once! It is the one bright oasis in the desert of my last year on earth.

I have read the papers since my arrival in America. He is not captured yet. I also see that he has not completed his work. Will he ever do so? I pray God that it may not come to pass.

Will he ever be discovered? Knowing the man as I do, I am inclined to think not.

It is all over. Day is dawning. I must rest. I turn down my lamp, dip my pen in the ink for the last supply necessary to write my last words, and go to bed. Before this time to-morrow I shall have solved the mystery of the hereafter. The black dog in the back yard is still howling. He will not howl this time to-morrow.

[FINIS.]

The Whitechapel Horrors

A Conjectural Story relating the Facts

Concerning Four of the Murders.

They Were Committed by an American While in a Condition of Hypnotism - Weird and Thrilling Story of Unconscious Crime.

Special to the Indianapolis Journal

London, Nov. 24.—The Whitechapel murders have yielded numerous theories, emanating from the police and others, but nothing conjectural has taken such readable form as an article by the *Pall Mall Gazette*. It is a piece of fiction, avowedly, and yet its ingenuity seems to recommend it to the Londoners about as strongly as though it were the truth. It makes out the Whitechapel assassin to be an American by his own confession, and it is complete as follows:

I.

My name is Charles Kowlder, and I am an American. I have come to London for rest and recreation. I have a business errand, however, else I would probably not be here, for a New Yorker engaged in a hurried pursuit of fame or money is not apt to lose time without making some sort of excuse to himself. But the trivial mission is already as good as done, and on this day and hour in August, 1888, I am waiting in a physician's ante-room. I desire to be told what is the matter with me, and I hope to get the information trustworthily and beneficially. Others have brought in their ailments ahead of me, so that we are a party of a dozen or more, seated in a dismal wooden room, for the walls are paneled heavily in oak. I over-hear one woman say to another that she feels as though she were in a big box, and the response is the suggestion that we are all in a huge coffin. The joke is grim, and the maker of it is lugubrious. I surmise that she has a fatal malady, and that inclosure for burial is, to her, an early certainty. We are a cheerless group—excepting myself. The sombreness of the room and the gloom of its occupants do not weigh down my spirits. I am mentally buoyant. The trouble with me seems to be physical fatigue. Before taking the present relief from my very busy employments, I went home from every day's work so weary that my steps were a trifle uncertain, and my nerves and muscles were slightly beyond control. Sometimes my brain was exhausted, too, but the depression of spirits was so transient that with an hour or two of rest I would rebound into higher animation than before. So it seemed folly to waste time in a vacation. It was only when a matter came up that necessitated a transatlantic trip by somebody from our establishment, and when I bethought me that I could use the period of physical relaxation without any abatement of mental tensity, that I decided upon the voyage. What I mean is that I intended to occupy my time in devising schemes and laying out plans, so that my ne-glect of New York labor should possibly be a gain in fortune, after all.

While I sit awaiting my turn for an interview with the physician I am not thinking of my health. I am projecting in my mind something to do when I get back to America. The calculations generally distract me from my surroundings, so that when the servant says, "It is you, now, sir," there is a dazed instant before I am aware of the place and why I am here. I enter the physician's own apartment. He is a sedate, clean-shaven old man, and he wears black clothes of so clerical an aspect that I feel like a Roman Catholic at a confessional. He motions me to a seat at one side of a table and takes one at the other.

"How do you do?" he inquires.

"First rate," I respond, with quickness; "never better."

Then it strikes me that I must seem absurd for calling on a doctor without any complaint to make. Be he expresses no surprise. He is imperturbable. He gazes critically into my face and waits silently for me to explain.

"To tell you the truth," I go on, "I shouldn't have visited you at all if I had not promised my family physician to do so. I am a New Yorker, and I have come abroad to rest. But I can't conceive that I require anything else. I feel, as we would say in my country, like a fighting-cock–like the American eagle, ready to flap his wings and crow a challenge to the British lion. Even your fog doesn't depress me. It rather exhilarates me, I think. Anyhow I was never lighter-hearted, brighter-minded, or more volatile than I am at this minute. So I feel like apologizing for this needless intrusion, paying your fee, and getting out."

I am customarily a vivacious man, but now I am uncommonly voluble and exclamatory. But the physician doesn't show that he is impressed by any singularity in my address. He quietly and tersely puts many questions, which I answer with loquacious readiness, and I am conscious of rising into a gayety of manner not to be expected in a patient while consulting a doctor.

"Perhaps my buoyancy puzzles you," I at length remark. "I have heard of malingering patients, but don't think that I am the reverse of that—that I am forcing an appearance of feeling remarkably well. It is unaffected and spontaneous, I assure you."

"I am afraid it is," says the doctor, gravely.

"Afraid it is?" I amazedly echo.

"Yes; that is what I mean. Your exaltation, is unhealthy mental excitement. It is one of the symptoms which, undoubtedly, led your physician in New York to send you to me. I am a specialist in nervous diseases. You did not know that? Well, my fame isn't world-wide, but I know as much about human nerves as can be learned. You manifest what may be early symptoms of general paresis."

"Why, that is softening of the brain!" I exclaim, half amused and half amazed. "Nonsense; I beg your pardon, but it seems absurd to say that my intellect isn't acute."

"Too acute, my dear sir. Exhilaration of the mind is a bad sign, taken in connection with the physical fatigue, uncertainty of motion, and other things that you have described to me. You are threatened with general paresis, induced by that over-taxation of brain which is so common to you Americans."

"And it is incurable?"

"General paresis is incurable—yes. I do not say that you have it. It is impending. Your only escape from it, in my opinion, lies in absolute rest. By that I don't mean avoidance of physical fatigue as much as respite from mental activity. It would be well if you could think of nothing whatever during the next three months. I sometimes think we shall discover a means of suspending mentality, in order to recuperate brains by positive disuse, but we haven't hit upon it yet. The best we can do is to advise our patients to ease their minds to permit themselves no fixedness of thought—to abstain from planning, devising, and executing—to keep out of troubles—to occupy their minds as trivially as possible. You must do that."

A smile of incredulity is my silent response. That is an offense to the physician, and for the first time in our dialogue he looks and speaks as though personally interested.

"If you will act on my advice," and he rises to his feet, rests his hands on the table, and leans over toward me and emphasizes every word, "you may become a well man in three months. If you disobey me you will by that time be well along into a hopeless imbecility, which will rapidly develop into insanity and lead quickly to certain death."

Now I am shocked, indeed, and I am conscious that my smile only remains as a sort of facial paralysis. So volatile is my fancy, however, that with the words of a possible doom still in my ears my humor floats lightly off to a recollection of the fixed, unmeaning grin which we see in the ballet girl. But I stop my smiling, nevertheless, and promise to do as this professional advisor tells me to. I thank him, pay him, and bid him good day.

Then I walk to my hotel. The medical man's diagnosis has impressed me deeply, and yet the upward tendency of my good spirits fights against the sense of peril that would sink them down into reasonable depression. I comprehend fully all that has been said to me, and I go over in my mind the symptoms upon which his warning is based. I feel as though I have brought away from his office some weighty burden in place of my unladen condition on going there. But the sensation seems physical rather than mental, and I detect a tendency to be jocose with myself on the subject.

On coming into my room at the hotel I am reminded by the sight of a London newspaper lying on the table that I have neglected to order a New York journal to be mailed regularly to me, as I had intended. So I sit down to write the necessary letter. For what term shall I make the subscription? Three months will cover my stay in London, as I have planned. Besides, and the thought comes like an unpleasant blow, shall I be able longer than that to read at all? Nonsense! Medical specialists are always alarmists. I am all right, or shall be as soon as rested. But I shall keep obediently quiet. After writing the brief missive I am inclined to use my pen further.

So, with a first light motive of recreation, and a second one of seriously making a record, I write this account of the day's episode. After this is done I pick up the London newspaper carelessly and glance over the columns that are in so many respects different from those of New York journals. Then my eye fixes upon headlines that are quite American in style. They belong to an account of the murder of Polly Nichols in Whitechapel. I read the narrative interestedly, because it reveals to me not only an uncommonly brutal murder, but gives to me an insight of such low life in London as has no counterpart in the greatest city of the other hemisphere.

II.

It was yesterday that I made my visit to the physician. It is today that I am thinking how I shall keep my business projects out of my mind, in order to get the mental quietude which, if the specialist is not mistaken, alone can save me from madness. You can lay down your hands, and say to them that they shall be idle. They will obey your will. But you cannot compel your brain to cease action, rational or otherwise, as long as you live. What shall I do as a means of distraction? The account of the murder of Polly Nichols still lies before me. I read it all over again. She was a vagrant of the streets of Whitechapel. In America we would have called her a tramp, from her homeless mode of life. But we have no female tramps in that country. Our unsheltered and sodden wanderers are men. The worst and poorest of our women are not like these Whitechapel wretches. I make up my mind, of a sudden, to spend the day in seeing the neighborhood of Buck's Row, where Polly was slaughtered. The Whitechapel Road, along which I walk in my quest of grim diversion is, in some respects, like the Bowery, a thoroughfare which runs through the most populous and impoverished part of New York. I find a similar rush and whirl of retail trade, and a like variegation of people, but more of personalised vice. The zig-zag and puzzle of small streets and intricate courts, too, are strange to a New Yorker's eyes. In wandering through them I come across exhibits of squalor and depravity such as are happily scarcer in New York, and where, when they do exist, they are kept more nearly out of sight. At length I made my way to Buck's Row. The police are in possession of the place, and I am brusquely excluded; but I obtain a sight of the still blood stained pavement where the body of Polly was found. By an exercise of Yankee inquisitiveness and perseverance, I at length get at the policeman who discovered the remains. I put to him, in the form of questions, sections of the account that I have twice read of the crime, and get answers in monosyllables of assent or denial. The information leaves the murder a mystery. The officer in his patrol passed through Buck's Row, as he had done a quarter of an hour previously. Then he saw nothing unusual. Now he found Polly lying flat. He kicked her, and said, "Come on, old girl, you can't sleep here, you know." He could not awaken her. Only the trump of Gabriel can do that, for she was dead. Her murderer had stabbed and slashed her furiously. Her front teeth were knocked out, too, and her face badly bruised. Her hands bore the marks of a desperate struggle. The accepted theory, I learn, is that Polly quarrelled with some drunken man, was struck by him, and, when she fought back, was cut to death with a knife wielded by a suddenly infuriated scoundrel.

The hours spent in Whitechapel will surely relieve me of the mental stress of preoccupation for an equal number of days. The general scenes in that quarter of London, the phases of unlucky life, the special commotion caused by the murder, are all new and strange to an American. There is something horribly engrossing, moreover, in the extravagant violence of the deed. The homicide was such a butchery, and there was in it such an expenditure of fiendish frenzy, that one feels he must contribute something toward the detection of the perpetrator. If no more had been done to Polly than to kill her, there would be nothing in the matter to make a foreigner think twice about it, but the either wanton or mysteriously purposed mutilation makes it a terrible fascination. I am sure that I do not, at this writing, lack a subject outside of my own affairs for thought.

III.

My mind has not been off the slaughter of Polly Nichols. I have engrossed myself completely in the case. The theories of explanation that I have read have multiplied into others of my own. I have studied the murder in every accessible detail, critically examining everything pertaining to it that could be seen or heard. No separately considered part of the crime has yielded anything definite as to who was the murderer, or why. I have spent days in Whitechapel, seeking original sources of information, but without avail. I have been able, by special favor, to see the maltreated corpse. The sight made me shiver, but conveyed nothing to my intelligence. Returning to my room after these vain detective efforts, I have viewed the case at a distance and as a whole, trying to deduce something at least credible as an explanation.

Today I take up a London paper and see that Annie Chapman has been murdered in much the same manner as Polly Nichols. She was a courtesan, too, and she has also become a dissected corpse. I read how she had not had the four pence, last night, with which to pay for a bed in a miserable lodging house; how she went into the street to get a pittance by customary degradation, and how she was found, early this morning, dead, like the other woman. The similarity of the crime strikes me strangely. As I glance along the account, the new murder seems so exactly counterpart of the other that I instinctively look at the date of the journal to see if I have not picked up a back number by mistake. No, this is a duplication of the other crime.

I peruse the matter rapidly, but carefully. As my eyes go from word to word, and sentence to sentence, comprehension seems to keep ahead of perusal. Are the facts so precisely repetitious that the second narrative is substantially a fresh version of the first? That does not prove so on reading again. The generalities of the dreadful deeds are the same, but the particulars are not. The sensation is peculiar, like that which most persons have experienced when, upon seeing or hearing something, they feel as though they have seen or heard precisely that thing before. Scientific men have explained these mental phenomena, I believe, by telling that they are kind of reflex action of the mind. The mental comprehension is quicker than our consciousness of it. The right of sound reaches the brain sooner than we physically know it by means of eyes or ears—like a flash of lightning and its more slowly arriving peal of thunder. That may be the right theory or not. Less rationalistic is the belief that the souls of men sometimes leave their bodies during sleep, and go with their thoughts to distant places, to return with knowledge that fades to the slightest imaginable impression when they awake. Did my mental being go to sleep walking in Whitechapel last night, and witness the killing of Annie Chapman? Ridiculous! I have had this vague sense of prior experience before. It is a sensationary freak that is not uncommon to persons in good health, and why should I be alarmed by it, unless I accept it as a sign of progress toward that aberration of intellect which the diagnosis of the physician pointed out as a possibility. That view of it startles me, and I consider the matter as carefully as I calmly can. I cannot persuade myself that my mind was quite normal while reading the newspaper report of the Annie Chapman case. I am sure that my cognizance of the printed lines outran my perusal, if only for the space of an eye's glance. This was certainly a more acute manifestation of reflex mentality—if that is the clearest phrase to use—that I had ever known to happen in myself. Is this proof that I am in an unduly impressionable state? That my brain is already diseased? That I am well along in the period of unhealthy volatility which precedes the insanity of paresis? I have read some of the literature of that malady, since my interview with the expert alienist, and have therefrom learned that an exceeding delicacy of psychological activity is apt to precede the first stages of imbecility. Instances are on record wherein the victims became clairvoyant, seemingly, and performed wonders of second-sight more inexplicable than any of the tricks of the showmen.

What am I to do? Nothing, as nearly as possible. That was the physician's advice. I cannot take off my head, put it safely away from consciousness, and so let it lie oblivious until rested. I must carry it around affixed to the top of my spinal column, connected with every nerve in my organization, aware of everything that goes on around me, and thoughtful all the time. It is only in this last respect that it can be controlled. I can fix my mind on something else than affairs of selfish consequence, and thus displace worry by a less exhausting kind of thinking. I will pay attention to the Whitechapel murders.

IV.

I have witnessed four murders in Whitechapel. The assertion is here set down solemnly, and for the present secretly, although I hope to soon make a sure and safe disclosure. I could not expect, under the circumstances, to convince the authorities or the public of a truth which has but slowly commanded my own credence. The revelation came to me dimly in the case of Annie Chapman, and has become clearer and clearer until today, the 2nd of October, I write the declaration positively that I have seen four of the Whitechapel tragedies. My knowledge, so marvelously acquired, enables me to say that the murders of Emma Elizabeth Smith, in April, and Martha Tabram, in August, do not belong to the series that have become shudderingly famous. They were doubtless homicides by separate men. The butchery of Polly Nichols was the real origin of the subsequent ones about which I know. The faint conviction if the murder of Annie Chapman was already in my mind, like a shadow of memory, as I have already described, the instant that I saw the published account. I was puzzled by it, and I attributed it to my peculiar mental condition; but for awhile it was not followed by any intellectual disturbance, and I began to believe that all danger to my sanity had passed away. I devoted myself assiduously to the scant evidence left for detective work in the Nichols and Chapman cases, not because I anticipated successful results, but in order to occupy myself with a subject which should not tax me overmuch. I am now aware that I made a mistake. I was more deeply absorbed than I imagined. What I regarded as a pastime became a fascination, and I fatigued my body with investigation, while I overwrought my brain with theorizing. Possessing myself by individual effort with all the facts that could be obtained by patient energy, and then placing them under minute consideration, I worked harder than I had done in those New York occupations from which I had fled for respite. The murder at Gateshead, in the north of England, with its peculiar mutilation of the body, has convinced the police that the hand of the Whitechapel fiend wielded the knife there. That may or may not be the fact. I did not make a journey of investigation, and I had no second sight of it. It was not until Sept. 26, several days after the Gateshead happening, that anything singular happened to me. On awakening in the morning, I recalled a dream, in which I seemed to have found myself in a place that was entirely strange. I am now aware that it was the site of the projected Metropolitan Opera House.

The vision was lurid enough for reality, which I now know it to have been, but it was left to me fragmentarily. What I retained when awake was like a series of instantaneous views, taken with winks of the eyes instead of the flashes of the camera, but separately clear and distinct. They represented a woman of the pave skulking into the dark shadows of the abandoned foundations of the opera house. She was a slatternly sot, and her vagrant personality was sharply impressed upon me. She had a man for a companion, but he was indistinct, as though out of the focus in which she was centered. There was maudlin endearment by the woman, for she seemed drunk, and she clung to her companion for support as much as for rough caress. Suddenly a knife was reached into the space covered clearly by my lens of sight, and it was held by the hand of the shadowy man, which extended out of gloom like the materialized member of a ghost in a spiritualistic séance. The weapon was struck straight into the heart of the woman, and her fall had barely brought her to the ground before the man set about his awful mutilation. The doing was in the light, and I saw it distinctly, but the doer was in the dark, so that his deed was stamped upon my mind, while his identity made no impress. I had never dreamt so startlingly. It was almost a surprise to me that I did not find in that day's journals an account of an assassination like that of my dream, which thereupon I pronounced an imaginary experience of a sleeper.

The murders of Elizabeth Stride and Catherine Eddowes, both in the first hour of Sunday morning, Sept. 30, brought a well-nigh paralyzing shock, which at first made me believe that I had reached the threatened dementia; but a visit to the physician and a demand of him to seek carefully for signs of hallucination, assured me that I was not yet a maniac. He was surprised by my questions, and I did not hint to him my reason for making them. That can here be told. I awoke that morning quivering in mind and body, with a second dream, in which I had seen one woman's throat cut in Berners street, and another butchered with dreadful elaboration in Mitre square. In my frequent visits to Whitechapel I had seen these places, and so they were not new to me in my dream, as the Thames Embankment had been. Again my vision was astoundingly distinct as to the women, and what was done to them, but no more than in the previous instance did I get other than a vague view of the perpetrator of the deeds. Regarding it all as a nightmare, wrought by my excited imagination, and caused by what I now regarded as too close application to my amateur detective whim. I resolved to ease myself of concern in the Whitechapel murders. I fell asleep again, and did not reawaken until nearly noon. Then I had a breakfast in my room, and was almost through with it when there were cries of newsboys in the street below. "Another Whitechapel Horror," they shouted. I got a paper, and there read accounts of the two murders exactly as I had dreamed them. I was amazed and stunned. As soon as I recovered a degree of self-possession, I made the call on the doctor, after which I tried to convince myself that the whole matter of the nightmare was fanciful—that the reading of the newspaper suggested it to a mind diseased, and that the printed narrative was really what first brought the facts to me. Indicative as this was of mental unsoundness, it was less revolting than the idea of supernaturalness.

But the demonstration that has irrefutably come to-day makes me out a clairvoyant witness of the Whitechapel murders. My visit to the physician was surely a tangible occurrence. It is equally certain that the cause of my resorting to him was my supposed dreams, one of which had not been realized. But here in print is disclosed the discovery of a woman's remains on the site of the Metropolitan Opera House, a place which I knew nothing about, but which in the description agrees exactly with my vision. The position in which the body lay when found, and its wanton disfigurement, were precisely as I had seen them in my sleep. It must be that my discernment was there when the tragedy happened, although I lay here abed three miles distant.

What shall I do with this knowledge? If I go with it to the authorities I will be deemed a lunatic, or else suspected of complicity in the crimes.

V.

I am the Whitechapel murderer. The woeful character of my confession should carry conviction of its truth. But I have a mind diseased, and, therefore, must prove that I am not an imaginary assassin. Let me go on, then, as calmly as I can, with my self-condemnation.

In already excluding from the series of Whitechapel crimes the isolated homicides of April and August I was right. As to the murderous dissection of Polly Nichols, that was the single deed of an undiscovered man, so far as I can tell. But the appalling use of the knife on Annie Chapman, Elizabeth Stride, Catherine Eddowes, and the unidentified woman at the Thames Embankment, was my work. The evidence against me in those cases is circumstantial, I admit, but it is not so in the instance of Mary Jane Kelly, who was killed in Martin's Court on the night of Nov. 8.

You will doubt and marvel as you read, but you will be finally convinced. Would to God you could find reason to acquit me, but that is impossible.

Another dream. An awakening before it was all over leaves it more clearly in my memory than its predecessors. I witnessed the encounter of Mary Jane Kelly and a man in a Whitechapel thoroughfare. The time was about 2 o'clock at night, but the street was still peopled, and everybody was in my view clearly, except Mary's companion. I seemed to recall my previous failure to discern the face of the assassin, and to endeavor this time to descry his face, but although his form was palpable, his head was invisible. My sight followed the pair as they went together to the court, and into the woman's poor room, and it remained with them during two hours. It was all pantomime. I saw her lips move in speech and laughter, for they caroused over a bottle of gin, but not a sound did I hear. My vision was restricted to my eyes, seemingly, and was not accompanied by anything auricular.

Conscious of a desire to see the man's face, I strained my eyes for it, but his countenance was the one blank spot in the picture. I was expectant of the climax of that miserable, mocking, revelry. I knew that the poor creature was to be slain by her fiendish visitor. "Could I but look into his face," I thought, "or follow him clairvoyantly after the deed, what a triumph for justice would be mine." My detestation of his purpose, and my dread of witnessing the stabbing, were as real as life. But the astral illumination would not fall upon his features, brightly as it revealed everything else in the room. The covert preparations of the murderer to strike the mortal blow were dimly revealed to me, and I vaguely saw him drawing a knife stealthily from his pocket. The pair were on the low, rickety bed that formed a part of the scant furniture. The woman was unsuspicious. She did not detect his design, and probably was never conscious of its execution, for her heart was pierced by the first stab, and she died with a few convulsive struggles. Then the dissection characteristic of these crimes was begun. I gazed in terror and revolt at the sanguinary work.

The hands and forearms of the infamous operator were in plain view. Looking at them keenly, with an intention of finding marks of possible identification, I saw that there was a ring on one of the fingers. It had an amethyst set in peculiar fashion. I recognized it instantly.

It was my own.

As by a stroke from an electric battery I was awakened. I was not abed in my room, but was there in Mary Jane Kelley's apartment, with a red, dripping knife in my hand, and my own atrocity lying hideously before me. I had found the Whitechapel murderer!

There was no guilt in my deeds. They were not committed by my own volition. Too intense study of the murder of Polly Nichols, at a time when my mind was in an abnormal condition, produced hypnotism. I have reasoned that out easily enough since my discovery. Just how I perpetrated the murders I cannot confess, because I know no more about them than I have here written. They occurred when I was in a curious state of somnambulism and lunacy. My actions were imitative, evidently, of what I had conceived as the manner of the assassination of Polly Nichols. It is through no fear of earthly punishment that I try to make out this defense of irresponsibility, for I shall be beyond the reach of human justice before this writing becomes public.

What I did immediately after my arousal to normal consciousness was to escape from Martin's Court, return to my hotel and take my departure from London.

Conjectural Note

After reading both stories in this volume a few times, and conducting research for the biographical sketch on Edward Oliver Tilburn, I have concluded that Tilburn could very well have written the anonymous story "The Whitechapel Horrors." While I have no definitive proof for that conjecture, many things indicate that he authored the work. First, there are similarities in the plots of *The Whitechapel Mystery* and "The Whitechapel Horrors": a New Yorker travels to London to commit the murders, and the Ripper commits the crimes while he's in a hypnotic state.

Second, the story was written while the Ripper murders were taking place and Tilburn had a track record for writing fictional works about current news events (e.g. *The Great Cronin Mystery* and *The Fateful Hand*).

Third, "The Whitechapel Horrors" was published in two Midwestern newspapers, The *Indianapolis Journal* and the *Chicago Tribune*, and Tilburn was either living or working in Indiana and the Chicago area during the years 1887 and 1888. "The Whitechapel Horrors" appeared in those newspapers in late November, 1888— of course, a writer living outside the Midwest could have submitted the story, but authors tend to submit to publications with which they are familiar.

Fourth, Tilburn alleges that he wrote several anonymous stories for Chicago area newspapers and "The Whitechapel Horrors" could very well be one of those stories.

Finally, the phrase "unconscious crime" was used in the subtitle for "The Whitechapel Horrors" and Tilburn would publish a novel in 1891 with the title *An Unconscious Crime*. Although that story had nothing to do with hypnotism, the phrase itself wasn't commonly used in publications in the 19th century (when results were filtered for the 19th century, the phrase appeared less than 40 times in a Google Books search, and less than 350 times in Newspapers.com).

Readers, what do you think?

Was Tilburn the author of "The Whitechapel Horrors"? Send your ideas to **HypnoRipper@gmail.com**, and they may appear in a future, updated edition of this book.

TILBURNE, EDWARD O., traveler, author, actor and theatrical manager, secretary Chamber of Commerce, Tulsa, born in Philadelphia, Pa., June 4, 1864, son of Edward and Mary Tilburne. Went to Yale University where he received Ph. D. degree, in 1887. Mr. Tilburne has been a great traveler, and twice encircled the globe in the interest of educational illustrated lectures. For a number of years he was literary editor of the Rand McNally Publishing Company of Chicago. Also an author and has published in all twenty-six books. He was assistant secretary of World's Fair at Chicago, and has been at the head of publicity work in San Diego, Cal., during the exposition at that place in 1915. Is a Mason, an Elk and Odd Fellow and a K. of P.

Biographical Information on Edward Oliver Tilburn

(aka N.T. Oliver, Ned Oliver,
Nevada Ned, and Edward Tilburne)

When I started this book, I planned on having just a brief biographical note about the author of *The Whitechapel Mystery*, but the more I searched for information about "N.T. Oliver," the more fascinated I became with his colorful life. His life story would make a great movie; after all, few people can resist the charms of a charismatic con man, and E.O. Tilburn was most definitely a con man, as well as being a great self-promoter. But Tilburn was also a very talented man; he possessed musical and acting skills, he was a gifted public speaker and writer, and he earned some praise both as a preacher and as an advocate for business owners and employers when he served as secretary for several cities' chambers of commerce. One does wonder though, why a man with so much intelligence and ability, felt the need to embezzle or turn to selling snake oil medicines, fraudulent medical devices, and phony real estate offers.

Much of the biographical information on Tilburn is taken from two articles he wrote about late 19th-century traveling medicine shows (articles appeared in the *Saturday Evening Post* on September 14, and October 19, 1929) and from an entry on him in the book *Progressive Men of the State of Montana*. These sources provided the skeleton of his biography, and the rest was filled in by genealogical sources and old newspaper articles. Newspaper articles were especially fruitful, for they provided a chronology of Tilburn's life and threw light on his many unethical and criminal transgressions. I searched many newspaper databases, but the ones yielding the most useful results were:

Chronicling America **https://chroniclingamerica.loc.gov/**
FultonHistory.com **https://fultonhistory.com/Fulton.html**
California Digital Newspaper Collection **https://cdnc.ucr.edu/**
Newspapers.com **https://www.newspapers.com/**.

Early Life

Edward Oliver Tilburn was born on June 4, 1859, in Philadelphia, Pennsylvania. His father, Edward Tilburn, was a Civil War veteran who earned his living as a bookkeeper and accountant. His mother, Mary Elizabeth Bailey, a native of Leeds, England, was brought to America when she was a young child, when her family settled in Baltimore, Maryland. Mary Tilburn died in 1873, when her son Edward was fourteen years old. E.O. Tilburn had a younger brother, Upton, and a younger half-sister named Kate (Tilburn's entry from the *Progressive Men of the State of Montana* stated that his parents had four children; genealogical research did reveal two other younger, unnamed half-sisters). Edward and his family lived with his grandmother in Philadelphia, until he was five years old, and then Edward was sent to live with a Baptist minister (Rev. N.B. Baldwin) in Colmar, Pennsylvania, until he was 11, receiving his education up to this time at private schools. He then attended Pepperell Academy, a private school for boys in Massachusetts, and at 16 entered Yale University where he studied a full classical course load with the intent of becoming a minister. Tilburn claimed throughout his life that he graduated from Yale, but a search through lists of Yale graduates turned up no proof of him having done so (Source: *Resources on Yale History: Alumni Information* **https://guides.library.yale.edu/yalehistory/alumni**).

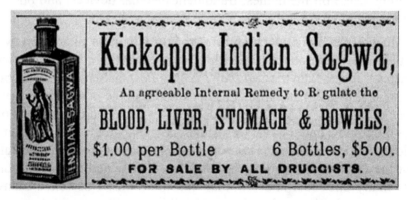

Tilburn the Snake Oil Salesman

During his high school and college years, Tilburn was active in musical and theatrical performances, and his love of the stage led him to leave Yale to pursue a career as a musician and actor. This change in life course was against the wishes of his family and friends, so at their request he dropped the name Tilburn and took on the name of Oliver, and for the next 15 years he would be known to the world as either Ned Oliver, N.T. Oliver, or Nevada Ned.

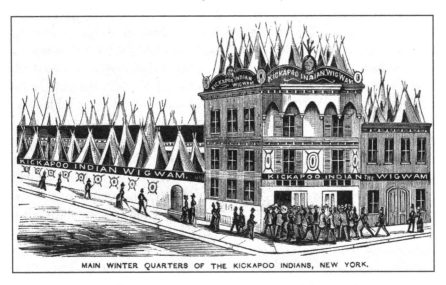

MAIN WINTER QUARTERS OF THE KICKAPOO INDIANS, NEW YORK.

Upon leaving Yale, Tilburn worked as a musician in the Sweatman & Fraser's Minstrels in Philadelphia, and he would later move on to perform with Rollin Howard's traveling show, working under the name "Ned Oliver" (Rollin Howard was an American minstrel performer, best known for his female blackface impersonations). In the fall of 1879, Tilburn joined Dr. E. H. Flagg to help him promote his liver pads and liniment—Tilburn (i.e. Ned Oliver) would play the banjo alongside two other entertainers, while a "doctor" would try and peddle the liver pads and the liniment to the crowd (the liver pad was a medicated bag which was clamped over the stomach; it was believed that the stomach provided a more effective way for the body to absorb the medicine due to the stomach skin's 50,000,000 pores). Around this same time, Tilburn took a brief break from traveling entertainment shows and promoting liver pads, and he started a sham company called the American Laundry Association, with his grandmother in Philadelphia as the unwitting company president and his sister an equally unaware company secretary. Tilburn would deliver lectures on laundry history in chiefly Black churches to an audience of African American women, and offer them a reduced rate on his newly formed company's overpriced clothes irons.

Tilburn's big break as a showman came in 1881 when he teamed up with John Healy and Charles "Texas Charlie" Bigelow to form the Kickapoo Indian Medicine Company, a traveling show that would eventually become the largest medicine show in America. The three-some formed the medicine company to sell Kickapoo Indian Sagwa, a mixture of alcohol and herbs that claimed to be "blood-making, blood-cleansing, and life-sustaining" (the company would also go on to add other Kickapoo products such as Kickapoo Indian Cough Cure, Kickapoo Indian Worm Killer, and Kickapoo Indian Prairie Plant—an herbal remedy for "all forms of female weakness"). Sagwa was promoted as the treatment that saved the life of Bigelow when he got deathly ill during a visit to the Kickapoo tribe while he was working as a government scout in Indian Territory. When Bigelow regained his health, he pleaded with the Kickapoo to divulge the recipe for Sagwa and to show him how it was made, and then with this knowledge he could establish the Kickapoo Indian Medicine Company and provide Sagwa to the public. The Sagwa promotion story sounded good to predominantly white audiences during that time, but it was totally fabricated.

Big Injuns in Town.

A row of tents has been pitched at the foot of Briggs street, on Cowden, five being gaudily painted imitations of Indian tepees, occupied by Kickapoo Indians from the Fox and Sac reservation and gymnastic performers, and as April showers bring May flowers, so the red man of the forest attracts a large crowd. N. T. Oliver, whose pseudonym is "Nevada Ned," an intelligent, shrewd gentleman, is the manager of the aggregation, which gives free exhibitions and advertises a patent medicine that cures everything. A large crowd of spectators took in the show last night. Between these exhibitions and Barnum's circus the small boy will have his hands full.

By playing on the mystique of the Indian as a natural healer/physician, the Kickapoo Company hoped to sell thousands of bottles of Sagwa; the Company even referred to its headquarters in New Haven, Connecticut, as the "Principal Wigwam" to further promote its Indian image. The main promotional tool would be traveling entertainment shows built around bogus Indian ceremonies, such as war dances, marriages and pow-wows, and to this end, the Company would hire hundreds of Indians, none of them, by the way, Kickapoo. Some of the "Indians" were actually Mexicans, "half-breeds," or white men dressed up as Indians. One of the main stars of the show was "Nevada Ned," the name Tilburn would go by in all his

Indian medicine show acts. Nevada Ned would be attired in buckskins, wearing a wide-brimmed hat that covered a head of long flowing hair. In a typical performance, Nevada Ned would introduce the show's cast of Indians to the crowd, and they would grunt their acknowledgements back to him, then one of the Indians would give a speech in Kickapoo, which Nevada Ned would translate into English. Nevada Ned would next lecture the crowd on the health benefits of Kickapoo Sagwa, and then the Indians and Ned would circulate among the audience to sell the various Kickapoo medicine products.

The Kickapoo Company shows would also incorporate other types of diversions, such as simulated Indian raids with Nevada Ned coming to the rescue of the people being attacked. Tilburn was highly skilled with a rifle, so shows would occasionally feature an exhibition of Nevada Ned's marksmanship, having him shoot the tip of a cigar in an actor's mouth, using a mirror to hit a target, et cetera.

For the next 10 years, Tilburn would work on and off again for Healy and Bigelow's Kickapoo Indian Medicine Company. At times, Tilburn thought he was too smart to need partners, so he would venture off on his own as Nevada Ned, but he would eventually return to Healy & Bigelow—sometimes as a performer, but often as a company manager. Tilburn would also work as a promoter and manager for Hamlin's Wizard Oil, another patent medicine company that used entertainment to sell its products. In between jobs working for medicine companies, Tilburn would on occasion turn to acting. One of the bigger acting gigs he landed was the title role in a Western drama called "The Ranch King." Tilburn saw the part as the beginning of a great acting career; full of swagger and having visions of fame, he sold his solo show and its horses back to Healy & Bigelow. "The Ranch King" was set against a theatrical backdrop of cattle ranches and mining towns, and it provided a perfect forum for Nevada Ned to flaunt his Western image and to show off his exceptional sharpshooting abilities. Tilburn awoke one morning to find a note from Joseph Clifton, the stage manager for "The Ranch King;"

Clifton's note accused Tilburn of coming on to his wife, May Treat, an actress in "The Ranch King." Tilburn admitted that May did have to sit on his lap in a scene of "The Ranch King," but he insisted that they had "as little sentimental interest in each other as two cigar-store Indians." Needless to say, Nevada Ned's lead role in "The Ranch King" was short-lived.

Tilburn's traveling medicine show years must have been exhilarating to him, and more than likely, quite lucrative as well. But there was also a dark period during those years, when he found himself addicted to cocaine. The addiction starting when he was fighting off a bout of catarrh and used a salesman's catarrh powder for relief. Tilburn found the powder's power extraordinary, and credited menthol as the curative substance. But one of the powder's main ingredients was cocaine, so unknowingly he became an addict. Tilburn would spend several unpleasant months dealing with his cocaine craving, and he would credit his overcoming the addiction through a combination of moral strength, a rigorous physical regime, and a patient wife.

Tilburn the Author

Tilburn's writing career didn't fit into a tightly set time period, as was the case for his years spent as a traveling medicine show performer. The majority of his published works were issued between the years 1888 and 1900, but he would still be writing and publishing all the way up to the early 1920s (it should be noted that Tilburn probably wrote many promotional pamphlets for the Kickapoo Indian Medicine Company but these works never credited authors). His first published books were detective and western novels, written under the pseudonym "N.T. Oliver," and most of these came out of two publishing houses: Laird & Lee and Rand McNally. It's hard to know exactly how many novels Tilburn wrote since he claims to have written many fictional works anonymously. He alleges that in collaboration with John Postgate he wrote 12 detective stories, which were first serialized in a Chicago newspaper and afterwards published in book form.

Tilburn tells the story of one of his anonymous publications, in the January 1929 article he authored for the *Saturday Evening Post*. Tilburn writes that Laird & Lee wired him the following message:

"BODY OF DOCTOR CRONIN JUST FOUND IN A CATCH BASIN. CAN YOU WRITE US 50,000 WORD NOVEL? MUST HAVE WRITTEN WITHIN SEVEN DAYS. NEWSPAPER CLIPPINGS BEING MAILED YOU TODAY BY SPECIAL DELIVERY."

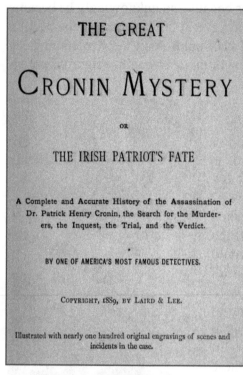

THE GREAT

CRONIN MYSTERY

OR

THE IRISH PATRIOT'S FATE

A Complete and Accurate History of the Assassination of
Dr. Patrick Henry Cronin, the Search for the Murderers, the Inquest, the Trial, and the Verdict.

BY ONE OF AMERICA'S MOST FAMOUS DETECTIVES.

COPYRIGHT, 1889, BY LAIRD & LEE.

Illustrated with nearly one hundred original engravings of scenes and
incidents in the case.

His telegraphed reply was: "Big job. How much?" The answer was: "Five hundred dollars on delivery of the manuscript."

Doctor Patrick Henry Cronin was murdered on May 4, 1889, by a band of assassins affiliated with an Irish republican organization called *Clan na Gael.* Newspapers headlines were filled with the news that Cronin's body had been found jammed into a Chicago sewer, and an army of police detectives were sent out to find the murderers. It was Tilburn's task to stitch together the facts along with a fictional solution to the crime. Tilburn was under a tight deadline, and to make the writing task even more difficult he was still responsible for putting on a Kickapoo show each night. Writing in longhand continuously he ground out a 62,000-word book, entitled *The Great Cronin Mystery, or, The Irish Patriot's Fate*, the book's author would be listed on the title page as "by One of America's Most Famous Detectives." Tilburn had written the book over the course of four days and nights, and he never gave a second look at any page of the manuscript. He mailed it out to Laird & Lee and they sent it out to the printer without any editing work; the book was illustrated with images borrowed from newspaper articles.

Laird & Lee published more than works of fiction, and like many large book publishers, they found cookbooks to be both profitable and a reliable source of income. "Doctor" N.T. Oliver would co-author a combination cookbook/medical advice book with Jennie Adrienne Hansey. Hansey would provide the recipes for the book and Dr. N.T. Oliver would provide the hygienic and medical advice. Their first foray into this type of book came out in 1894 and was entitled *Dr. N.T. Oliver's Treasured Secrets: The Century Cook Book, a Carefully Selected List of Household Recipes*. The book's title page broke the book down further into its two parts, the first being "The Century Cook Book" by Jennie A. Hansey and the second being the "Thoroughly Practical and Entirely Original Family Medical Adviser" by Dr. N.T. Oliver. The book must have been a fairly good seller, for Laird & Lee would publish several updated editions of it. Tilburn would also co-author a similar book with William H. Lee, entitled *Lee's Priceless Recipes*; this book also went through several editions.

In 1900, Tilburn co-authored a fictional work, *The Autobiography of a Quack*, with the Century Company, but only his co-author's name (Silas Weir Mitchell) would appear on the book. The story itself deals with a death bed confession of a corrupt doctor who made his living by peddling fake remedies, electromagnetic treatments, and other nostrums.

Tilburn must have done extensive writing when he was a preacher and for the years he worked as secretary for various cities' chambers of commerce, but most of these writings were internal and never meant for wider distribution. His public writing pen was mostly silent from 1902 until the time of his death in 1940, but in 1915 he did submit a manuscript for a stage play entitled *An Adventure in Justice*, to the Oliver Morosco Play Reading bureau. Oliver Morosco was an American theatrical producer, director, writer, and theater owner whose Play Reading bureau would seek out manuscripts for possible stage presentation. More than a thousand manuscripts were submitted to the bureau in 1915, and Tilburn's *An Adventure in Justice* was among the 20 that were recommended for production, but his play never ended up being performed or published. The last books published in his life came out in 1921 and were products of the Christian New Thought movement. Both of these books were published in Los

Angeles by the Universal Property Partnership, their titles being: *Whatsoever a Man Soweth* and *Principles and Practice of Christian Psychology*.

Tilburn the Preacher

In 1891, Edward Oliver Tilburn found God. In a newspaper article ("Nevada Ned Converted," *Galveston Daily News*, March 1, 1891, p.22) Tilburn stated that he never troubled himself about religion, nor did he think much about religious subjects, even though his parents were devout Christians. He never considered himself an atheist, but he doubted the inspiration of the Bible and was skeptical about many of the claims made by the holy book. He always believed there was some supreme power, but he did not give much thought to the idea of heaven and hell, nor did he care that he was living a heathenish lifestyle.

This was the state of his spiritual life, until he came to Weatherford, Texas, in early 1891. Tilburn could never quite pinpoint what led him to his spiritual transformation. All he knew was that one day, Mr. Fred Bargy, a colleague of his, was singing a song on the street that impressed him in a way he could not explain. From that time on, he was troubled about the song, and the feelings it elicited, and he became so affected

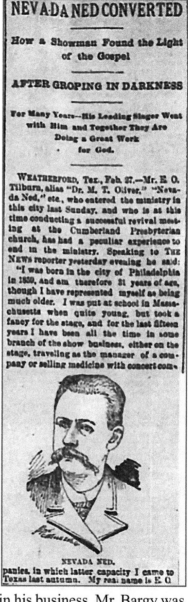

NEVADA NED CONVERTED

How a Showman Found the Light of the Gospel

AFTER GROPING IN DARKNESS

For Many Years--His Leading Singer Went with Him and Together They Are Doing a Great Work for God.

WEATHERFORD, Tex., Feb. 27.--Mr. E. O. Tilburn, alias "Dr. M. T. Oliver," "Nevada Ned," etc., who entered the ministry in this city last Sunday, and who is at this time conducting a successful revival meeting at the Cumberland Presbyterian church, has had a peculiar experience to end in the ministry. Speaking to THE NEWS reporter yesterday evening he said: "I was born in the city of Philadelphia in 1859, and am therefore 31 years of age, though I have represented myself as being much older. I was put at school in Massachusetts when quite young, but took a fancy for the stage, and for the last fifteen years I have been all the time in some branch of the show business, either on the stage, traveling as the manager of a company or selling medicine with concert companies, in which latter capacity I came to Texas last autumn. My real name is E. O.

NEVADA NED.

by it that he couldn't take any interest in his business. Mr. Bargy was invited to sing in church on a particular occasion and Tilburn was persuaded to attend. Tilburn spoke to a Rev. W. G. Templeton there about his feeling and the thought that he may be getting a spiritual calling to the ministry. Some time went by, but Tilburn still couldn't shake the feeling that he was being guided by God to become a minister, so he wrote to Rev. Templeton about it. Templeton replied that Tilburn should "burn all his bridges behind him" and to trust in God. Tilburn claimed to have taken the Reverend's advice, and that he turned his business over to one of the people in his company and had nothing further to do with it. Tilburn's intention was to devote himself to evangelical work and that he would use the remainder of his life to secure conversions to the cause of Christ. Tilburn went on to say in the newspaper article that "I quit a paying business to follow the dictates of my conscience without a guarantee of so much as a living, but I feel better that I have made the determination, and believe that the Lord will provide. Yes, I have written a good deal, but most of my work was of the sensational detective kind, written for the money they brought me, and I did not feel honored by their authorship."

After his conversion to Christianity in 1891, Tilburn started almost immediately to preach the Gospel in Texas, chiefly around the city of Sherman. Newspaper coverage of Tilburn's life is pretty sparse for the time period between 1892 and 1894, so it's hard to know exactly how active he was in his religious pursuits during the early 1890s. According to his entry in the *Progressive Men of the State of Montana*, he entered the McCormick Seminary in Chicago to pursue a course

REV. E. O. TILBURN Ph. D.

of study in theology, though the entry's information says he started at McCormick in 1889 which would predate his conversion by two years. Tilburn's name does appear in a directory of the Cumberland

Presbyterian Church in 1894 and lists him as being a licentiate in Texas, so he definitely was working on becoming a certified minister. The *Progressive Men of the State of Montana* entry also claims that Tilburn lost his voice in 1891 and he was obliged to give up preaching for three years, although this seems odd, because several newspaper articles have him working for the Hamlin's Wizard Oil Company during the period of 1892 to 1894, and his work for Wizard Oil included speaking in front of large groups of people ("Dr. Oliver's" lectures upon the wonders of Hamlin's Wizard Oil medicines would often be given to an audience of over 1,000 spectators). It's unclear how Tilburn's work for Hamlin's Wizard Oil assisted him in bringing souls to Christ, and one can only wonder if the several works of sensational fiction he published after his conversion made him feel "honored by their authorship."

REV. EDWARD O. TILBURN.

Tonawanda Minister, Who Has Resigned to Become Pastor of Forest Ave. Christian Church of Buffalo.

Rev. Tilburn more than likely continued to minister to the people of Sherman, Texas until 1895 when he relocated to Wanatah, Indiana. For the next four years, Tilburn would work for several churches in Indiana, chiefly in the cities of Princeton and Washington. In April 1899, Tilburn became the pastor of the Christian Tabernacle in Butte, Montana; he would serve there until November 1901. Tilburn next accepted a call to head a church in Tonawanda, near Buffalo, in New York. While serving as a pastor there, he had a narrow escape from drowning while swimming in Lake Ontario, off the shores of Olcott, New York; he had dislocated his shoulder when he was some distance from shore, but

NARROW ESCAPE.

Rev. E. O. Tilburn Dislocated Shoulder While Bathing.

SANK IN SIX FEET OF WATER

And Crawled Along the Bottom Until He Was Near Enough to the Shore to Get His Head Above Water—Might Easily Have Drowned

managed somehow to get himself back to shallow waters. Tilburn also garnered a fair amount of national press during his time in Tonawanda when he gave out trading stamps to all people who attended his church service. His promotional scheme appeared to pay off when hundreds of people took him up on his offer. In December 1903, Tilburn resigned from his Tonawanda church, and transferred to the nearby, Forrest Avenue Christian Church of Buffalo. His next move would take him to a church in Warsaw, Indiana, in the fall of 1904, and from there to a congregation in Mishawaka, Indiana, in the summer of 1905.

In April 1907, Tilburn would find himself back again in Butte, Montana, this time at the Shortridge Memorial Christian church. In the fall of 1908, Tilburn must have tired of being a preacher, for he left Butte and headed to Texas to join forces with Dr. J.L. Berry, better known as the "Phenomenal La Fayette." Berry was in Texas, giving public demonstrations of his work on bloodless surgery, and Tilburn (now going under the name "Dr. Tilburne") was lecturing on topics dealing with the soul and the body (Dr. Berry would be prosecuted in the spring of 1909 for violations against the Texas medical practice act). Shortly after returning to Butte from his Texas lecture tour, Tilburn resigned the pastorate of the Shortridge Memorial Church. His resignation was accepted by the church's board and another pastor was appointed to succeed him. A few months later, Tilburn returned to Butte seeking to be reinstated as pastor, and he asked the board to reconsider its action in accepting his resignation. The board refused his request, so Tilburn was forced to find another preaching position. Around March 1909 he found one, and he became the pastor of the Christian church in Linton, Indiana—this would be his last move as a preacher.

By the fall of 1909 the entire country would know of the Reverend E.O. Tilburn. Newspapers across the nation would be filled with articles carrying titles along the lines of: "Rev. E.O. Tilburn Wanted by Police," "The Linton Scandal," "Preacher Elopes With Girl," and "Rev. E.O. Tilburn Faces Charge of Embezzlement." It appears Tilburn became smitten with Mary Smith, a 20-year-old organist and choir singer in his congregation (Tilburn was 50 at the time). Hearsay had it that Tilburn was supposed to be giving Miss Smith lessons in elocution. It was said that they frequently met alone in the pastor's study and in the library hall until the librarian, becoming suspicious, forbade them meeting alone in the hall any longer. There was also talk that Tilburn's wife and daughter had moved out of their house in Linton, and relocated back to a house in Butte, leading many to think that the family must have been having trouble, and that the separation was due to the attention the Reverend was paying to Miss Smith.

LINTON SCANDAL

Pastor of the Church There Accused of Fleeing with One of the Pretty Sisters.

Linton gossips are rolling a dainty morsel under their tongues these days. It is charged that Rev. Tilburn, pastor of the First Christian church, has eloped with pretty Mary Smith, who has been singing in his choir. Two weeks ago the pastor left stating that he was going to help a brother minister in a revival at Bicknell, and about the same time the young lady left, presumably to visit friends in Bloomington. It is said that they both are now in Chicago. The minister leaves a wife and family, who are visiting in Butte, Mont. The church board has declared the position held by the pastor vacant.

Mary Smith left her home on September 11, 1909, ostensibly to pay a visit to friends in Bloomington, Indiana, where she had been attending college. By a strange coincidence, Rev. Tilburn was supposed to be assisting a fellow minister at a revival meeting in Bicknell, Indiana—yet neither would end up staying where they said they would be. Instead the two met at Bloomington, and from there went on to Chicago, where they would spend the night. The next day the couple headed for Lawrence, Kansas, and eventually the pair would find their way to California. To complicate the couple's flight, Tilburn was being accused of embezzling several hundreds of dollars from his church's building fund. Authorities across the

LOOKING FOR COUPLE.

Plymouth Officials Notified to Watch for Minister and Girl of Linton, Ind.

There are two people prominent in the social world of Linton, Indiana, whom the police authorities are anxious to locate. Sheriff Voreis has received full descriptions of the parties, the descriptions being accompanied by photographs. They are Rev. Edward Oliver Tilburn, Ph. D., and Miss Mary Smith. The former is about 6 feet in height, weight 185 pounds, smooth shaven, fifty years old, broad shouldered, slightly stooped, hair very light color, cut Henry Ward Beecher style, blue eyes, magnetic appearance, usually carries a cane.

Miss Mary Smith is a vocal and instrumental musician of considerable ability, and also possesses elocutionary talent. She is a dainty, petite bit of humanity. Her height is four feet, weght 90 pounds, age 20 years, dark auburn hair, large brown eyes, left eye slightly crossed, both eyes slightly almond shaped

country were sent lookout notices for Tilburn, and the citizens of Linton raised money to offer a reward for any person providing information on Mary Smith's whereabouts; Mary's father was offering a separate reward as well—it seemed inevitable that the fugitive couple would be apprehended in a short time.

A short time turned out to be three months, and over that period of time all kinds of rumors floated. It was said that Tilburn had divorced his wife, and that he had married Miss Smith while they were together in Chicago. Someone supposedly had spotted Tilburn getting aboard a ship at New York, accompanied by a "boy" who was really Miss Smith in disguise, and there were many other sightings of the couple being at places they had never visited. One source even stated that Tilburn was an acknowledged hypnotist, though no other source ever mentioned Tilburn having anything to do with hypnotism (except for his using it as a theme in *The Whitechapel Mystery*). A few newspaper articles said it was thought that Tilburn made a practice of fleecing churches throughout the country, although none of the churches that Tilburn had pastored at confirmed those assertions publicly.

The couple were finally located when the Reverend W.C. Hull, a pastor at a church in Pasadena, recognized Tilburn's face. Rev. Hull had learned of the theft of money through a denominational publication, and he recalled the fact that many years ago he had at times seen Tilburn in Tonawanda, New York. While living in Pasadena, Tilburn assumed the surname of Osborne and obtained a job as a sightseeing guide, and Mary Smith would find employment as a piano player at a Pasadena theater. When Tilburn was arrested he was in the uniform

MINISTER REARRESTED

Girl With Whom Tilburn Eloped Files Charge Against Him.

of a tourist guide and was in the middle of distributing advertisements for a trolley trip to sightseers. Miss Smith would later be located in the Hotel Carlton in Pasadena, the place the couple had been living since October. A sheriff from Indiana with extradition papers was sent to California to retrieve Tilburn, and he soon found himself on a train, heading home to face a judge and jury on his embezzlement charge.

While Tilburn was in custody at Pasadena, a *Chicago Tribune* article reported that he had made the following statement:

"I can think of nothing upon which a criminal complaint would be based. The only transaction I have pending in Linton is with a relative. I borrowed $500 from a man there. He took a mortgage and the note is not due for a year."

"I worked hard at Linton. I started collections for a new church and my daughter, Mrs. F.S. Potter of Butte, Mont., has receipts showing every cent turned into the church. My wife and I disagreed and there was a separation. I was divorced in Linton two months before my departure."

"I left the ministry because it proved irksome. Finally I decided to leave the ministry and departed. My last sermon was on socialism. It created a row. I left that night for Chicago. With me was Mary Smith, my present wife, whom I married in Chicago."

PASTOR SAYS FLOCK STILL OWES MONEY

Linton Church Members Declare Expenditures Were Not Ordered by Board.

(Note: no proof of either his divorce or marriage to Mary Smith could be found).

Mary Smith was one of the first witnesses to be called to testify at Tilburn's trial. She provided information about her rendezvous with Tilburn at Bloomington, and how they went together to Chicago, and from there on to Kansas. She also stated that at some point Tilburn received information stating that the people in Linton were

PASTOR FREED FROM JAIL

INDIANA PREACHER, AFTER LONG WAIT, SQUARES CHURCH EMBEZZLEMENT CHARGE.

CASH SETTLEMENT WITH GIRL

Divine Who Eloped with Choir Singer Is Suddenly Flush with $100 Bills.

incensed and that trouble was brewing as members of his congregation suspected that the two of them were together. Tilburn then told her that she had better return home, but she refused, and the couple then continued on to California. While in California, Smith said, Tilburn took out a roll of money amounting to $200 and said in her presence, "I can beat the best of them, and if I am arrested and sent to prison for embezzlement I will kill every one that has anything to do with it." She said, however, that when Tilburn was arrested afterward he expressed surprise, saying that he did not know why he was being arrested, for he was not aware of any crime he had committed.

Tilburn's legal team was intent on proving that the church at Linton owed the Rev. Tilburn more money than he was alleged to have embezzled, and that some of the money he supposedly stole, was actually given to him by permission by the church's financial secretary. When Tilburn took the stand, he calmly stated that any money he had collected for the church's building fund had been turned over to the secretary, and any money he had borrowed had been taken with no felonious intent.

The jury for the trial spent several hours in deliberations, but the end result was a hung jury, 10 standing for conviction and 2 for acquittal. The prosecutor in the case then filed a written motion to dismiss the indictment, which a judge sustained, so Tilburn was released from jail. Shortly after the end of the trial, Mary Smith brought paternity charges against Tilburn, but he quickly settled the claim against him with her family (monetary payment amount was never divulged), and all charges against him were dropped. Tilburn was now free and clear of all legal allegations against him, but he was also well aware that his days as a preacher were most assuredly over, and that he would have to find another way to make a living.

Tilburn the Chamber of Commerce Secretary

Even if it was true that Tilburn had come to find ministry work "irksome" as some reported, his adulterous and monetary misdeeds definitely precluded him from finding employment as a minister in any case. Former Indiana parishioners of his sent copies of newspaper articles about him to many local members of the Christian churches at which Tilburn was once pastor; denominational newsletters would also highlight his moral failings, and that, coupled with word-of-mouth accusations, would more than likely have resulted in lifetime banishment from preaching. (It is noteworthy that around the time of his fling with Mary Smith, Tilburn inexplicably started adding an "e" to the end of his surname. Occasionally newspapers would inadvertently misspell his last name as Tilburne, but starting sometime in 1909 it becomes quite obvious that he intentionally started using the surname "Tilburne." Perhaps he was looking for a new identity, but an additional "e" placed at the end of one's name seems pretty slim cover indeed.)

A few months after the end of his trial, Tilburn would find himself back in California, giving a series of free lectures at the Booklovers' Hall in San Diego. Tilburn, now referring to himself as Dr. Edward Tilburne, Ph.D, D.S., was offering a series of five lectures dealing with metaphysics and "divine science" and these lectures were presented over the course of a couple of weeks in November 1910. In late December 1910, Tilburn would offer a paid admission lecture at the Booklovers' Hall, entitled "A Christmas Tide with Dickens." In 1911, Tilburn spent much of his time managing a Buffalo and Pawnee Bill Wild West Show, but at the tail end of that year he found employment as an organizer for the Order of Panama. The Order of Panama was an organization whose chief purpose was to assist in promoting the city

NEW CHAMBER OF COMMERCE SECRETARY

Edward Oliver Tilburne of San Diego Was Chosen Today

of San Diego for the upcoming Panama California Exposition, set to be held there in 1915. Tilburn simultaneously held a paid position with the Department of Publicity and Exploitation of the San Diego Exposition, and would for a short time work for the industrial department of the San Diego Chamber of Commerce. In 1914, Tilburn must have been bitten by the acting bug, for he found himself work

ORDER OF PANAMA TO BE ORGANIZED

Charter Members Will Hold Dinner and Meeting on Friday

The Order of Panama is the latest institution to play an important part in the history of the Panama-California exposition. It is composed of leading citizens of San Diego, who will take over the management of future annual celebrations to be held leading up to the exposition, such as the parades and carnival of last July.

E. O. Tilburne, as organizer of the Order of Panama, has secured a large membership and has his offices in the headquarters of the exposition.

Announcement cards have been

as an actor with the Wright Huntington Players in St. Paul, Minnesota, and would spend two seasons performing at the Shubert Theater there.

In June 1915 Tilburn would land his first job as a secretary for a chamber of commerce. It's too bad that history can't provide us with a copy of the résumé he submitted to the city of Tulsa, Oklahoma, for the position. We know from some Tulsa newspaper articles that he claimed to have been a general advance representative of Buffalo Bill for 10 years, but except for a few months in 1911, there's no record of him being employed that long by Buffalo Bill. He also claimed to have had some affiliation with New Orlean's Mardi Gras, but there's little evidence that he spent much, if any, time in Louisiana. You can be sure that his résumé contained the dubious claim of having a doctorate degree from Yale, and just as sure that it made no mention of the 17 years he spent as a minister. But his recent work for the city of San Diego, coupled with his assorted truths and half-truths about his work experience, must have been enough to impress his new employer.

SEC'Y TILBURNE TO BUILD HOME

Fell in Love With City at First Sight, and Intends to Stick.

That Edward O. Tilburne, new secretary of the Chamber of Commerce, has become a thorough Tulsan and intends to "stay a while" was shown yesterday when he purchased a lot in Park Hill, just south of Irving boulevard, and let the contract for a splendid home of the California bungalow type, work on which is to start at once.

Tilburn definitely gave the people of Tulsa the impression that he loved their city and was intending to "stay a while" when he purchased a lot in a recently developed part of the city and was planning on having a home built on it. But 11 months after taking the job in Tulsa, he tendered his resignation. The excuse he gave the city board for leaving was the ill health of his wife and because he wanted to better himself financially during the next six months, previous to his permanent return to California to live. It should be noted that Tilburn's usual excuse for leaving any position was the ill health of his wives. He left several jobs as a preacher for that reason; he even left his first church in Butte because he said the high altitude was making his wife ill, yet he would take another position as minister at a different church in Butte a few years later (he was married to the same woman for both moves—so much for caring about his wife's aversion to high altitudes). Even though Tilburn only stayed a short time at Tulsa, the folks there seemed to have thought he did a good job because they threw him a banquet upon his departure, and the speeches at that event only reflected regret at losing such a great man as Tilburn.

Tilburn's next stop as secretary for a chamber of commerce would be in Bartlesville, Oklahoma. Tilburn was actually brought in as a consultant to advise the city of Bartlesville about some planning issues, and when the topic concerning the selection of a secretary for the chamber of commerce was brought up at an advisory

> This paper has had a good deal to say regarding the management of the Chamber of Commerce ever since the "New Life Day" was pulled off and E. O. Tilburne took up the secretaryship. Knowing something of his business qualifications and what he had done in the past as a town builder, it was just natural that we predict the final outcome, which came to pass sooner than we had expected. Bartlesville got stung in more ways than one by the coming of Mr. Tilbourne and loses nothing, in a business way, in his departure. He failed in every proposition he took hold of and gained nothing for the city. We doubt very much that any are sorry that he has chosen to seek pastures "greener."

meeting, Tilburn was informed that many different people had been considered for the position but all were rejected. A person present at the meeting had a thought—why not offer the job to Tilburn? Tilburn was offered the position on the spot, a salary offer was discussed, and in a few minutes Tilburn had made up his mind to accept the city's offer.

The city of Bartlesville was ecstatic that Tilburn had been selected to lead their city's chamber of commerce. Bartlesville always seemed to be in a constant state of stagnation and it was hoped that Tilburn would bring it out of the economic doldrums and make it one of the premier cities in northern Oklahoma. Tilburn was invited to speak at the city's "New Life Day," which would feature decorated streets, a grand parade, band concerts, and all other types of fanfare to reflect Bartlesville's newfound hope in its promising future. But when Tilburn accepted the job at Bartlesville, he must have failed to inform the city's officials that he was only planning on staying there six months before making a permanent move to California (Tilburn did let the folks in Tulsa know that this was his long-term plan). The people of Bartlesville seemed to have been incensed when it became known that Tilburn was leaving them after such a short time. This editorial, which appeared in the local paper (*The Independent*, January 5, 1917, p.2), summed up the feeling of the majority of Bartlesville's citizens, as well as reflecting the skepticism the newspaper editors had about Tilburn from the beginning:

"This paper has had a good deal to say regarding the management of the Chamber of Commerce ever since the "New Life Day" was pulled off and E.O. Tilburne took up the secretaryship. Knowing something of his business qualifications and what he had done in the past as a town builder, it was natural that we predict the final outcome, which came to pass sooner than we had expected. Bartlesville got stung in more ways than one by the coming of Mr. Tilburne and loses nothing, in a business way, in his departure. He failed in every proposition he took hold of and gained nothing for the city. We doubt very much that any are sorry that he has chosen to seek pastures 'Greener.'"

Tilburn, no doubt, considered California a more favorable place to live than Oklahoma, and he seemed to be pretty hell-bent on returning to the Golden State, but the newspaper record provides little insight into what he planned on doing once he relocated there. An article that appeared in the *San Diego Union* on December 24, 1916, informs its readers that E.O. Tilburne, well known to San Diegans because of his connection with the Panama California Exposition, had returned to San Diego to stay. "The best reason for leaving San Diego is to come back to it," he told a *Union* reporter. He went on to tell the reporter, "The old town looks good to one who has been away as long as I have and I don't care if they make me stay here the remainder of my life."

An advertisement for the "Sunset Senario Service" appeared in a March, 1917 issue of the *Screamer*, a movie studio newspaper that was published in Los Angeles. The Sunset Senario Service provided editorial and promotional assistance to aspiring screenwriters and playwrights. Edward O. Tilburne is listed in the advertisement as a person "who tells you how to dispose of a scenario." The only other person named in the ad is a David Lindeman, so it's probably safe to assume the company was a two-man operation run by Tilburn and Lindeman. The ad seems to have only appeared once in the *Screamer*, and the company itself does not appear in any San Diego or Los Angeles business directories for the time period.

Tilburn's experimentation with the business of assisting aspiring screenwriters must have not panned out, because in early February 1918 he would find himself back in the familiar role of chamber of commerce secretary, this time for the city of San Pedro. Tilburn had beaten out two other qualified candidates for the San Pedro position; a member of the city's executive committee said, "Just now we need a big man for the place for we have big things to do," and the rest of the committee agreed that Tilburn was the "big man" San Pedro needed to accomplish the "big things." As it turned out, the big things may have been too big for the big man—Tilburn would resign after just four months on the job. San Pedro would be Tilburn's chamber of commerce swan song.

California Scheming

Real Estate Scamming

A newspaper article in the July 6, 1918, issue of the San Pedro *News-Pilot* informs us that Tilburn wished to be relieved of his position as chamber of commerce secretary because he had accepted a position with the Emil Firth realty firm. Southern California was experiencing tremendous population growth in the first half of the 20th century, and the burgeoning population in the area had many ambitious people seeking their fortune in the world of real estate, and Tilburn appears to have been one of those people. There is no record to inform us how long Tilburn stayed with Emil Firth, but by 1920 Tilburn had joined forces with E. E. Shafer to form the Shafer & Tilburne real estate company. However, by the end of 1921 the company must have gone out of business, because its name no longer appeared in either business directories or newspaper advertisements.

Tilburn's failed venture with Mr. Shafer doesn't appear to have discouraged him from continuing his pursuit of making money via real estate because by early 1922 he would be a major partner in the Kirkpatrick Brothers' Syndicate. The Kirkpatrick Brothers' Syndicate was a trust company that purchased valuable oil-laden lands in the Santa Fe Springs region of California, and then sold units of that land to oil speculators. Tilburn acted as lecturer and promoter for the syndicate, often passing himself off either as a geologist or as a former federal judge (several ads referred to him as "Judge Tilburne"). The Bible figured prominently in Tilburn's syndicate lectures, and his scripture-filled speeches were intended to provide evidence of trust and good faith between the syndicate and any potential oil land purchasers.

The tactics used by the Kirkpatrick Brothers' Syndicate caught the eyes of federal investigators, and in July 1924 the four organizers and promoters of the syndicate, Charles H. Kirkpatrick,

> # Our Third
> # Big Success
> will be
> ## Kirkpatrick Syndicate No. 2
> ### Santa Fe Springs Opening Friday, Nov. 3, 1922
>
> Success in two propositions, why not in the third? The only sale close in that is absolutely proven and, think of it, a well now going down!
>
> Briefly our proposition is: To drill two wells on this proven tract out of the sale of units. Other development and other wells also included to the unit buyers.
>
> $100 per interest and approved by the corporation commission.
>
> Dr. Edwin O. Tilburn will deliver a lecture on the development and record of the field, giving detail and methods of procedure relative to all other unit propositions in the field. Dr. Tilburn has made a study along these lines and on account of being connected previously with more successful sales syndicates than any other lecturer, his discussion will be good and in one or two cases to the point.
>
> *If you own units in Santa Fe Springs come out and learn how well you are off. If you don't own units it will do you good to know how much you have lost.*
>
> Long Beach Office, 135 E. Ocean Ave. Phone 633-271
> ## McLean & Rowse, Mgrs.

> Judge E. O. Tilburne, geologist and oil promoter, has sufficiently recovered from his cold to be present at the meeting of the Lynwood Communities Oil and Refining association. The $100 shares, of which there will be 2200, have not been selling so rapidly as they should and the judge has put May 20 as the date in which he must have the 2000 promotion shares sold. The buyers can pay $25 down and have until June 1 to pay the remaining $75.

W.O. Kirkpatrick, Willis A. Cates, and E.O. Tilburne, were arrested and indicted on federal charges of using the U. S. mail to defraud. According to the indictment, the four men made false representations through lectures, letters, and financial statements; they were alleged to have obtained nearly $1,000,000 from investors by misrepresenting the value of their oil units. They were also charged with failing to comply with permit conditions and with having secret contracts with drilling contractors for illicit rebates. Tilburn and his associates were freed on $5,000 bond each; newspaper research did not reveal how much jail time (if any) Tilburn served for his part in the oil fraud scheme, or how much he had to pay in fines. His legal entanglements with the federal government over the oil land fraud did seem to extinguish any dreams he had of getting wealthy through real estate.

Lecturing

If there was one thing that Edward Oliver Tilburn enjoyed doing, it was talking in front of large groups of people. It didn't matter if he was acting on stage or selling Indian remedies, real estate, or the teachings of Jesus Christ—the man thrived when speaking to crowds. Tilburn offered hundreds of lectures over the course of the 1920s and early 1930s. Some of his lectures were targeted to specific groups, such as those lectures he used to win over gullible investors in the Kirkpatrick Brothers' Syndicate scam, but most of his lectures were open to the public and were advertised widely in newspapers. The newspaper ads for Tilburn's lectures would list him as being a scientist, Christian psychologist, psychoanalyst, teacher, author, and philosopher. The majority of his public lecture topics can best be described as a combination of Christian psychology and Western esotericism. The following are a sampling of some titles of his lectures: "Are You Successful? If Not: Why Not?"; "The

Phenomenal Man Coming to Santa Ana to Give Free Public Lectures on Health, Eternal Youth, Science of Living and Prosperity to All. Two Weeks, Commencing Sunday, 8 P.M., Elks' Hall.

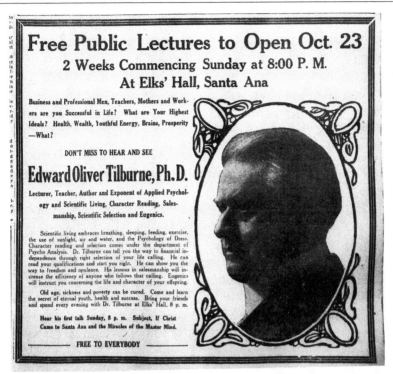

Free Public Lectures to Open Oct. 23

2 Weeks Commencing Sunday at 8:00 P. M.
At Elks' Hall, Santa Ana

Business and Professional Men, Teachers, Mothers and Workers are you Successful in Life? What are Your Highest Ideals? Health, Wealth, Youthful Energy, Brains, Prosperity —What?

DON'T MISS TO HEAR AND SEE

Edward Oliver Tilburne, Ph. D.

Lecturer, Teacher, Author and Exponent of Applied Psychology and Scientific Living, Character Reading, Salesmanship, Scientific Selection and Eugenics.

Scientific living embraces breathing, sleeping, feeding, exercise, the use of sunlight, air and water, and the Psychology of Dress. Character reading and selection comes under the department of Psycho Analysis. Dr. Tilburne can tell you the way to financial independence through right selection of your life calling. He can read your qualifications and start you right. He can show you the way to freedom and opulence. His lessons in salesmanship will increase the efficiency of anyone who follows that calling. Eugenics will instruct you concerning the life and character of your offspring.

Old age, sickness and poverty can be cured. Come and learn the secret of eternal youth, health and success. Bring your friends and spend every evening with Dr. Tilburne at Elks' Hall, 8 p. m.

Hear his first talk Sunday, 8 p. m. Subject, If Christ Came to Santa Ana and the Miracles of the Master Mind.

——— FREE TO EVERYBODY ———

Mission and Miracles of Jesus," "The Hidden Mystery of Sleep and Dreams," "How to Read People on Sight," "You Are a Supreme Miracle," "The Way to Perfect and Permanent Health," "The Law of Universal Prosperity," "Life Forces and How to Use Them," "The Ruling Instinct and the Inner Urge."

Tilburn garnered high praise as a lecturer, and some of the acclamations he received were so glowing it makes one wonder if Tilburn himself didn't provide the content for some of the newspaper articles about his public lectures. For example, an article that appeared in the October 21, 1921 issue of the *Santa Ana Register* describes Tilburn as "the acknowledged leader in Christian psychology and an orator in the class of Robert J. Ingersoll, William Jennings Bryan, and the world's greatest platform speakers, he delivers a message illuminated by picturesque phrase backed by absolute sincerity and fearless thought that reaches the hearts and minds of his hearers and transforms the lives of those who hear and practice." This same newspaper article informed its readers that "enthusiastic audiences attended the Free Lectures given by Edward Oliver Tilburne in Riverside and many of the sick and afflicted arose and proclaimed they had been cured or benefitted by the words spoken from the lips of Dr. Tilburne while he was lecturing. Mr. Andrew Robinson stated he had been suffering from asthma for years but since he had attended the Free Lectures he had been cured by the Faith of the spoken words. One little woman all crippled up with rheumatism, remarked that it seemed like a miracle to her as her condition was improved by attending the lectures." So Tilburn was not only a great orator, but apparently, a faith healer as well.

In 1923, Tilburn took his educative pursuits beyond just lecturing—he founded his own college. An advertisement in the January 13, 1923, issue of the *Los Angeles Evening Express* announced the opening of the College of Applied Sciences. The first classes of the College of Applied Sciences were to be held on Wednesday, January 24, 1923, and "Permanently Thereafter Teaching and Practicing the SCIENCE OF LIFE: Psychology—Metaphysics—Physical Culture. The only institution of its kind in America. Dr. Edward Oliver Tilburne, Founder." Other ads for Tilburn's College would state that its classrooms were "elaborately and fully equipped at great expense for

THINK! This is to annuonce the opening of the

COLLEGE OF APPLIED SCIENCES

337½ SOUTH HILL ST.

WEDNESDAY, JANUARY 24, 1923

3 p. m. to 10 p. m., and Permanently Thereafter Teaching and Practicing the

SCIENCE OF LIFE

Psychology—Metaphysics—Physical Culture. The only institution of its kind in America. Dr. Edward Oliver Tilburne, Founder.

lectures, classes and actual demonstration of the co-related Sciences that, when combined, teach and demonstrate THE TRUE SCIENCE OF BEING." The College of Applied Sciences' faculty consisted of several lecturers and practitioners who taught on topics such as: comparative religions, practical psychology, ancient and modern languages, physiology and hygiene, numerology, and physical science and culture. Beyond scant newspaper advertisements, little information exists about Tilburn's College of Applied Sciences. Did it offer a degree for students? If so, was it a two- or four-year degree, or perhaps

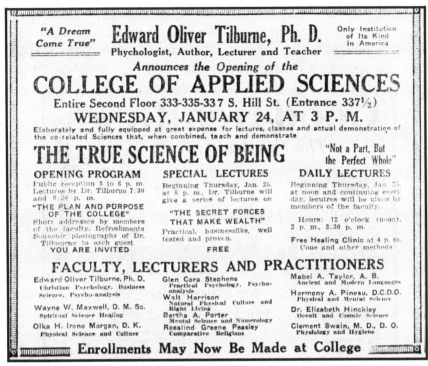

just a certificate? But even if the College of Applied Sciences had offered a degree no student probably ever received a diploma because the college itself lasted less than two years.

Medical Quackery Redux

Sometime during the latter portion of 1926, Tilburn would find himself adapting a page out of his old playbook of selling phony medical products, but instead of peddling Sagwa and liver pads, the focus of his new sales endeavor would be on a highly hyped product called I-ON-A-CO. The "I-on-a-co" (or just "Ionaco") was an electromagnetic therapeutic device developed by Henry Gaylord Wilshire. Gaylord Wilshire (he didn't use his first name) was a real estate developer, publisher, and socialist who helped turn Long Beach, California into a seaside resort and developed Wilshire Boulevard in Los Angeles. According to research by Donald G. Davis ("The Ionaco of Gaylord Wilshire" *Southern California Quarterly*, Vol. 49 (Dec. 1967) pp.425-453) the Ionaco was created by Wilshire to cure his own ailments. Wilshire suffered from severe headaches, and though he sought relief from many doctors and specialists, neither they nor the many remedies he tried brought him any comfort.

Wilshire was known as a tinkerer, so no one thought it was strange when he started experimenting with electric currents as a possible therapeutic application for pain relief. But his device, the Ionaco, was not Wilshire's own discovery; he based his invention on the

work of Otto Warburg, a German biologist who demonstrated the fact that the iron in human blood acted as a carrier of the oxygen from the blood to the body's tissues. The Ionaco's magnetic field was supposed to increase the body's absorption of oxygen to free the body from toxic diseases. Wilshire started work on his therapeutic "life belt" in 1910, but it wasn't until 1925 that he perfected the device to the point that he felt that it cured his condition. Believing that

his device really did help him, Wilshire started giving the devices to his friends and relatives, and many of them reported positive results as well.

The Ionaco itself was a simple coil of insulated 22-gauge wire which weighed about 6.5 pounds and was worth about $3.50 in 1926. The Ionaco generated a weak magnetic current when a plug at one end of the wire was attached to an electric light socket. The device also had a smaller wire coil with a flashlight globe that would light up when placed close to the thicker wire coil. The exterior of the Ionaco wire belt was covered by a thick layer of leather and the diameter of the apparatus was roughly 18 inches. The Ionaco was used by placing this "magic horse collar" (as it was commonly referred to) over the neck, around the waist, or around the legs of the person seeking relief from their affliction (the Ionaco claimed to cure everything from constipation to cancer). To commercialize the device, Wilshire established the Iona Company in Los Angeles. As with many products based on quackery, the Ionaco's main advertising asset was testimonials. The testimonials were published in

Good for 3 FREE
I-ON-A-CO Demonstrations

CLIP this advertisement, and present it to the nearest authorized I-ON-A-CO office listed below. Judge by your own experience the remarkable efficacy of the I-ON-A-CO in restoring health. This offer is free. You will not be obligated in any way. Make this simple, delightful test now.

E. O. TILBURNE, 332 E. Colorado St., Pasadena.
Phone: Wake. 6356

E. O. TILBURNE, 125 W. Main St., Room 203
Alhambra

newspaper ads and also aired on the radio. Wilshire's Iona Company would use regional distributors to publicize the Ionaco (retail price for the unit was $65, equivalent to approximately $950 in 2020). The distributors would promote the device by demonstrations and door-to-door sales. The device could be purchased outright or on credit for $5 (equivalent to $72 in 2020) a month.

The snake oil salesman in Tilburn must have been attracted to the idea of Wilshire's electromagnetic device, and that attraction led him to become an Ionaco distributor in early November 1926. An advertisement for the Ionaco which ran in the November 11, 1926, issue of the *Los Angeles Evening Express* lists Dr. E.O. Tilburne as one of several authorized distributors for the Ionaco in the southern California area. A few weeks later, in the *Pasadena Post*, Tilburn would start running his own individual ads for the product, and the phrase "DR. E. O. TILBURNE" printed in large font, would stand out prominently in the ads. The blatant use of "Dr." before his name would land Tilburn in legal hot water, and he would be arrested and charged in December 1926, with practicing medicine without a valid license from the Board of Medical Examiners of the state of California. He pleaded not guilty and was held on $500 bail until his preliminary hearing, which was held later in December, 1926. An investigator for the California Medical Board was the only witness at the hearing and the investigator testified that Tilburn called himself Dr. Tilburne unlawfully, and that he had given treatment to people without proper authority. An Ionaco belt, pamphlets, and newspaper advertisements were used as exhibits by the prosecution. Tilburne offered no defense at his hearing, but his attorney said he would show in Superior Court that his client had never given treatment as charged. At his court appearance, Tilburn avoided the more serious charge of providing medical treatment, but he admitted that he called himself doctor in violation of the law, and filed an application for probation with the Superior Court judge. Being on probation didn't stop Tilburn from being a distributor for the Ionaco, but when he ran an advertisement for the product in February 1927, the prefix "Dr." was missing, and just plain old "E.O. Tilburne" appeared in the ad.

During the years 1926 and 1927, many organizations started to investigate the Ionaco's health claims and most of the investigations found the claims made by the device's manufacturer and distributors to be false or deceptive. When Wilshire ran a full-page ad in the *Los Angeles Times* challenging the medical community to investigate the Ionaco, Arthur J. Cramp of the American Medical Association responded with an article that analyzed the claims regarding the device. The bad press coming from critical reviews of the Ionaco would lead to a decline in sales, and when Wilshire died in September 1927, the Iona Company dissolved, though sellers continued to promote the Ionaco throughout the 1930s and early 1940s. Tilburn ceased running ads for the Ionaco in early 1927 and appeared to have stopped distributing the device around the time of Wilshire's death. But five years later, Tilburn would again find himself promoting a product with questionable health claims. A 1932 Los Angeles city directory lists Edward O. Tilburne as a manager for the Mineral-Kur Institute. The Mineral-Kur Institute sold a therapeutic mineral concoction which claimed to offer "proven 100% relief to sufferers from stomach, kidney or liver troubles, rheumatism, neuritis, blood, skin, or nerve diseases, female disorders, goiter, piles and inflammation of the rectum, tumors and abnormal growths." The Mineral-Kur Institute was a bit player in the fraudulent medicine arena, and Tilburn's affiliation with the company appears to have been short-lived.

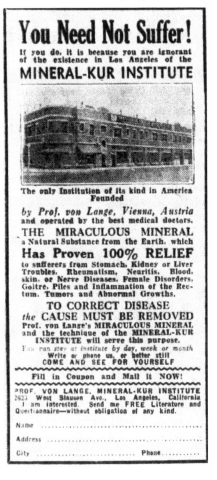

Biographical Loose Ends

E.O. Tilburn was a very untrustworthy chronicler of his own life. He played very loosely with the truth, and many of the reliable parts of his life story are only available because of the extensive newspaper coverage of his various career activities and the reporting on his numerous wrongdoings. But the newspaper articles about Tilburn provide very little information or insight into his personality or personal life; diaries and correspondence are useful to researchers looking for such details, but Tilburn or his family members don't appear to have kept such documents—if they did, those items have either been destroyed or yet to find their way into any library or historical society's archives. The following information on Tilburn's wives and offspring has been gleaned from newspapers, books, websites, and genealogical sources.

According to Tilburn's entry in the *Progressive Men of the State of Montana* he was married February 26, 1881, to Ave Marie Wagner, a native of Germany and a relative of the musical composer Richard Wagner. Her family immigrated to the United States when she was seven years old and they settled in Baltimore, Maryland. During the early years of their marriage, the Tilburns weren't going by that surname. Instead, Edward was commonly known to the public as either N.T. Oliver or Nevada Ned; his wife never used her first name Ave but preferred to be called either Marie or Mary. Marie performed for a short time in a few of Nevada Ned's shows; a newspaper ad for a "Nevada Ned Novelties" performance that took place in Bangor, Maine, in January 1885 lists several novelty acts and "Novelty No. 2" was a "Marie Oliver, wonderful female rifle shot, who sights with an ordinary hand mirror, snuffs a candle and equals in skill and dexterity any of the shots now traveling." Marie appears to have stopped performing just around the time she began to have children, though her name would appear in an ad for a Nevada Ned show as late as 1891. Marie and Edward had three children together: a girl named Gertrude Lillian born in Philadelphia on November 26, 1885; a son named Albert Roanoke, born in New Albany, Indiana, on November 13, 1887; and, a third, unnamed child who died either during childbirth or in very early childhood. While Edward Tilburn received much coverage by the press, both as a medicine show performer and as a prominent clergyman, his wife got very little mention in newspapers, and when she did, it was as "Mrs. E.O. Tilburn" and the references to her were usually about her either giving or attending a social event. Marie received some unwanted attention during the time her husband went missing with Mary Smith, but she kept a low profile during this period and she let her son-in-law be the family contact with the press. After Edward left her and started a new life for himself in California, Marie continued to live close to her daughter in Montana. Marie's name did appear in a May 9, 1910, article in an Anaconda, Montana newspaper which reported that Marie and her granddaughter narrowly escaped harm when a runaway horse carriage almost ran them over.

Marie must have been estranged from her brother, Louis Wagner, because he contacted the editors of the *Anaconda Standard* in March of 1922, seeking their assistance in helping him track down his sister. The paper would publish a brief notice in its March 23rd issue, entitled "Mrs. Mary Tilbourne [sic] is Sought in Butte." Wagner, who lived in Maryland, had not seen Marie since 1886, and an uncle of theirs had recently died leaving a legacy to himself and Marie, and he was anxious to get in touch with her if she was still living in order that the estate could be settled—it's unknown if Wagner was successful in his quest to get in contact with his sister. Toward the end of her life, Marie relocated to be near her son, first in San Fernando, California and then on to New York City. She died in the Bronx and was buried in Fresh Pond Crematory on March 23, 1926.

Very little information could be found on the Tilburns' daughter, Gertrude Lillian (she normally went by the name Lillian). Her name does appear several times in newspapers during the period Tilburn was a preacher, but these mentions were all very brief and usually in reference to her involvement in church related activities, such as singing in the choir, or assisting her father with religious programs. Her wedding ceremony had a fairly lengthy write-up in a couple of Montana newspapers (she married Dr. Franklyn Harrington Potter, a dentist on August 27, 1908) but overall, Tilburn's daughter received very little attention from news reporters. Lillian had three husbands over the course of her lifetime. Her second marriage was to Stanley C. Conrad, which ended in divorce, partly, because Mr. Conrad discovered that Lillian had lied about her age prior to their marriage—she claimed to be at least six years younger than she actually was ("Accountant Wins Decree of Divorce" *Los Angeles Daily News*, March 14, 1933, p.2—Stanley's name is incorrectly listed as Seamley in the article). Her third marriage was to a man named Ernest Jenewein. Lillian Tilburn died in Los Angeles on September 1, 1959, and is buried in Rose Hill Memorial Park in Whittier, California.

In contrast to their daughter, the Tilburns' son, Albert Roanoke, garnered a fair amount of media attention over the course of his life-time, especially the later portion of his life when he became fairly famous as both a magazine illustrator and a painter. Due to their father's involvement in operating patent medicine and Wild West shows, the early part of his and his sister's childhood were spent traveling across large sections of the United States. Albert was a talented singer, and his fine baritone voice led him to participate in many public recitals in his father's churches. He spent several years in Europe studying vocal music with the intention of becoming a pro-fessional singer, but upon his return to the United States he instead turned to acting. Albert performed with several theatrical companies from 1911 to 1916, and his work with the Washington Square Players earned favorable reviews in both the *Washington Post* and the *New York Times*. On February 9, 1911, he married Celine Rousseau; the couple had two sons together, Edward (born in 1913) and Leopold (born in 1915). In 1917 Albert joined the United States Naval Reserve and was trained in the operation of dirigibles for U. S. coastal air defense. On July 2, 1919, he was a crew member on-board the Navy dirigible C-8 when it exploded while attempting to make an emergency landing near Baltimore, Maryland. Everyone on board the dirigible survived the explosion, but several nearby houses were destroyed and over 70 people among a crowd of curi-ous onlookers were severely burned in the disaster. After leaving the Naval Reserve in 1922, Albert spent the next couple of years traveling to Cuba and between countries in both Central and South America, when he was employed, first by the Tobacco Products Export Corporation, and then by the United Fruit Company. In 1924 he relocated to New York City and founded a real estate firm with two partners. When the Great Depression arrived, Albert closed his business but continued to work as a real estate broker. In 1934 he became a building manager for a large apartment complex. In 1935 he began to sell illustrations to pulp magazines but continued to work as a building manager as well. By 1938 Albert was selling his illustrations to magazines such as *Weird Tales* and *Short Stories* and the money he made from these publications enabled him to become a full-time illustrator. Around 1950 he retired from illustration and began to devote his time to painting scenes of the Old West. Albert would credit his interest in painting western scenes to his boyhood experience of traveling with his father in his Wild West shows. His reputation as a western artist developed quickly, considering that as early as 1952 his western paintings would be exhibited in group shows alongside the genre's more acclaimed artists, such as Frederick Remington and George Catlin. Albert died on January 22, 1965, at the age of 77, and is buried in Arlington National Cemetery next to his wife Celine.

Before moving on to E.O. Tilburn's second marriage, it should be mentioned that in all likelihood Tilburn had a child with Mary Smith. It's possible that Mary was lying about being pregnant, but the speed in which Tilburn settled her claim against him seems to validate her accusation. If Mary was indeed pregnant and carried the baby to term, there are no genealogical records or newspaper accounts that lead us to know what happened to the child.

On September 22, 1910, E.O. Tilburn married Bertha Aukema. No record of Tilburn divorcing his first wife could be located, and if he did in fact fail to get a divorce, then bigamy can be added to his list of legal transgressions. As to Bertha Aukema, very little information on her could be found. Genealogical sources reveal that Bertha was born on September 18, 1877, in the Netherlands, and that she arrived in the United States in 1890 at the age of 13. She lived in Iowa until 1905, and in Idaho for a while after that. She married Tilburn in Almeda, California, but how the two of them met is unknown. Had Bertha been acquainted with Tilburn prior to his running off with Mary Smith? If not, why a 33-year-old woman would want to marry a 51-year-old man she hardly knew, and who had recently (his trial in Indiana had just ended in April 1910) been found guilty of adultery, hit with a paternity suit, and charged with embezzlement, is puzzling. Perhaps, the two had known each other for some length of time, but even given that, Tilburn had so much social baggage that a pause before getting legally entwined with such a person would seem a prudent move. It's possible that Bertha had no idea about Tilburn's past (this was long before the advent of the Internet, after all), and that his charismatic personality won her over, and his lies kept her in the dark about his various iniquities, but it's also possible that she knew all about Tilburn's past and married him anyway.

As with Tilburn's first wife Marie, Bertha's name was rarely mentioned in newspapers, and if it was, it was usually tied to some social event as well. For example, at the 1913 Tournament of Roses Parade in Pasadena, a newspaper article tells us that Bertha was seated upon top of an Order of Panama float, on a throne, where she represented the spirit of San Diego's progress. In a more serious news article that appeared on February 14, 1930, in the *Pasadena Post*, readers were informed that Charles Stickle, a suspended Pasadena school teacher spent the night in the city jail awaiting arraignment in justice court on charges of performing lewd acts with a boy under the age of 14, and that Bertha A. Tilburne and two other friends of the accused teacher furnished bail. Bertha's name would also appear along with her husband's in a November 10, 1927, *Los Angeles Times* article discussing a legal judgment in their favor—the couple was awarded several thousand dollars in a damage suit they had brought against James Burton of the Burton Transfer and Storage Company. The suit was filed because of an accident that occurred on March 14, 1921, when a car occupied by the Tilburns collided with a truck owned by Burton.

It couldn't have been easy, either for Bertha or Marie, being married to E.O. Tilburn. For one thing, con men tend to move frequently since frequent relocation keeps a swindler's criminality from being discovered. Marie was constantly on the move when she was married to Tilburn, both during the years he was working for traveling medicine shows, and then for all the time he spent as a preacher (Tilburn relocated at least 11 times during the 17 years he was a minister). Bertha would also find herself living in many different places, especially in the early years of her marriage to Tilburn. Con artists are notorious for their "disappearing acts," and people who disappear for days or even weeks at a time are usually up to no good. An article that appeared in the *Anaconda Standard* (November 17, 1909, p.9) during the time that Tilburn went missing with Mary Smith, reveals that it wasn't unusual for Tilburn to disappear for long periods of time. The article quotes Tilburn's son-in-law, Franklyn Potter, as saying, "Last winter Mr. Tilburn said one day to his wife that he was going away for a while. He said he didn't know where he was going and that was all the information she had …. I wouldn't be at all surprised to hear any day that he had taken it into his head to go to Europe or anywhere else. He might be in Alaska or China. We haven't the slightest idea where he is. He was a great traveler and inclined to wander."

By all accounts, Tilburn was incredibly personable and charming—the kind of man that would be easy to like, easy to believe, and easy to love, and more than likely, Marie and Bertha interpreted Tilburn's lies in more forgiving ways because they loved him, but it's not hard to imagine married life to a con man as being a life full of deception and empty promises.

Tilburn's Final Years

Even aging didn't appear to have lessened Tilburn's love of lecturing. He was in his 70s in the early 1930s, and still presenting lectures in the Los Angeles city area. One lecture he gave (under the pretense of being a physicist!) in February 1931, was entitled "You Who, What and Why?" and dealt with Einstein's theory of relativity. Other lectures, given around the same time, carried titles such as: "Sick People and What Makes Them Sick," "What Part Has Christianity with War," "Why Grow Old," and one aptly named "Criminals and What Makes Them." Besides lecturing in 1931, Tilburn was starting to take an interest in the market for California grapefruits. In an article that appeared in the June 1, 1931, issue of the *Calexico Chronicle,* "Doctor" E.O. Tilburne

Eugenic Sex Talk Tonight At Elks Hall 7:30 p. m. and How To Read People At Sight.

Dr. Tilburne is giving human analysis at the St. Ann's Inn every day between the hours of 10 a. m. and 3 p. m. Do you love your work? Do you know your strong points? Do you know what you are best fitted for? Do you want to know what has prevented you being a greater success?

Modern Science has proven that the traits and tendencies of every person are indelibly written in the shape of the body, head and face.

is cited as having been interested in California grapefruit production for some time and that he had considerable correspondence with the El Centro Chamber of Commerce and with the management of the Desert Citrus Exchange about the topic. Tilburn believed that there

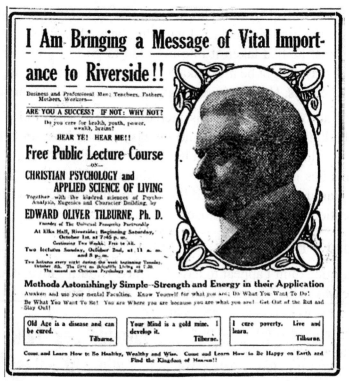

would be a ready market for California grapefruit and its byproducts if only the appropriate canning facilities were constructed. In 1932 Tilburn was employed as a manager for the Mineral-Kur Institute according to a Los Angeles city directory, and a 1933 South Pasadena city directory lists Tilburn as being retired. We know that Tilburn had some serious medical issues to contend with in 1933 because Tim "Banjo" Sullivan (a colleague of Tilburn in his medical showman days) informed the readers of *The Billboard* in its May 6, 1933, issue that he learned "Nevada Ned has been in the hospital in Los Angeles, having had three very serious complications. He is just out of confinement and doing nicely." Sullivan's brief disclosure about Tilburn's hospitalization didn't mention any more in the way of details, so we don't know what Tilburn's health issues entailed. The brief mention in *Billboard* regarding his health was the last bit of newspaper coverage Tilburn received during his lifetime.

Edward Oliver Tilburn died on January 9, 1940, and the only newspaper that informed the world of his passing was the *Los Angeles*

Times (January 10, 1940, p.35), and it provided only this very brief death notice:

"Tilburne, Edward O. Tilburne, Forest Lawn Mortuary in charge"

The notice contained no information about funeral services, or any mention of his surviving wife and children. An obituary, or a lengthy death notice, is an optional way to pay a public tribute to a deceased person, and it is very understandable why Bertha would have chosen not to have had one for her husband—writing an obituary about a colorful lawbreaker would be a real challenge. Tilburn's death notice didn't even mention that he had a surviving spouse, and that informational lacuna does start to make you wonder about Bertha and Edward's relationship. Surmising the happiness status of any couple's marriage is a precarious exercise, but an unavoidable one when a person is married to a con artist. Con men manipulate all the people around them, including their significant others. Tilburn was an expert at telling lies, and he probably knew the right proportion of truth to weave into his falsehoods to make a story believable to his spouses, but years of marriage to a liar must be both emotionally and mentally draining, and when the death of the lying spouse occurs, it wouldn't be surprising to find that the surviving spouse would feel a sense of freedom and relief. Bertha Tilburne passed away on February 19, 1954, in Pasadena, California; her death notice made no mention about her late husband, and it was either her wish, or the wishes of her surviving family members (she had a brother and two sisters), that she not be buried next to Edward Tilburn. Bertha's remains are buried in Mountain View Cemetery and Mausoleum in Altadena, California.

E.O. Tilburn was indeed a man who possessed broad general knowledge, superior intelligence, acting ability and resourcefulness—he could have been an excellent businessman, lawyer, doctor, or a success in almost any line of work, had he chosen to hone his craft instead of his graft. There was nothing stopping him from becoming an outstanding real estate broker, or chamber of commerce secretary; he could have applied himself to become proficient in either of those professions, but he spent his energy on learning how to impersonate a professional in those occupations instead.

By most newspaper accounts, Tilburn was well thought of as a minister, and he amassed a fair amount of praise for his motivational preaching and for his ability to fundraise for his churches. What drew Tilburn to become a man of the cloth? A person with good character and a love for Christ should be a requirement for entry into Christian ministry, and Tilburn claimed in 1891 that the Lord called him to leave his sinful life and assist in shepherding God's flock on Earth. It would be nice to give Tilburn the benefit of the doubt about his sincerity in wanting to preach the good news of Jesus Christ, but given his questionable ethics prior to his becoming a minister, his behavior while he was one (adultery and embezzlement), and his using the Bible as a means to help him swindle people out of their money in the Kirkpatrick Brothers' Syndicate fraud scheme, it would be naïve to do so. Con artists like to seek positions in careers with high respectability, so it's easy to see why they might be drawn to camouflage themselves in the form of a cleric. A charismatic public speaker with the ability to convince people that he's been called by God to lead them, has it made in the shade. Most con men will start their faux clerical careers at a small church, and then start moving from church to church, and from state to state, going on to larger churches where they can gain more power and influence, and Tilburn most definitely followed that pattern. The only church that publicly accused Tilburn of stealing church funds was the one he pastored at in Linton, Indiana, but it wouldn't be shocking to discover that he stole money from all of the congregations he ministered to. Tilburn made the decision to leave the ministry when he chose to run off with Mary Smith, but had he wanted to, he more than likely could have duped the faithful for the rest of his life.

Tilburn seemed to have been fairly successful as an author, so why didn't he just make writing his full-time occupation? One reason could be that it's very difficult to make a living off being an author, and that was just as true in the late 19th century, as it is today. There are only a small number of people who make a decent living as an author; most published authors have other jobs or just struggle to get by on what they make from their writing. While some of Tilburn's publications met with success, especially his cookbooks, most of his fictional works probably had middling sales and produced short-term royalties. Another reason why Tilburn didn't make writing his vocation could be that good writing requires hard work, and con artists would rather spend their energies on financial scheming and deception, than on working hard. Tilburn could be a lazy writer at times; he admitted that his book, *The Great Cronin Mystery* was slapdash and not properly edited. Another book of his, *The Fateful Hand; or, Saved by Lightning,* received the following review in the August 8, 1896 issue of the *Scranton Tribune*:

"Talking about enterprise, here, from Laird & Lee, Chicago, comes a novel of 200 pages constructed around the incident of the St. Louis cyclone, which happened only two months ago. It is called *The Fateful Hand, or, Saved by Lightning* and its author is one Dr. N.T. Oliver. Dr. Oliver evidently started out to write an original story, but as he got pressed for time, he simply took his scissors and clipped whole columns of cyclone material from the St. Louis papers. Hence the story is merely incidental. On the whole this scheme impresses us favorably. Good newspaper writing is invariably preferable to bad novel writing."

To be fair to Tilburn, both *The Great Cronin Mystery* and *The Fateful Hand* were time sensitive publications that didn't lend themselves to thoughtful and well-crafted sentences since they had to be written in a hurry. These two publications are insightful in that they reveal that Tilburn cared more about money than providing his readers with quality writing, but we don't need these examples to point out that Tilburn was a mercenary when it came to his publishing endeavors. He told the world that directly in 1891 with this quote from the article "Nevada Ned Converted": "Yes, I have written a good deal, but most of my work was of the sensational detective kind, written for the money they brought me, and I did not feel honored by their authorship." It should be pointed out that *The Fateful Hand* was published in 1896, and Tilburn was five years into his Christian ministry by then.

Snake oil salesmanship appears to have been Tilburn's true calling in life. He spent all of his 20s and the early part of his 30s peddling liver pads, Sagwa, and other sham medicines, before plying his conniving ways to preaching, running cities' chambers of commerce, and selling real estate. But he would eventually return to his true lifework when he was 67 years old and he became a purveyor of Whilshire's magic horse collar, the Ionaco. Even when Tilburn was in his 70s, he couldn't turn down the temptation of hawking the spurious medical products produced by the Mineral-Kur Institute.

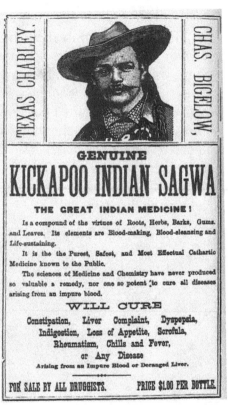

Whereas it is possible to map out the generic behavior of pickpockets, tracing patterns and supplying copious examples without necessarily referring to individuals, confidence men are after all artists laden with idiosyncrasies that distinguish their work. There are styles, schools, trends, evolutions, innovations, reactions, triumphs, failures. And it takes much more than cupidity and unscrupulousness to make a con artist. The best possess a combination of superior intelligence, broad general knowledge, acting ability, resourcefulness, physical vigor, and improvisational skills that would have propelled them to the top of any profession."

Quotation from Luc Sante's introduction in David Maurer's
The Big Con: The Story of the Confidence Man.

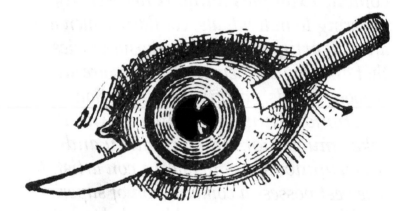

Acknowledgements

This book is indebted to many. Special thanks to David Bertuca for all his work on the book's layout and cover design, and to Rob Sajda for providing artwork for the book's cover and many interior pages.

Thanks also to Rebecca Frost for her examination of the mindset of the protagonists in the two tales included in the *Hypno-Ripper*, and for emphasizing that even though these two stories are old, they can still resonate with the modern crime reader. I am also grateful to Mary Soom for all the genealogical information she provided me on Edward Tilburn, and to Karlen Chase who proofread the manuscript.

I would also like to thank all the libraries, archives, and commercial and non-profit organizations that have so painstakingly scanned old newspapers and made them available to the public; without access to online historical newspaper collections I would never have discovered the short tale "The Whitechapel Horrors," or had any inkling of the rascally Edward Oliver Tilburn.—DKH

Also Available...

Death by Suggestion *gathers together twenty-two stories from the 19th and early 20th century where hypnotism is used to cause death—either intentionally or by accident. Revenge is a motive for many of the stories, but this anthology also contains tales where characters die because they have a suicide wish, or they need to kill an abusive or unwanted spouse, or they just really enjoy inflicting pain on others. This volume also includes an intro-duction which provides a brief history of hypnotism as well as a listing of real-life cases where the* use of hypnotism led to (or allegedly led to) death.—Back cover

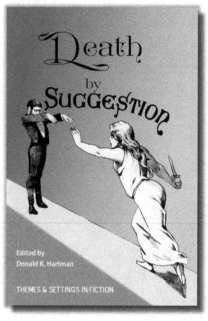

"Donald K. Hartman's DEATH BY SUGGESTION, is a melange of crime fiction featuring stabbings, clifftop suicides, hangings and the odd strangulation. Hartman offers an admirable introduction, exploring the history of hypnotism and defining the terms 'mesmerism' and 'hypnotism.' He discusses the positive and negative applications of hypnotism today before looking at modern criminal cases as well as those well-reported cases relating to his selection of stories."

—*TIMES LITERARY SUPPLEMENT*, January 15, 2019, p.30

Available from
Amazon and Barnes & Noble
in print and on Kindle

CPSIA information can be obtained
at www.ICGtesting.com
Printed in the USA
LVHW010935230821
695886LV00002B/228